HIS INFERNO

S.K MAY

Other works by S.K May

Whispers Series
Whispers in the Blood
Whispers from the Curse
Whispers within the world

Heirs Series
The Hidden Heirs (returning 2026)
The Returned Heirs
Untitled Book 3

The Coven and the Marked Series
His Inferno

TRIGGER WARNINGS

ASSAULT

DEATH

GORE

EXPLICIT LANGUAGE

EXPLICIT SPICE

ABUSE/SEXUAL ASSAULT

TRAUMATIC ENDING THAT MAY END IN YOU THROWING YOUR BOOK OR
KINDLE.

Pronunciation Guide

Morteferi - More-tea-fur-i
Arcanum - Are-can-um
Arcansire - Are-can-sir
Shadowmere - Shadow-meer

Dedication

This is for those who love the men who'd burn the world for their women, the magic that lingers in fantasy and the escape that only books can give you.

igna eros quis urna. Nunc viverra imperdiet enim. Fusce est. Vivamus a tellus. bitant morbi tristique senectus et netus et malesuada fames ac turpis egestas. Pr nummy pede. Mauris et orci. Aenean nec lorem. In porttitor. Donec laoreet no spendisse dui purus, scelerisque at, vulputate vitae, pretium mattis, nunc. n venenatis eleifend. Ut nonummy. Fusce aliquet pede non pede. Suspe llentesque magna. Integer nulla. Donec blandit feugiat ligula. Done perdiet euismod, purus ipsum pretiunt metus, in lacinia nulla nisl eget sap

Donec ut est in lectus consequat consequat. Etiam eget dui. Aliqua em in nunc porta tristique. Proin nec augue. Quisque aliquam tem bitant morbi tristique senectus et netus et malesuada fames ac tur ecenas odio dolor, vulputate vel, auctor ac, accumsan id, felis. is. Pellentesque porttitor, velit lacinia egestas auctor, diam gue magna vel quam erat nectus

in nunc por
ctus et netus
ac. Sed at lor
eros tempus ar
ante Morbi
ectus et metus,
iaculis nibh, vi
Cras non magn
Donec elit es
ultrices lobortis
pis egestas.

massa eget
magna. Pellentesque eos. Done
magna. Maecenas odio dolor, vulputate eos. Done
Pellentesque porttitor, velit lacinia egestas auctor et, conse
vulputate augue magna vel risus. Cras a non magna vel ante adipiscing magnis di
aliquam erat volutpat. Integer ultrices lobortis eros. Pellentesque habitant morbi Etiam a
malesuada fames ac turpis egestas. Proin semper, ante vitae sollicitudin posuere
scelerisque nunc massa eget pede. Sed velit urna, interdum vel, ultricies vel, fauc cus, se
consectetuer eget consequat quis, tempus quis wisi.
Pellentesque habitant morbi tristique senectus et netus et malesuada fam
semper, ante vitae sollicitudin posuere, metus quam iaculis nibh, vitae sceleri
In in nunc. Class aptent taciti sociosqu ad litora torquent per conubia nostra, per in
Sed velit urna, interdum vel, ultricies vel, faucibus at, quam. Donec elit est, con
ullamcorper fringilla eros. Fusce in sapien eu purus dapibus commodo. Cum sociis natoque
quis, tempus quis, wisi.
parturient montes, nascetur ridiculus mus. Cras faucibus condimentum odio. Sed ac ligula.
ligula et tellus ullamcorper ultrices. In fermentum, lorem non cursus porttitor, diam urna a
interdum wisi nisl nec nisl, ut tincidunt volutpat urna. Mauris eleifend nulla eget mauris. Sed
Curabitur posuere quam vel nibh. Cras dapibus dapibus nisl. Vestibulum quis dolor a felis congue
pede purus, iaculis sit tempus eget egestas quis. Curabitur non eros. Nullam hendrer
Fusce lacus, est quis lacinia pretium, pede metus molestie lacus, at gravida wisi ante
porttitor, diam urna accumsan lacus, sed interdum wisi nibh nec nisl. Ut tincidunt vo
Lorem ipsum dolor sit amet, consectetuer adipiscing elit. Maecenas porttitor congue mass

Prologue

Magic lingers in every corner, a birthright for only those fortunate enough. It flows, unseen, unchallenged—except when it does not. Those left unmarked are cast into shadows, unworthy.

When the sun turns black and the sky drinks the last light, the world will shake. From embers and ruin, a Firebound One shall rise—their fate sealed in fire, their heart torn by unseen forces. Beside them, one without ordinary power shall appear—not as their equal, but their unmaking.

They tread the twilight path, inked in blood and whispers. They hold no spells, no gifts of might, yet within them drums a force unknown. Through them, the Firebound One will grasp a truth long buried: power is not always conjured, nor wielded.

Chapter One

The Future

Drake

The elevator beeped, opening onto the dimly lit hallway that led to the hidden basement beneath the house. The room that technically didn't exist. This house had been in the family for generations, and I doubted that I would ever sell it. My Arcanum, my second, Jackson Malak, stood at the door, the longer strands of his brown hair pulled back off his face. Power vibrated through my chest. I was ready to burn this fucker to ash, but not before torturing him for answers; we had lost too many mages lately.

All at the hands of the *Morteferi*, the hunters, the fucking arseholes who believed we were nothing but a scourge on this earth. Yet they used the same power to kill us whenever it was convenient for them. Their attacks lately had increased; we had lost three mages just this week. That was too many for my liking. Being the High Mage came with its challenges, especially when it came to protecting my people. The Vita Flamma was the strongest Coven in Australia. Traditionally, groups only accepted those blessed with a single elemental gift—Air, Fire, Water, or Earth. I welcomed them all, believing our diversity made us stronger and without limitation.I could feel my Fire magic brimming under the surface, weaponised and ready to get the answers that I needed. I rolled my sleeves up, my tattoos on display. Every one of them told a story about the person I had become. Mages used tattoos to show their power and their conquests. Some Mages would participate in the barbaric The Hexed Gallows. I partook when I was a younger man, before the tragic death of my mother. I had a reputation that had stuck with me, and everybody knew that I wasn't a man to be trifled with.

Jackson opened the door. The peasant was tied to the chair, his long hair hanging over his shoulders. The stench of piss lingered in the air. We liked to leave them to think for a few days before interrogating them for further information. We barely got answers before they attacked another Mage. I checked the binds that made him powerless.

"His name is Callum, according to his wallet. Quite a rookie move for a Morteferi." Jackson's voice echoed through the dungeon.

"Yes indeed." I flicked a flame between my fingers, enjoying the thrill of magic that surged through my body. The complete control over such a destructive and dark force. Fire magic was the most powerful of all; we could destroy any other power if used appropriately. Some Fire Mages had been killed by Morteferi's simple Air magic. They would suffocate them; those that had succumbed had yet to learn how to harness the air to keep the flame alight.

"Tell me, Callum, what do you know?" I snarled, wishing that their kind didn't exist.

"N…n…no…nothin," he stuttered, unable to lift his head fully. I left out a low chuckle.

"Callum, I don't beat around the bush. Tell me what I want to know about the Morteferi's movements or…"

"Or what?" he snapped, lifting his head to meet my eyes.

"Callum, have you ever felt your body melting from the inside out? You see, I start with a toenail, a small flame placed underneath. That is all I need for it to burn the nerves. But the problem is…the flame will attach and slowly make its way through your entire foot, frying all those nerve endings, causing your foot to feel like it is being stabbed by a thousand tiny knives. It will slowly climb up your leg while turning what is left of your foot to ash. The choice is yours, but once it starts, there is no way of stopping it unless you give me the information that I want. Then I will make it quick. What do you choose?"

"Nobody is that fucked up."

A manic laugh escaped my mouth, and I flicked the flame between my fingers into the air, igniting the ceiling and warming the room within seconds. I was accustomed to the heat. This was the moment that Jackson normally left. He was a Water user and only here if I needed a quick cool down, so to speak.

I pulled a flame from the ceiling, bending down and inserting the flame into his big toe. I watched the toe ignite before it surrendered under the surface of the skin. Callum kicked his leg, but it was futile. The flame had already killed the nerves in his toe, slowly making its way down the other toes before his entire foot had been consumed.

"Make it stop!" Callum shouted. He bounced his blackening foot, small pieces of his skin floating into the air. His screams echoed in the room, increasing my enjoyment at seeing my words become truth and watching his internal struggle. I wondered how much longer he would la—

"Fine, end it, please."

"I told you, Callum, I can't stop what has already been started; I can only finish it quickly for you. Tell me what you know and I'll make it swift."

"They are planning…fucking hell, on attack…ing—" His foot was completely black now, with his calf slowly losing its colour. "EverFlame."

I moved to snap my fingers, stopping myself with a sly smile. He didn't deserve relief. I turned, making my way toward the exit, his screams getting louder, gut-wrenching noises that would cause any normal person to offer leniency. I left him to his torture, looking at my Arcanum and stretching out my shoulders.

"You are messed up, Drake."

I shrugged him off, knowing that sometimes, business required hands to be a little dirty. "Warn the EverFlame of an imminent attack," I demanded of my second.

"Will do, but we must discuss another important matter," he stated, with a small head bow out of respect.

I nodded and headed upstairs, with Jackson following close behind. The smell of ash lingered in the air. I returned to my office, leaning back in my chair, and Jackson sat opposite me.

"Sir, you need an heir. With the increase in attacks, the Coven council is growing anxious."

My chair creaked as I turned to my Arcanum. Jackson was the only person allowed to speak to me so candidly. We grew up together, we fought together, chased women together, but he settled down about five years ago and had a beautiful son with a perfect wife. I had no desire to take a wife; they were troublesome and wanted what I could never give them. *My love.*

His brow lifted in anticipation of my answer. I ran my hand through my thick black hair before rubbing it over the scar on my forehead. He would have a selection of women in mind. One of the perks of being a High Mage was that I could have whichever woman I wanted; they desired the power, the royal life, per se.

"Whom do you have in mind?" Jackson scratched his chin, his nervous tick. "Even you don't know." I chuckled at his awkwardness.

"You have two choices: marry inside the coven or marry an outsider." My chair squeaked once again. I needed to get the bloody thing fixed.

"The inside. They know the expectations and are raised in the life. An outsider will need to be taught or, worse yet, trained. I have no desire to assimilate a needy woman into the correct way of Coven life. Let's try an insider first. Bring me a selection of all the daughters twenty-eight or over."

"Twenty-eight, Drake?" he questioned, and I quirked an eyebrow at him.

"I won't go any younger." I refused to have a massive age gap with my future wife, even though I had avoided being married.

"You know that a lot of the daughters will be married at that age. Most are, after the age of twenty-two." I knew this; it was my aim.

"I am sure there will be one more than happy to serve their Mage." I grinned. "Speaking of, can you send in Melinda? I need to work out this excess energy." My cock was already hard thinking about her dick sucking skills. Jackson shook his head, opening the door and calling out for her.

She sashayed into the room, getting to her knees and unbuckling my pants.

"Ready to serve your High Mage?" I questioned, pushing her head a little further, feeling my knob hit the back of her throat, and listening to those magical sounds. I watched her head rise and fall, taking every inch of it. Wrapping my fingers around her platinum blonde ponytail to control her rhythm.

She had no real prospects, and her family was trustworthy, but I would keep her close for now. "Good girl, suck it harder!" I growled, forcing it a little farther to ensure it coated the back of her throat.

CHAPTER TWO

HAPPY BIRTHDAY

DANIELLA

Today was like any other day. I hated birthdays. My phone beeped to remind me of my own birth. July 16th, 2000. Twenty-eight today. I'd had no family since they kicked me out ten years ago, after disgracing them by getting pregnant out of wedlock. But that wasn't the worst part. The baby daddy didn't belong to the organisation, as I called it, though it was probably more appropriate to call it a cult. This meant they couldn't hide it under the rug with a quickie wedding. Their supposed only choice was to excommunicate me. I worried about my poor sister and brother, who would have been forced into a marriage by now. One that *makes the family strong*— the words my father lived by. I gave my son up for adoption, which was the hardest decision of my life, but I received regular photo updates from his adoptive parents. He had the cheekiest face, and his smile reminded me of his father, who was dead. That would be a fun conversation to have one day. The man I loved was killed for getting me pregnant.

Since being kicked out with no money, I'd managed to find my feet. After spending some time homeless, I got myself a job at a café, put myself through university, and became a teacher. I worked in a small town with a population of three thousand. Most people knew each other, and I preferred it that way. Nobody knew who I really was, and nobody cared. They saw me as the happy, funny, pretty red-haired high school teacher known as Miss Daniella Duncan. I kept my first name, but changed my last to avoid my past. I never wanted to see my parents again. It was mutual.

Coffee Life had the best coffee in the whole town. I entered through the glass door with my heels clacking against the wooden boards. Next to the counter was an oval indoor garden, which added to the beauty and the quirk of coffee and life in one. People smiled when I entered; they all knew Miss Duncan.

"DANI!" Brett shouted, his mouth opened wide to say more.

I raised my finger at him in warning. "Don't you dare start. You know I don't celebrate." His face fell when I went to pay. His blond hair covered his face as he shook his head. I placed my hand on his in apology.

"If you won't allow me to sing, you at least get a free one today." He beamed with his hazel eyes.

"I won't fight you on that." I sat on the stool near the window, checking my work emails. None from parents, which generally meant a good start. Brett brought over the coffee with a white paper bag.

"Brett…"

He raised his hand, and my mouth closed instantly. "My present to you. Let me know what you think of my new creation. Also, look over my left shoulder. A stranger from out of town, and he is delicious. I would be on my knees begging for him."

Grabbing my coffee, I stood and slyly peered over his shoulder. The man was delicious indeed. Thick black hair, dark eyes, and olive skin with what appeared to be a slight scar on his eyebrow. His broad shoulders were barely contained under his expensive suit. I was surprised he could fit through the door. I noticed his eyes were focused solely on me, a small smirk playing at his lips. A small collection of tattoos hidden under his shirt. He smelled of danger and hot, dirty sex. Warning bells sounded in my brain.

I tore my eyes away, kissing Brett's cheek. "See you tomorrow," I whispered.

"See you tonight. I'm taking you out for a drink."

"Brett," I groaned, allowing my shoulders to drop. He knew I hated birthdays.

"When was the last time you went out and enjoyed yourself?" He had a point. I never did. I feared being seen.

"One drink," I warned him, daring to look at Mr. Tall, Dark, and Handsome once more.

Brett clapped his hands with a small squeal. "Also, your outfit is on point. Those heels and that dress. No wonder you're being ogled." Brett winked at me, and I rolled my eyes at his enthusiasm.

"I'm going now." I couldn't stop myself from glancing back to look at the stranger. He almost seemed familiar. He raised his cup, and my cheeks flushed with embarrassment before I jumped into my car and sped away.

Chapter Three

More Information Required

Drake

Not many girls fit my criteria. I had a selection of three: a Matthews, a Sinclair, or a Romano. Isabella Matthews was a meek woman; she would be eaten alive. I considered her rather plain, even with a full face done up. Maria Sinclair had deep green eyes and a wonderful figure that I could picture sinking inside of to create an heir. There was no picture for Daniella Romano.

"Why does she have no picture?" I flicked through her file. There was only her date of birth. No mention of higher education. Everything else was completely blank. "Why is there nothing on this girl?" I glanced around at Jackson and Marcus. Both avoided looking in my direction.

"She got pregnant out of wedlock and was excommunicated." Jackson rubbed the back of his neck. Nothing could make this girl more perfect; she went against the norm, and I would enjoy her fight. She fought the system, and I needed someone strong – someone who can stand up for herself.

"Where is she now?" I was intrigued by how someone managed to escape the organisation. We kept to ourselves; we had to for the sake of our survival, and covens had rules. If anyone broke those rules, they were excommunicated. A baby out of wedlock wasn't worthy of this. I pondered the circumstances.

"Her stepmother doesn't know, the baby daddy is dead, and the baby is a question mark." Jackson shrugged. The lack of information about this girl frustrated me. "Not sure what she had or if she even had the baby. I suppose at least she is fertile." His smile was unnerving.

I cleared my throat. "Find her. I want to see this one in person." I slammed the folder down, eager to know what this girl looked like.

✦

Marcus found Daniella later that day; this girl couldn't be more perfect as my wife. She had strength; she made herself something from nothing. I went for a drive to her small town, and after her bank statements showed she visited the same café every morning, I planted myself there with my tablet to work. Even though I ran an entire coven, I still had to earn a wage in the real world.

My grandfather started a concreting business, which had flourished since, and was the most sought-after in Australia. Mages were taught basic skills to help assimilate into society to make money for the coven. Every person had to contribute to the coven in some way. Those on the council were given a senior management position, with many other smaller ones. I had to keep those under my care looked after.

I stared at the photo of Daniella in my hand. No social media, no dating profiles. She was scared and stayed away from anything that could be linked to finding her. Her mother was a beauty. I remember meeting her years ago.

The bell chimed, and I glanced up to see a stunning woman enter with red hair that flowed down her back. Her grey eyes were hypnotic, and she had curves and a perfect arse. Her boots sat just below her knee, complementing a charcoal woollen dress, and I noted her breasts would fit nicely in my palms. My cock hardened at the very sight of her. Pure fucking perfection. Her smile lit up the room, and I couldn't tear my eyes away. I watched her intently, at her small gestures. When she touched the man behind the counter, rage surged through my body. I wanted to rip him to pieces. She showed no interest in him, yet she agreed to drinks later. Her eyes found mine, her face pensive. I wondered if she remembered me. I had visited her house once, never meeting her. I knew now she was mine, and I would take her as my wife.

Chapter Four

Party Time

Daniella

The meeting went long, as it normally did, with some of my colleagues asking stupid questions that had already been answered. There was always one who asked the same question, in different ways, hoping to get a different response. I swear they did it on purpose. The politics that came with being a teacher, was just bullshit. At least growing up within the organisation taught me one thing about politics: you follow the rules or you are dead. If only we could implement that ideology here, except not death, more you're fired. I chuckled. Sam nudged me to stop, her eyes glaring as I rolled mine back at her. I sighed before continuing to doodle in my notebook. I just wanted to be home and relax. Finally, our principal clapped his hands in his casual manner, which I swear was to cover his anxiety more than to get people's attention.

"I almost forgot we have a new staff member joining us. Kris, who came all the way from Melbourne. Let's give him a warm country welcome." He gestured behind us, holding out his arm and motioning for him to come to the front.

Everybody clapped. I was particularly tired today after a restless sleep last night, plagued with thoughts of my siblings and hoping they were alright. A swift elbow to the ribs shook me from my thoughts. I turned to glare at Sam when I noticed her reason. Teachers were expected to dress professionally, but the man before us was skirting that very fine line.

His white shirt was unbuttoned a little too far, revealing a toned chest. He crossed his arms, showing off his thick forearms and bulging biceps, which threatened to rip the seams of his clothes. His intense hazel eyes locked onto mine.

"Daniella, he is fucking finnnnne." She drew out the word.

"Everyone, this is Kris Fields. He is our newest English teacher here at our illustrious college and will be teaching plenty of eager young minds in the years to come. I need volunteers or a mentor to help him settle into our school."

Sam's hand shot in the air. I rolled my eyes. That honestly didn't shock me. "I would offer, but considering I am head of English and literacy, I think it is important to separate, but Daniella has a very nurturing personality."

I wasn't a violent person, but in that moment, I really wanted to punch Sam in the fucking head. What the hell was she thinking? This wasn't a dating pool; she couldn't pimp me out because she had a husband and family. I clenched my fists before forcing a smile on my face. Sam had a leadership position, and talking over her in this moment would look dreadful to my boss.

"Sounds like a great idea," I said politely, giving Sam an angry look, who plastered an innocent smile on her face, like butter wouldn't melt.

"Thanks, Dani. I think that about wraps it up. Any questions, send an email. Go home. We have taken enough of your time tonight, and you can come in early tomorrow." Everyone laughed at his comment. He was way too casual to be a principal, but it worked, surprisingly. I stood, stretching my legs out, when Sam pushed me playfully.

"Are you about done?" I walked back to our office, throwing my book on the desk and plonking onto my chair. "I might have zoned out during that meeting after the twenty inane questions, but you had no right to volunteer me for that position." I clicked my pen fiercely, listening to the constant noise in my ear, wondering if it would break.

"It's only because I love you. Now, come on, we have dinner and then we are going out for drinks. Brett told me you agreed."

"I hate the way you guys gang up against me." I poked my tongue out at her.

"It's only because we want what is best for you. Now go home"—she flapped her hand in front of her nose—"have a shower 'cause you smell, and meet me at six." I went to sniff myself before realising she was only joking. I threw my pen at her for laughing at me, before she grabbed her bag and left.

I waited a few moments before packing my stuff. A knock broke my focus, and I peered up to see Kris enter. A small smile on his face while he stood awkwardly in the doorway.

"You sure look thrilled to be my mentor." There was a hint of humour in his voice before he cleared his throat.

"Sorry, it's not that. Sam has the best intentions, but honestly, she can be, excuse my language, a fucking idiot sometimes. I'll be your mentor." I pointed to the empty desk in the corner. "This will be your desk. Feel free to bring your stuff in tomorrow or even tonight. I'm not sure what time the office closes, but you still might have some time."

I continued packing. "Are you going somewhere?" he asked, watching me throw more items in my bag.

"Yes, sorry. I'm not trying to be rude." I paused, my eyes meeting his. "I'm going out with Sam and a few others tonight. It's just to the local pub, the only one in town, and you are welcome to join us. No pressure, of course."

"Wow, first day here and already getting asked out on a date," he said, and I was unable to read if it was a joke or serious.

"What? No, I'm not." I noticed the smirk on his face, and I watched his hand reach up to rub his chin. "Oh, it's going to be like that, is it?"

He nodded. "I'll see you tonight, Dani."

"Sounds good. Maybe try to wear a shirt that is your actual size. The locals might not like all that out in the open."

He threw his head back and laughed. I spun on my heel and left for my car.

I unlocked my phone, hoping to receive a message from my siblings, just once. If they did, it would be disastrous for them, but I wished for it. Not necessarily my father, but I wished for them. The engine purred to life, and I drove my seven minutes home. I noticed a bouquet of red roses at my door. I parked my car in the garage before heading to the door to bring them inside. They were stunning. I had never received flowers like this. I placed them into a vase while searching for a note, but came up empty. It was probably Sam and Brett, who both wanted me to move on and start dating again. I popped outside to check the letterbox, and it was empty, but the roses inspired words for a song in my head.

The roses wilting in the winter air, a reminder that I walk alone, my steps echoing in the dark, the only place I've ever known.

I sighed before smelling their delicious aroma. I hated how my brain automatically thought of magic. Witches were born with one of the specialities—Fire, Water, Earth, and Air. My family was Earth or Water. I didn't need to linger on the idea of what I missed out on. I had a new life, a better life. Even if my heart yearned for more. I never felt complete.

I showered and searched through my robe for an outfit. I could hear Sam's voice in my head, telling me to dress a little more provocatively, and tonight, I would. For tonight, I would be brave.

Chapter Five

Chance Encounter

Drake

I watched her arse sway to the music; the tight black dress left little to the imagination. I salivated at the thought of her sitting on my face. I imagined her tits bouncing while she rode my cock. I had never been harder in my life. There was something about her, an allure, a magnetism that didn't seem possible. I downed another whiskey before a full-figured young woman walked over, her face covered with a mischievous smile and her hair in a bun.

"She's hot, horny, and single. You should go and tap that." I snorted at her remark, whoring her friend out in that manner.

"I didn't realise I needed your permission," I said, solely focused on my soon-to-be wife.

She slid onto the stool beside me as the bartender filled my glass before pouring her another two. "She wants it, but she's too shy, and the best part is, our toilets are rather spacious. Big enough for two people." She winked suggestively.

"You're cheap and disgusting to speak of your friend in that way. She has class, something you'll never have," I snapped at her, my anger only growing stronger at the degrading way she spoke about her.

She glared at me. "You're a creep." She attempted to throw her glass at me, but Marcus grabbed her arm. I waved at him, wordlessly ordering him to escort her away. Nobody knew who I was here, and I rather liked it.

Her friend was right, I needed to sink deep into her cunt and feel it clench around me, milking every drop of my cum. Daniella made her way to the bathroom, and I moved quickly. I waited outside. I wasn't thinking; I only knew I needed to be inside her. My cock couldn't take any more; it ached to feel her. She stumbled out of the toilet, falling into my arms. Her eyes found mine before she smiled, reaching up and kissing my lips. I groaned at the taste of her strawberry gloss.

"Hello, handsome," she whispered, her breath erratic. Her eyes told me exactly what she needed. I motioned to the door she just exited from, taking her hand and kissing it. "Shall we?" she purred, leading the way. I motioned for another guard, Vince, to stand watch.

"I need to warn you, I can't be gentle." She giggled and locked the door to the toilet. Her eyes lingered over my groin, my cock straining to be free.

"Shall we bring him out to play?"

This was either her or the alcohol talking with confidence. I worried, but I watched her walk and listened to her words; she wasn't drunk, just tipsy. I pulled her hand, and she landed against my frame.

"I have to ask, how badly do you want it?" My hands roamed down her body, squeezing that perfect arse.

"So fucking badly." She admitted.

I kissed her, licking her lips to open that sweet mouth. I looked forward to the day she would wrap her mouth around my cock. I groaned at the thought, my lips moving down her jaw to her neck as I nibbled into the crease.

Her hands played with my hair. I had never experienced a touch that turned me on more, and I'd had plenty of pussy. I couldn't hold back any longer. I spun her around, her arse pressing against my cock. I wished I could ram inside her right now.

Kissing the back of her neck, my hand slid down her body, feeling the seam of her underwear. "Take them off," I growled.

She moved quickly, pulling them off and flinging them to the floor. My hand found its way down, rubbing her cunt to find just how wet she was for me. "You're fucking perfect." I plunged a finger inside; her tight pussy could have swallowed it whole. My cock hardened further before I picked up a steady rhythm. Her moans filled the air, and I pushed another finger in. "That's right, moan louder, princess. That's a good girl." She tightened further, as if it were possible, before her release. I unbuckled my belt, pushing her legs wider before thrusting inside. She felt better than I imagined—warm, soft, and so fucking tight. I had to force myself to hold back my release. I considered wrapping him, but this girl would be my wife. She could milk me dry. I brought my hand up to grab her throat, forcing her to look in the mirror. "Watch yourself as you take my dick like a good little slut." Something flashed in her eyes before she gritted her teeth.

"I'm not a slut." She shook her shoulders and body. "We're done. Get out of me." Her voice sounded broken, weak. She pulled her dress down and ran from the room. I stood, holding my hard dick in my hands. I pulled my pants up, leaving the toilet before scanning the bar, but she had already left. I nodded to Marcus, who simply shrugged.

What the hell happened?

CHAPTER SIX

THE NEXT DAY

DANIELLA

I wanted it last night, but hearing that word — the one I hate more than anything: *slut*. Before I even got pregnant, my father called me a slut every single day. I heard it more than I love you. I shuddered at the thought of the pain I endured from him daily. I walked into my office, forcing a fake smile on my face and removing my sunglasses.

"Good morning, everyone." My hangover lingered, but the life of an adult meant you had to carry on. There was no rest for the wicked.

"Morning, Dani. I heard you had some fun last night." Neil wriggled his eyebrows suggestively.

"Um, is that not sexual harassment, Neil?" I mumbled, plonking my bag onto my desk.

The door opened, breaking my thoughts and interrupting the conversation.

"And here is our degenerate staffroom, filled with misfits, and you met Daniella last night. Your mentor, who should have shown you around the school this morning." Sam winked at me. Our office was hardly ever professional, but we didn't have to be perfect all the time. "Everyone, this is Kris Fields. He was introduced at the staff meeting last night. As our illustrious principal announced, he is our newest English teacher here at our wonderful college."

Nate coughed, coffee coming out of his nose. He stood and offered his hand, introducing himself. All others followed before I stood and strolled over, offering my hand as all the others had before me.

"Hello again. Sorry about missing the tour this morning. I am feeling a little under the weather."

Returning the handshake, his grip was strong. I could feel a pulse under his skin. An odd sensation I had never felt before. His auburn hair was short, wavy, and to his ears. It was unruly and not perfectly styled. He wore the same outfit as yesterday—grey slacks and a white shirt with several buttons undone, revealing a sculpted chest and just enough hair to draw the eye without distraction. A sparkle drew my eyes to his necklace, the 'Eye of Horus'.

"Yes, did you enjoy the celebrations last night? Sorry about my non-attendance. I wanted to rest before my first big day here." He rubbed his hands together eagerly.

I brushed off his concern without a wave. Then something shimmered. It was subtle. My eyes narrowed at the sight, as though it was dragging my attention toward it.

"That's…odd." I stepped closer, pointing at the black chain where a faint golden symbol flickered, almost shimmering against the dark metal.

"I found it at a market and thought it looked cool." He shrugged nonchalantly.

"Wait, you don't know anything about the Eye of Horus?" I queried. Why would he wear something without understanding the meaning? My witchy brain always went nuts on people who didn't understand the power that surrounded them.

"Nah, what does it mean?" he asked, his voice low and edged with a kind of curiosity, like he already knew. He picked it up, toying with it between his thick fingers and manicured nails. I noticed how close we were—his presence pressing in just enough to make me step back, needing a breath of space. That's when his cologne hit me, masculine and, wow, seductive. It smelt like a forest after a storm, but something else lingered, a spice. It was dangerous, lingering between us, overwhelming my senses. I glanced up, noticing a faint twinkle in his eyes. I couldn't decipher it, but it wasn't innocent.

"It is a symbol of protection, healing, power, and restoration. It is connected to the myth of Horus, who lost his eye during a battle. The eye was eventually restored and became a symbol of wholeness and renewal."

"NERD!" Sam shouted, and I rolled my eyes and took a seat.

"Welcome, Kris." Sam liked to eclipse the room with her boisterous attitude, while I preferred to work on my own and keep to myself. I only spoke to Sam because we shared the same dark humour. "See you all at lunch," I said, standing and leaving for first period.

✦

I taught for the first four periods before heading out for a yard duty, the fresh air helping to alleviate the thumping in my head. The sun beamed down, warming my body from head to toe. I was forever grateful for the way the earth could give you exactly what you needed. The Wiccan part of me could live off whatever she gave us. I never enjoyed the way the Coven would act like we were superior to other beings, and by that, I meant all of them. Not just humans, but other supernatural creatures too.

The ones that arrived after dark, the ones that hunted and preyed on the innocent. It didn't help that I never declared any powers. The night before my transcendence into my powers, I discovered the baby growing in my belly. I knew I couldn't stay. I knew I had an out, and I was taking it. John, my baby's father, and I ran. I never expected my father to find us. John sacrificed himself for me, and I would always cherish him for that.

John was the only man who showed me real kindness. I wrote a letter to our son about it. I knew he might inherit powers because he had a mixed bloodline, but I didn't care. He was safe, and that was all I needed to know. My phone buzzed. I knew the number; it was one I could never forget. I switched my phone off. I didn't need this, not today, not with my head hurting.

"Penny for your thoughts?" A deep voice cut through the fog in my brain.

I spun to see Kris behind me, wearing the same fluorescent orange vest and glasses. I smiled before continuing to walk.

"How has your day been so far? Sorry if Sam has been driving you insane in the office. She means well, if not a little over the top. I'm sure you've noticed that already."

"I think it's a little hard not to notice." He chuckled before I joined him. He cleared his throat. "The day has been good. The kids are certainly not what I expected. So many of them are kind, while others are very much country bumpkins whose sole focus

is to farm. Not that there's anything wrong with that, just…"
He paused, clicking his finger while trying to find the polite
words.

"It's different from the city. Trust me, I get it. I grew up in
the city before moving out here. I prefer the community." I
took a deep breath, smelling the fresh air.

"Oh, whereabouts?" he queried, and part of me worried, while
the other pushed aside the doubt. Making new friends wasn't
necessarily a bad thing.

"I grew up in Balwyn. Shhh, don't tell the others." I winked
at him.

"Ah, I was Canterbury."

I poked my nose toward the sky. "Oh, Canterbury, yes, yes
indeed," I said with a posh accent.

The bell rang, and we walked back to our office. Not speaking,
just moving, our steps in sync. I buried myself in marking for
the rest of the afternoon, but my brain continually thought back
to my lack of magical powers. My mother was an Earth power
while my father had Water. I never showed promise in either.
Even when compared to my brother, who seemed to master their
skills at an early age. I often wondered if I had been adopted, but
I looked exactly like my mother; her beauty incomparable. Men
sought her for years before she agreed to be with my father. I wish
she'd never died in childbirth. I never had the chance to know

her. My stepmother raised me, and I'll always be grateful to her, even though she never protected me from him.

"Dani…Dani…DANI!" I turned to see Sam yelling at me. I smiled at her.

"Yeah, what's up?" I put my pen down before I followed her eyes, staring at the page. The edge of the paper appeared black, almost like it had been burnt.

"What the hell is that?" she asked.

"I have no idea. Maybe I had something on my hand." I inspected it closer, but came up empty. How odd. "Anyway, was that all you wanted?"

"No." She pushed my arm playfully. "How did it go last night?"

My thoughts drifted to last night in my slightly tipsy state, his strong hands on my body, his rough voice. He was sexy as hell, exactly what I needed to clean out the cobwebs, even if it lasted barely a minute. I'd only been with three men, and his was by far the thickest out of them all. I had never felt so full. His touch lit my body on fire.

"Yeah, fine." I brushed it off. How could I explain that he called me the one word that brought back my nightmares? A reminder of the innocence that I lost, the innocence that could never be returned.

"Fine, no, Dani. He was a fine specimen; he was the type of man that you would get on your knees for. He could contort my body to do whatever he wanted. There is nothing fine about that. I mean, his voice was just pure sin, the tattoos he hid added to the red flag, a danger warning, but I would have done anything for a piece of that fine arse."

My cheeks blushed. "Sam, you're so crude sometimes. I don't know how you speak so dirty, but we started, and he said something…and I stopped and ran home. He…he just triggered a memory, and no, I don't want to talk about it. I won't ever see him again, and I don't ever want to."

"Alright, alright. I won't. I just wanted you to let loose for one night, be someone a little more carefree, and just let go and enjoy."

A small smile spread over my face. "I know, Sam, and I appreciate you, but sometimes, those days are just too hard." She turned back to her work; she would never understand what I knew. Sam stood up and left the office to attend a leadership meeting.

"You can have fun without letting go," Kris's voice echoed behind me, and I bit my pen while spinning to see his face.

"Oh, really?" I quirked my brow at him.

"Yeah, maybe after I settle in, I could show you how." Blood rushed to my cheeks, the lack of makeup today probably making me look like a fucking glowing red light.

CHAPTER SEVEN

DADDY DOWRY

DRAKE

I thrummed my fingers on the desk. I wasn't a patient man, and Giuseppe tested this patience. Nico opened the door. Giuseppe used to be a powerful man, but he trusted the wrong people and cost my business thousands. The council never treated him the same again. His short stature and protruding gut made me wonder how he produced a daughter as beautiful as Daniella.

"What's the meaning of this, Drake? I detest being summoned." Giuseppe unfastened the buttons on his suit jacket while I rubbed the scar on my lip, a reminder of somebody's strong hand when I was a boy.

"Sit." I sat straighter to assert my dominance over this meagre man. I motioned to the chair. Giuseppe glared at me before I moved to stand, my arms flexing in anger. Fear flashed over his features as he plonked on his fat arse, the chair squeaking in pain.

"Now, we need to discuss your daughter, Daniella." I cleared my throat, getting closer to achieving my goal.

"I have no such daughter by that name. I have a son, Bracken, and a daughter named Willow." His words were devoid of emotion, and I pondered why. She only had a baby. It didn't seem like a massive issue for this type of contempt.

"Giuseppe, I am aware that Daniella is your daughter, and I have no time for your bullshit. Are you willing to speak or will you continue with this idiotic façade?" I stood, making my way over to the drinks trolley and pouring myself a glass of scotch. He lifted his hand, and I smirked; he wouldn't be getting any of my premium liquor.

"What about her? I sent her away for her crimes against the Coven. She shamed us by fucking an outsider."

"Now, I may not be as old as you, but I don't remember seeing those rules. The child wouldn't be allowed inside the Coven unless it showed promise of sharing the mother's gift. It's not a reason to banish your child unless there's more that you have yet to reveal?" I questioned, lifting the liquor to my lips and savouring the taste on my tongue.

He shook his head. "What do you want with her?" he asked, ignoring my remark, which told me he was hiding something. Interesting. I wondered what it could be.

"As you're aware, the council has declared that I need an heir. I need a child to continue my bloodline as High Mage. I've selected Daniella to be my wife. I called you here to discuss a dowry." I didn't quite understand why I had to pay a dowry to my bride's family to marry her. Should it not be enough that I was taking responsibility for her from this moment on? She would be mine.

"I would appreciate it if you could pay off the loan on my house," he said, fidgeting with his buttons.

"How much?"

"Only one hundred thousand." I scoffed at that small amount. It was almost a bargain when I thought of just how good her arse looked in that tight black dress the other day. I was hard again, and I briefly thought about how tight her pussy was. I bit into my lip to stop the dirty thoughts of wanting her juices on my face.

I cleared my throat. "Done. Anything else?"

"No, I'm happy with that."

"Excellent. It shall be deposited into your account tomorrow. What else can you tell me about your daughter?" I asked him, sitting up straighter. If he had any insight into my future wife, it might help me gain her favour. She ran away from me while I was balls deep inside her. It wasn't the norm, and had never happened to me in the past.

"I don't know much about her. She was always in trouble; she never listened to us. She was rude, abrupt, and promiscuous. There is no telling how many men she had lain with. When we discovered that she had a baby in her womb, I chose to excommunicate her. Just before her transcendence. A pity, really."

I sighed. It didn't tell me a lot. "All I hear is how much you don't know your daughter. I met her, and I've already discovered her strength and her willingness to strive for more. She worked hard for everything she has. That isn't the girl you describe. Are you aware that she educates the minds of young teens?"

"People change," he mumbled.

"Not that much." I pushed the envelope towards him, waiting for the signature to approve our union. I flicked my fingers to play with a flame between them, watching it roll over my knuckles. I'd rarely used the full extent of my Fire magic since my father's death. I had enough power without having to use it, but while Giuseppe and his family had Earth, Water, and Air magic, he was nowhere near as strong as I.

"What else are you not telling me?" I pressed for more.

I stood, allowing small flames to drop onto the table, slowly building in strength. His eyes focused solely on the fire that threatened to eat him alive. Sweat gathered on his brow, and I watched small droplets run down his cheek. "That's not sweat from fire, that's from fear. I don't play games. What else do I need to know about her? She will be my wife."

"Good luck. She'll fight you more than fuck you." Her father spat such hatred towards her. "She won't be able to satisfy you." He signed the documents, taking his copy and pushing the others toward me.

I slammed my fist on the table. "You dare speak of my wife in that manner again, and it'll be the last thing that you ever do. Get out of my office before I decide to no longer pay the dowry."

Giuseppe scampered away, and I snapped my fingers to extinguish the flames, smirking at his cowardice. No evidence of fire lingered. I needed to see what was going on with Daniella. I wondered what she was up to. I checked the GPS on her phone to discover that she was still at work. A woman had never had this effect on me, wanting to know where she was and why she had so many secrets. I would keep an eye on her tonight and collect her tomorrow to begin our life together.

I downed my chilled glass of scotch in preparation for alerting the council of the woman I had selected to be my wife. Daniella Romano—my little firecracker, *my inferno*, my newest obsession. Her father had agreed, and the dowry would be paid tomorrow. Tonight was simply a formality of my intentions with their approval, but I doubted any pushback. They knew not to question my judgements.

Marcus and Vince drove to our building on Collins Street, not hidden, but unknown to the human world. We parked in the underground car park. They waited in the car as Jackson and I pushed open the double doors, clapping as I entered. "Gentlemen, I have news. You requested that I find a wife to provide an heir and secure the future of our Coven. You'll be pleased with my selection of Giuseppe's daughter, Daniella Romano. She will be informed of this decision tomorrow. Now, what other matters must be discussed?"

I took a seat at the head of the table, leaning back in the chair and waiting for any trivial item they wished to discuss. The meetings were tedious but necessary, especially with the increase in attacks from the Morteferi. I wished they would just vanish. I expected the normal rush of questions and complaints, but only silence echoed through the large space containing the ten family members of the council. I glanced at my Arcanum, who shrugged, his brow creasing at the lack of whining from their mouths.

"What, are you shocked that I selected a wife sooner than you predicted?" I questioned, sitting straighter, unsure of what had rendered them so silent.

"I think it's more of who your selection is," Stefan Wood uttered, staring at the table, unable to meet my gaze as I glared at him.

"Please explain, Stefan." I stood, my hands firmly placed on the table. I could feel the flames threatening to envelope the entire room and burn these pathetic arseholes to the ground.

"Daniella was excommunicated for her crimes against the Coven, and you wish for her to return."

I stood aghast for a moment. Nobody had dared question me since I removed my tyrannical father from his position of power, and here stood an Earth user, questioning Daniella because of her unplanned pregnancy. I moved toward Stefan, whose eyes continued to stare into the table that he would probably prefer to be hiding under. My hands landed on the back of his leather chair, and I exhaled.

"Stefan, I always encourage those on the council to voice their opinions. I welcome it, even. But on this occasion, you've spoken about the woman whom I have selected to wed, the woman who will bear my children and will help run this Coven. What crimes has she committed against us?" I queried, knowing this to have come from Giuseppe.

"The laws state that those cast out may never return. Excommunication is reserved only for the gravest crimes committed against the Coven." His voice croaked.

I chuckled. "Oh, Stefan. My father would remove any member that the council requested, some without merit, and Daniella fits that category. She was excommunicated for conceiving a child with an outsider. It's hardly a breach of our rules. I think it was more embarrassment from her father than the actual crime committed. Or do you know of something that I don't?"

I stared at Giuseppe, at the smirk playing over his lips. He wanted to cause this disharmony within my council. He'd been sly since the day he'd been invited to join. I needed to send a message. Fire warmed my blood, ready for whatever I needed.

"Any Mage within the Coven should never lie with an outsider. A High Mage such as yourself should select a partner with more appropriate attributes. I believe Johannes's daughter is more suitable." My eyes snapped in his direction, and he raised his hands and shook his head.

I'd had enough of this shit; my hands erupted in flames. I slammed my hands onto Stefan's shoulders. The fire took control, and his screams filled the room before all that remained was the dirt that represented the piece of shit that he was.

"Does anybody else dare to question my choice?" All heads shook, and their lips remained tightly closed. I returned to my seat before I looked in the direction of Giuseppe, whose face was now devoid of that smirk. I had sent a message tonight; nobody would dare to question her again.

Chapter Eight

Pain From the Past

Daniella

I dumped my bags under the hall table. I had no intention of doing any work tonight. Being hungover and dealing with bratty kids was enough for me. I ordered a pizza and plopped myself onto the couch. This was where I would stay all night. I needed to watch trash TV and work on my songs.

I wondered if Sam's comment from earlier was right. Should I start dating again? I had so much baggage that I worried nobody would ever accept me. Even Sam had no idea who I was. I had no social media for this reason; I had to hide. The organisation had resources, and it was sheer luck that I hadn't already been discovered. I downloaded a dating app, but as soon as it asked for a photo, I threw my phone away. Absolutely pointless even trying to consider it. I grabbed the remote to put on something stupid and started to write.

The past keeps me in a cage, a lock I cannot break

The pain from those I should have trusted, I wish someone would see,

What is truly inside of me?

The doorbell rang, and throwing my journal down, I jumped up to answer the door. My stomach grumbled.

"Hello, Daniella. Or is it Dani now?"

I froze. My heart thumped harder in my chest, fear creeping through my system as the man I hated stood before me. A man I never wished to see again, the reason I ran away, the reason I did everything. Bile rose in my throat. My father stood before me; he had aged, and it didn't agree with him. His suit was too tight, but his hair had thinned on the sides. What was once sprinkled with grey was now fully white.

"You haven't aged well." I tried to slam the door, but he pushed himself into my apartment.

"You've done well for yourself. Finished a degree, bought a house, working full time. I expected less from you. Where's the bastard child? " I crossed my arms. I couldn't let his words hurt me.

"I never had it." Taking a deep breath at my lie, I continued, "Please, keep the insults coming. I'm used to your abuse, both physical and mental. How is your wife? Still a drunk with no idea of how fucking sick you are?" He moved closer. "Raise your hand to me and I will fucking kill you." My voice sounded foreign. He registered the threat and took a seat at my circular dining table.

"I suppose you have done something right." He nodded towards the red roses.

"What's that? Getting away from you and starting fresh?" I fired back.

He snorted while he observed the room around him, no doubt judging. "No, you managed to snag yourself a good husband."

"What the hell are you talking about? I'm not married. I'm not even dating anyone." I stayed close to the front door, ready to run if I needed to. An evil smirk played over his face, and I watched his eyes crinkle.

"Drake found you rather appealing and has requested your hand in marriage, and I agreed." He took out an envelope, placing it on the table and sliding it closer to me.

That name sounded familiar. "Who the fuck is Drake? I'm not an object to be sold."

"Daniella, you should know by now, the life in the Coven. You own nothing. I control your life." I snatched the envelope, opening it to see the man from the bar. His name and licence beside my own on a marriage licence form. He placed a black shiny ring box on the table. The man was too pathetic to even give me the ring himself. I ripped it to pieces, throwing it at my father.

"This means nothing," I noted, hoping he didn't see my fear.

"Are you that naïve to think it was the only copy? It has already been filed. You will be married this weekend." He stood, grabbing his lapels and fixing them. He appeared rather pleased with himself.

"Like hell I will. I won't turn up." I picked up the box, throwing it at him. I wasn't going to submit to the Coven's rules.

"Do you honestly think you can run from the High Mage?" He chuckled, his belly shifting with the movement, a grotesque display, but more from the man than his body.

"I ran from you and your resources." My heart thumped in my chest, the life I ran from suddenly catching up to me. My fists clenched. I wanted to hurt this man. How did this happen?

"Yes, but he found you in a day. Good luck, Daniella." He winked and moved toward the door.

"Go fuck yourself, Giuseppe. Go home to your fake happy home!" I shouted, my voice shaky.

"It became happy the moment you were gone," he snarked ineffectively.

"I doubt that. You didn't have a toy to play with anymore." He glared at me, but I'd never forget what he did to me. It lived with me every single day.

"He paid for you, and you *will* be the perfect wife."

"What happens if he discovers the truth about your dodgy deals? How you have worked against them?" I declared, he had to remember that I knew his secrets.

"You wouldn't dare." He gritted his teeth, but I had no fear of this man. I hadn't for years. He couldn't hurt me anymore. I was no longer a child.

"I would see you dead or excommunicated. The perfect wedding present," I snarled.

He closed the door. My heart shattered into a million pieces, and my knees buckled. The pain resurfaced, the buried memories. I thought I was past this.

Chapter Nine

Not the Life I Want.

Daniella

I knew I needed to run. I couldn't stay. I would forever be trapped. I had no idea how they found me. I had been so careful. I changed my name, changed everything. The sight of my father brought back all the fear of my past life. The control, the power, the murders. I climbed into the crawlspace in the roof, opening my safe and pulling out the money to run and hopefully start again. I wouldn't be able to say goodbye. I couldn't risk my friends' lives. His father was relentless, and Drake would be the same—ruthless and deadly.

I threw my suitcase down, dust filling the laundry. I jumped down and plopped it onto my bed, picking what little clothes I could. If they came looking for me, I wanted it to look as if I had been kidnapped rather than running away. It seemed more logical, but my head was scattered with thoughts and memories.

I had so much to do; half of me worried about my son, but I had no tie to him. The suitcase was packed. I would drive my car as far as I could before dumping it for another, and making my way on public transport. There seemed to be nobody around, no suspicious cars outside. I paced around the house for hours. I couldn't leave too early and risk people seeing me. It had to be when most were sleeping. The time ticked over to one a.m. The world was quiet, and the streets were silent.

I packed the car, standing in front of the home I had worked so hard for. I shook off my emotions; I couldn't be weak. I had a new life waiting for me. I would change my hair when I arrived at my new place, wherever that would be. Maybe I would try blonde. The car roared to life, and I moved it into drive, ready to start the journey. It almost felt too easy. Drake would surely have put people to watch me. I would take what I could. Goodbye, Trafalgar.

Driving further into the regional areas of Victoria, I looked for a small town to start over. I could drive for two to three hours before needing a nap or a break. Darkness surrounded me, but my mind raced, thinking about Sam.

I pulled over for a moment, my fingers hesitating over the screen, my eyes welling with tears. She annoyed me, but she was a good friend.

Thank you for being the best friend that I could ever ask for. You reminded me that I didn't have to hide the darkest parts of myself. I will forever be grateful for your friendship. Love always D xo

It was a calculated risk, but one I needed to take for my own sanity. I threw my phone out the window and continued to drive. My eyes began to flutter with exhaustion, and my coffee cup was dry. My GPS indicated a small motel not much further ahead, so I turned off the road and headed toward it. Thankfully, the lights were on, and they were still open. I pulled up, checking that I wasn't followed before hopping out. I entered the tiny office that smelt of mothballs.

The older gentleman glanced up. "How can we help you?"

"I need a room for one night." I kept it short and sweet, scanning the room and feeling vulnerable with the amount of curtainless windows in this office.

"That'll be one hundred dollars, and I'll need ya ID." He crossed his arms, his brow quirking. I should've been a little nicer.

"How about two hundred and no ID?" I counted the money for him to see before removing it from my wallet and holding it in the air.

He cast his eyes down, obviously noticing that there was more that I could give. "Three." He blew his nose and hocked up a log of phlegm. Gross. I'd be blocking the door tonight.

If I got to keep my safety and anonymity, fine. I slid the money over before taking the key. I locked the door and closed the curtain, leaving the lights and television off. Changing into pyjamas didn't seem worth the effort, so I slipped off my pants and climbed into bed. For a moment, I considered keeping my shoes on, but something about wearing them under the covers felt wrong.

I woke to the sun shining on my face, but unease curdled in my stomach, an odd sensation that I was being watched; I wasn't alone. The floor creaked, and I shot up with sleepy eyes to scan my surroundings.

"Good morning, Daniella." I knew that deep voice. I checked the time: nine a.m. My eyes adjusted to see his massive frame sitting on the dusty armchair with his legs crossed. His tattoos were hidden beneath his collar, there was a scar on his eyebrow, and his dark features exuded power. I noticed his position was further from the door. If I were quick, I could grab the keys and run. I left the money in the car for this reason. His eyes were trained on my every move. I stood slowly and turned toward him.

"What do you want?" I watched his finger rub the scar on his lip, his eyes sweeping over my naked legs. My body on full display, I wanted to use this to my advantage, if possible, but I doubted a powerful man like Drake would be so easily influenced by me. I pulled my hair off my face in preparation to make my move.

"I believe you are already aware"—he peered at my finger—"but I see no ring on your finger. Was it not good enough for you?" He smirked. I rolled my eyes at his cocky demeanour. I never opened the box that my father delivered yesterday.

"I cannot accept your proposal. It's very kind, but I'm quite alright being a single gal, floating my way through different men. I like to be free, and I don't want to be tied down. I'm a free spirit. A bit of a loosey goosey." His glare intensified, his eyes trained on my own before they shifted toward the keys, where my hands were inching closer to grab them and bolt.

"Daniella." His voice laced with a warning that I ignored, and I snatched the keys from the table and ran to the door, throwing it open, only to run into a solid mass. A hand wrapped around my throat, throwing me backwards onto the bed. "DO NOT touch her!" Drake shouted at the man. I scrambled to a corner before finding my feet to reassess what to do next.

My hands trembled as I lifted them, palms open, fingers shaking. Tears blurred my vision, and the cool air touched my cheeks. My breathing was shallow, my chest heaving with the sudden rush of adrenaline. I didn't want this life. *I didn't want this.* He had to know that I wasn't built for Coven life.

"This doesn't need to go any further. Just let me go, and I'll disappear. Just pretend you couldn't find me. I'm sure there is another who would happily take the place of your wife. To help you run the Coven. I'm not that girl. I refuse to be that girl." I closed my eyes, knowing that I had no choice; once you were selected by the High Mage, there was no escape. You were his.

Drake stepped forward, his long, powerful legs moving closer. I had to fight. I rejected the idea of becoming a prisoner to the toxic underworld. I watched his strides before I swung my leg; he gripped my calf, throwing it away. He reached down, wrapping his arms around my waist, and I thrashed like crazy. He threw me onto the bed. I lunged, managing to connect my fist to his face. He grabbed my wrists, forcing them above my head. His eyes filled with a darkness that threatened to consume my entire soul, but it didn't scare me; something else lingered in his gaze.

"Get off me." I raged in his grip, moving my body to release his hands.

"Careful, Daniella. I may get other ideas if you keep rubbing on me that way." A sly smile spread over his face. "It felt so good being inside you the other night." The temperature in the room was increasing.

Desire pooled for a moment, with memories flashing in my mind, but I shook my head. "You disgust me." I brought my knee up, feeling it connect with his balls. His grasp loosened enough to escape, so I rolled off the bed and ran to the bathroom, locking the door behind me. It had a tiny window. I climbed up the rail in the shower, forcing the window open while I listened to the pounding on the door behind me.

"DANIELLA!" Drake shouted, and I jumped down into the soft grass only to see that I'd landed in a courtyard. Trapped. Fuck.

"Fuck me," I muttered, searching for an exit. There were two doors, and I selected the one to the left, pounding my fists against it. "Help! Please, help me!" The door swung open, revealing Drake standing before me, his face flush with anger, heat radiating from his muscular stature. Cautiously stepping backwards, I watched as his eyes filled with fire, a fire I had to escape. I spun, but not before he grabbed the back of my neck, twisting my body and slamming me into his chest.

"Big mistake, *my inferno*." I hocked up and spat at him. He wiped it off, and I spotted a syringe in his hand. I squirmed in his grip. "Sweet dreams, Daniella." The needle pierced my skin, the liquid stinging as it entered my system. My eyes grew heavy before his lips landed on mine. "I will enjoy our wedding night." His voice was the last words I heard before darkness took me.

Chapter Ten

The Engagement Begins

Daniella

My head throbbed and my eyes burned. I rubbed them to remove the excess sleep. Stretching out, I registered the sweet smell of maple bacon and eggs, and my mouth salivated. I shot up quickly, remembering the events of yesterday, the headache now making sense—the lingering effects of the drug. The man who kidnapped me, the man forcing me to marry him, was cooking me breakfast.

"I've called your principal, and you've been given the week off work with no pay, but you're exempt from writing up your classes this week. You don't even need to plan them; it's all taken care of." His voice echoed while I lay in bed, processing his words, and I barely moved.

How the hell could this man just take control of my entire life? I knew it was possible—after all, they had resources that the average person couldn't even begin to comprehend—but I never imagined it would happen so fast. It had only been a day since the forced engagement. A single day since I failed to escape this nightmare. I reached for my phone, only to remember I threw it out of the car to avoid being tracked, which clearly helped.

What happened to my normal life?

"Breakfast is ready," Drake called out from the kitchen. It was unnerving how cheerful he seemed with this whole situation, but he'd managed to get exactly what he wanted. A wife, a breeder for his heir. It disgusted me how some aspects of the Coven were so old-fashioned.

I refused to move, hoping to sink into the mattress and disappear. Pulling the covers over my head to bury the day and what my life would slowly become, the doona was yanked from my hands, and a small squeal escaped my mouth. I scrambled to my knees until I gathered myself.

"Do you mind?" I growled at him only for a moment. Until my eyes noticed his lack of clothing.

He stood before me, his chest heaving with frustration, his glare enough to make me fall to my knees in submission. His tattooed chest was on full display, each marking showing his journey to High Mage. One tattoo stood out—a broken arrow through his heart. His large, muscular frame managed to make my mouth water, and a pool of wetness gathered below. I lasered in on his biceps, watching them flex while he threw the blanket away. His nostrils flared, and his eyes filled with fire. His inked sleeves had intricate patterns showcasing just how much power he had. One flick of a wrist, and I'd be dead.

"When I tell you to come to breakfast, you come to fucking breakfast. Do you understand?" His voice was tight, each word forced through clenched teeth. Rage simmered just beneath the surface, like he was barely holding himself together. His hand flexed and curled again, over and over, like he was trying to wring the anger out of them.

I plastered a smile on my face, portraying no fear. "You don't own me, and you never will. If I wish to lie in bed, I'll lie in my bloody bed. Do you understand me?" My voice was sweet but laced with the threat of being my own person.

He grabbed my face, lifting me from the bed like I weighed nothing, and brought me closer to him. I didn't struggle. I had to keep my head clear and never let anger control me. The words my mother would always whisper to me.

"You'll be my wife. From this moment on, I'll control your every thought. It would be wise to remember where you stand with your High Mage."

I snorted at him. "It would be wise to know that I was excommunicated from your organisation for a reason, and you're a fool if you think that I would come back in so willingly and be a people pleaser."

He sniggered. "I'll enjoy breaking that spirit." He brought me closer to him, his eyes dropping to my lips briefly.

"Not before I break yours. I'll have you on your knees by the end of the week." I bared my teeth at him, not wanting to submit to this powerful man. He dropped me back to the bed, proceeding to laugh loudly.

"Oh"—he rubbed the scar on his lip, a smirk playing over it—"that's a position I'd enjoy. You covering my face in your juices…" He paused to readjust himself. "But we can focus on our mutual breaking over breakfast. I won't have a weak wife. Come eat, now." My stomach decided at that moment to grumble with hunger. He lifted an eyebrow, that infuriating smirk spreading like he already knew he'd won.

"Fine, but get out of my room." He turned to leave before stopping at the door, peering over his shoulder.

"You sure enjoyed the snuggles last night." He clicked his tongue and left, his laughter wafting through my tiny house.

My face froze, my cheeks blushing from embarrassment. I did remember waking up and cuddling into his chest for warmth before rolling away quickly.

✦

I ignored Drake's orders, dressing myself in a black skirt with tights and a grey blouse before fixing my hair into a ponytail. The kitchen smelled amazing with the bacon sizzling in the pan. He plated the food and slid it over the island bench.

Drake pushed a coffee toward me. "Cappuccino with one sugar." He sounded incredibly proud of this achievement when he spotted my clothing. "What are you wearing?" The cheerful demeanour was gone within seconds. His eyes filled with rage and lust. I hoped at just how good these clothes clung to my body and the cleavage on display.

I purposely leaned forward to give him a better look, his eyes drifting for a moment before he glanced at the plate of food. "Ah, clothes. Is there something wrong with them?" I sat up, grabbed my coffee, and took a sip. He rubbed his hands over his face.

"Did you not hear what I said? You are not going to work this week." He crossed his arms, and I used the opportunity to sneak a peek at his flexing muscles.

"I did andddd…I chose to ignore it," I said, drawing out the word before taking another sip of the coffee. At least he could make a good cup. "My students have an upcoming assessment, and I cannot skip the classes because you demand something. I'll be going for that lesson, which is only period one and two. Then I can return home to be your perfect *Stepford* wife." His jaw ticked.

His phone vibrated on the counter, and he picked it up to take the call.

He stepped out of the kitchen and into the bedroom, closing the door behind him. I quickly grabbed my bag, downed my coffee, and snatched a piece of bacon. I opened the door to see a car filled with his men and another standing beside the front door. Not at all obvious that somebody needed protecting. The entire town would be talking about this, no doubt. Every day here was a slow news day.

"Excuse me," I said with the sweetest voice, pushing between them and walking to my car.

One stepped back inside to inform his boss. Time was running out, and I turned the car to start the engine. It turned over a second time, and I tried for a third. Drake came out holding up a tiny spark plug. I slammed my fists into the wheel.

I opened the door. "Are you fucking kidding me?" I shouted at him.

"You'll be driven to work where one of my men will escort you." I closed the door, forcibly making my way over to him.

"They will *not* be allowed to enter the school grounds. It's trespassing, and it doesn't matter about the organisation. You don't own this town; you'll be escorted off the premises." He crossed his arms, and I watched his man whisper in his ear. I needed to think quickly about this. "You can have men stationed outside the school at each of the exits. My class is within view of the main car park." The men nodded to one another. "Honestly, who would even bother to harm me in a public area? It would only reveal their very existence."

Drake threw the spark plug toward me, which I caught, and quirked a brow, showing he was impressed. "You can drive yourself if you can put this back in. If not, you'll be driven." I glared at him; he had no idea that I could do this. I popped the hood of the car and opened the garage door. He watched while I searched for the tools that I needed. Drake shook his head.

"Marcus, fix it for her," he grumbled, shaking his head and walking inside. I admired his butt and broad shoulders. He was a fine specimen, even if he was an arsehole and twenty years older than me. Marcus took the necessary tools and fixed the car before I started the ignition.

Drake came out again, holding up a thermos with a beaming smile. "Another coffee and an engagement ring for my future wife." I took the coffee from him, but looked away, not wanting to watch while he placed the ring on my finger. He grabbed my hand, his grip tightening, and I struggled against him. "Don't forget. The organisation isn't to be discussed." He mocked me with talking marks, but I refused to call it what it was—my way of distancing myself from what I was born into.

"I remember. I was raised in it. I'll just have to see how good my acting skills are compared to my friends at work. We fell madly in love." I pretended to fan myself. "He's the perfect man. How did I get so lucky? I don't deserve him." He rolled his eyes and wandered inside as I giggled.

I walked into my classroom, glancing at the men stationed at the closest exit. I wondered what threat occurred for my principal to allow this to happen. I strolled in, setting up the room and writing notes on the board. I wanted to avoid seeing Sam and the awkward questions. Even though I pretended to be with Drake, I honestly had no idea how to explain it to her. I was now engaged to a man I didn't know. If I dared to tell her the truth, and Drake discovered that, he would silence her. *Permanently.*

I explained the assessment task to my students, going around answering all their questions. The double period was nearly finished when I received a message from Sam through our teacher portal, asking me to come and see her. Not long after, I received an email from Drake, the email line: 'Home straight away.'

I would have around ten minutes to speak with Sam if I wanted to. I had to risk it. I rushed from class to my office, grabbing Sam's hand and pulling her into a separate classroom. I needed a friend. I had to tell her the truth.

"Whoa, slow down." She winked. "This is a little erratic for you, including that odd text the other day. I mean, what the hell is—"

I put my hand over her mouth. "I have a limited amount of time, but I have to tell you this. The handsome stranger, the one from the coffee shop, the one from the bar, is now my fiancé." I held my hand up. "Before you ask questions, let me get this out. He's the leader of, let's call it an organisation, a rather powerful organisation, if you catch my drift. How did I get mixed up in this? Funny story, I was born into it. I was excommunicated after falling pregnant outside of wedlock. I'd been in hiding until Drake found me. He needs a bride, or rather, a baby factory, and he sought me out. I have no choice, and before you say run away, I literally tried it, hence the cryptic text, but he was already watching me. Everything I do now is watched, every choice I make now is controlled. I shouldn't even be telling you this, but I need a friend because my life is literally about to be turned upside down."

"What, are you connected to the M.A.F.I.A.?" She spelled it out, afraid to say it aloud.

"Wait, what? No!" I realised my mistake. "No, it's like an underground Witch Coven. I call it the organisation for personal reasons."

"Wait, you're a Witch?" That was a loaded question, one I would answer another day, even though I didn't know how to answer it.

"I don't have time to explain this. Drake is expecting me home. It's complicated, and I promise that I will, but you can't repeat this to anybody. And I mean *anybody*," I said, emphasising the words for her to understand. She nodded. I could feel them coming, as if the ground was moving beneath my feet. "I have to go." I speed-walked to my desk, grabbed my bag, and rushed out the door to see his men almost enter.

"Is everything alright, Dani?" Kris asked, his brow creasing before he took note of the men about to walk into my office.

"Yep, fine." I waved goodbye, rushing toward them. I didn't need any more complications.

"You are late," the grumpy guard, Marcus, stated. I really had no care for his attitude. I walked past him, the brute who was close to six feet tall, broad, and had the same fuck off face that Drake wore. I wondered if they were related. Dark features and tattoos hidden beneath his perfectly tailored suit, long hair, and I mean longer than my own.

Chapter Eleven

The Need for Answers

Drake

"At least you have taste, Daniella," I mumbled while sipping my hot coffee and opening my tablet to check on my holdings and businesses, and complete any necessary work while I waited. I despised her house. It was tiny and not to my standard of opulence. That would change. We wouldn't stay here for long, just until she understood her place and agreed to her duty. I had enough men and power to keep us protected, *for now*. As long as the Morteferi never discovered us, we'd be fine. I wondered how Daniella had been able to hide so effectively. She had power. I could feel it when around her.

I tapped my fingers on the glass table, growing impatient while waiting for her to arrive home. My guards had alerted me that they were on the way. I boiled the kettle, then grabbed a mug, making her a coffee for her arrival. She entered with her boots echoing on the timber floors, and her tight skirt clung to that perfectly curved arse. I would her fuck in that tight hole one day. I couldn't wait to be inside every single part of her, to twist her body for my pleasure. To fill her with my seed. What the *fuck* was wrong with me?

"Can you stop staring at me like that?" she remarked, putting her bag down and pulling out her laptop. She spotted the coffee in my hand and strolled over, taking it from me before sitting at her circular dining table that could barely fit four people.

"I'm only admiring my future wife's curves." I provoked her, enjoying the bite in her response.

"You keep saying that like I'm going to agree." Her eyes darted to the rock now on her finger. It suited her, the large three-carat, princess-cut platinum engagement ring.

"And you keep fighting like you have a choice. You're better off just accepting your fate and following me into the bedroom where I'll fuck your brains out."

She spluttered, coffee coming out of her nose, and I smiled. She wiped away the mess, shaking her head to compose herself.

"Do you ever stop to consider that maybe I don't want to marry, and maybe I don't want any children?"

I noticed her answer avoided mention of her previous conception. "Daniella, I'm aware that you birthed your child. The thin scar down low revealed the truth. Do you want more children?" I asked her, knowing I couldn't force a child to come out of her. I only thought about my selfish need to have her as mine. But I also didn't care whether I had a child or not. This was purely an arrangement to placate the council. If it developed into a child, that would be beneficial.

"That's none of your business."

I smirked, knowing the answer to be yes. If not, at least a maybe. I examined the small movements she made while raising her cup to those luscious lips, taking a sip. I watched her throat bob as she swallowed her coffee. She placed it down, gently lifting the lid on her laptop and brushing the stray hair behind her ears. Daniella skirted around the conversation, yet I needed to understand the woman before me and the missing pieces of her. Giuseppe yielded no helpful information.

"Daniella, where are your markings?" I wondered why her soft skin had been untouched. Her father never spoke of her transcending into her power. "You never claimed your power, did you?" I queried, hesitantly taking a step closer, wanting to see what truths she would reveal.

"I…uh, um…no. My father discovered I was pregnant and didn't allow me to participate in the ceremony. I was excommunicated after that and never felt the need for them. I wanted…want no part of the organisation. I want my life exactly as it is. I'm just waiting for you to realise how much I don't give a fuck what you want." Her eyes filled with anger and rage, but not directed toward me.

"Daniella, what happened?" The words left my mouth before I even realised. My pulse quickened. What was it about her? The man who once kept his heart guarded now found himself wanting to know everything she hid beneath the sexy surface ."Do you ever stop talking?" She huffed in frustration, her grey eyes meeting mine, glaring at me to let it go, her red wavy hair flowing over her shoulder.

"I'm just trying to get to know my future wife," I quipped, like there was nothing more to this conversation.

"Oh my god, shut up." A small smile threatened to cover her face before she pushed it away.

"You shut up."

"Make me," she said before poking her tongue out at me.

"I can. Open wide and I'll shove my cock in your mouth, but even then, you might moan a little."

Her mouth dropped open. She glanced down at my cock, already hard and waiting for those lips to wrap around it. I walked over, closing it and kissing that soft spot just under her ear.

"Don't worry, Daniella, one day when you stop fighting the chemistry we have, you'll be dying to get on your knees to please me." She shivered, standing and pushing me hard in the chest. I stumbled slightly, laughing and watching her run into her room and slam the door shut.

My phone rang, breaking my thoughts. "Yep, what is it?" I answered.

"A few hunters were spotted."

"Where?" I asked, my jaw clenching in frustration. One day, they would leave us alone. I hoped. I needed to marry Daniella sooner rather than later and return to the safety of my home.

Chapter Twelve

Unspoken Words

Daniella

I wore Drake down and managed to convince him to allow me to go to work on Friday despite having Thursday off. The week had been crazy—my birthday on Monday, kidnapping on Tuesday, and by Wednesday, I was living with Drake. Thursday was just awkward, having to be around him all day. He strutted around with all of his sex appeal, whether it was in grey sweatpants or a tailored suit. His arrogance lingered in my tiny two-bedroom home. We barely managed to share a couch. I ended up sitting at the dining table to avoid being close to him.

Friday brought about report time, the rush to get all my marking done and online to send out to parents, where maybe about ten per cent of them would read it. Then the emails, asking why I'm not helping their child enough. Sorry that little Jamie prefers to throw pens rather than write with them. How I wish we could actually email the truth, just once. Students were always handing in assessment tasks late, or parents emailed about some nonsense excuse to cover for their child's inability to use time management, even with multiple reminders. Or even parents claiming they never received any emails from you despite the read receipts.

I sighed, marking another assessment that received a mark of forty per cent because they didn't read the instructions. I got up, grabbed my coffee cup and headed to the main staffroom to fill myself with more caffeine than I should have. My neck ached from hunching over a desk for the last two hours. Coffee, such a life saver, one scoop of Moccona and two sugars, the perfect blend. Now to fill it milk, which appeared beside me. Kris leaned against the counter, his arms crossed and his shirt way too snug. The definition hidden beneath, made it hard not to stare. He was hot.

"Where were you during the week? Didn't we have tentative plans?"

Heat rushed to my cheeks. My hands shook slightly while I stirred my coffee, accidentally spilling some over the side of the cup. He took the milk from the bench, returning it to the fridge.

"Yeah, I was out sick. Sorry about that." I turned, lifting the cup to my lips and taking a sip, watching as his eyes grazed over my body.

"That is new. Here I thought you were single. Did I lose another good one?" He chuckled, referring to my ring.

"It's complicated." I looked away from him, honestly having no idea how to answer him. How could I explain that just a few days ago I wasn't engaged — and now I was due to be married tomorrow, with none of my friends present? Drake forbade Sam from attending, stating that humans didn't need to understand or be part of the supernatural world.

"Was it the guy from the pub on your birthday Monday night?" Kris questioned, fingers tapping restlessly against the cup he held.

I tilted my head at him. "Wait, didn't you say you weren't there?"

"I might have lied. I got a bit nervous. I hid in the shadows like a creeper and just watched you. That dress on your body was…ahem." He dropped his arms and fiddled with his belt. "You looked sexy as hell."

"You're bringing out all the compliments today, aren't you?" I tried to keep myself composed. Never in my life had a man flirted with me this much. It was an odd feeling to be someone's centre of attention

"Just shooting my shot. Who was that guy? He looked way too serious for you."

I stood dumbfounded. I had no idea how to answer the question. Sam knew the truth, but what do I say? An old family friend? We dated years ago and reconnected? An arranged marriage? In the

21st century? That wasn't really plausible. It just didn't happen unless you were in some ridiculous romance novel. I opened my mouth to speak, but the door burst open, and our principal entered.

"Ah, Kris, how are you settling in?" he asked, ignoring me completely, which wasn't uncommon for him and probably out of fear of whatever Drake had threatened the other day.

I peered over my shoulder at Kris, the unspoken words between us lingering in the air. A man who finally seemed interested in me, someone who cared, and yet it would never happen. Tomorrow, I would marry another man and return to work on Monday as if nothing changed over the weekend. I sniffed and wiped my eyes, stopping the tears that wanted to spill out before holding my head high. I was his, but I would never give him every piece of me.

CHAPTER THIRTEEN

JUST LEAVE US ALONE

DRAKE

I let Daniella go to work against my better judgement, especially after the Morteferi attack yesterday and leaving one of their lackeys in her garage. I didn't want to deal with more animosity between us before we were due to be wed tomorrow. I spelled the garage with soundproofing. Though it didn't matter how much noise he made—nobody outside would ever hear the last screams that ever left his pathetic fucking mouth.

I checked in with my guards, and they noted that Daniella had left her office to venture inside the main building. I managed to sneak a tracking chip inside her ring, the best way to know where she was at all times of the day. *Ah, technology, you've made my job easier in almost every aspect.*

"Boss, are we ready?" Marcus asked, and I pushed myself off the couch, removing my suit jacket and shirt. I didn't want the smell of ash lingering, lest she discover the truth of what I had been doing in her garage all day.

"Let's do it. The fucker better have some answers for me because I am fucking over these attacks on our Coven."

I kicked the door hard, and the prisoner yelped, almost falling back on his chair. The four-pointed Star of Eve was drawn on the roof, a simple protection to prevent him from using his own magic. With the symbol of Eve being present, witches weren't able to use their magic against one another in a way that would cause harm.

"The story of your intelligence isn't a lie, I see." His eyes motioned to the roof and the symbol of Horus at his feet.

"No, I use what I must to ensure our survival."

"Your time is coming, Drake, as is for all of your pathetic fucking kind." The hunter snarled, like his words held weight.

I formed a ball of flame in my hand, bouncing it in the air a few times before throwing it at his head. It wasn't enough to harm him, but enough to scare the absolute fuck out of any sane person. His laughter filled the room. What was wrong with these hunters? Were they all a little psychotic?

"Is that all the great Drake has? A fireball? Oh, I'm shaking with fear." Rage consumed me, and the verge of reason and chaos lingered in the air.

"Fuck this." I entered the circle, knowing my magic would be useless inside, but this time, it was personal. My fist struck his face, and he fell backwards, two of his teeth sliding onto the concrete floor. "How is this, motherfucker?" Another strike, his eye now barely able to open. "I have two choices right now: beat you to a fucking pulp or beat you to the brink of death and leave you for your people to collect. With the message that I'm no longer holding back. If you want to keep coming for my people, I'll start hunting yours down one by *fucking* one. This has gone on for long enough, and your pathetic existence should have been erased long ago."

"Your ego will always be your biggest downfall, Drake. You never seem to look at the whole picture." He choked on his words, blood spilling from his mouth. This was pointless, I knew that now. I had wasted my energy on nothing. I threw him to the ground, hearing his head smack against it. He wouldn't live much longer.

"Take him out and leave him in a public place, somewhere they will have to use plenty of resources to cover it up." I waved my hand at him, watching my men lift the almost lifeless body out the front door and into the back of my SUV.

I hopped into the shower to wash away the blood literally on my hands. My thoughts drifted to Daniella and her sexy arse swaying to the music, and how tight her cunt was that night. Fuck, I wanted to bury myself inside her again. I grabbed my hard cock, rubbing it slowly at first, closing my eyes and picturing her luscious lips around it. Watching her tongue swirl around the knob like a fucking lollipop. Increasing my pace, I braced the wall with my other hand, groaning at the image of her head bobbing on my cock. The door creaked, and I opened one eye to see Daniella standing in the doorway, her eyes focused on my actions.

"Are you going to just stand there, or are you going to get on your knees for me?" I said, watching her wet her lips before scoffing and walking away. She wouldn't be able to deny her attraction toward me forever. Moments later, I blew my load and dried myself before pulling on a pair of grey sweatpants and heading to the kitchen.

Daniella sat at the kitchen table, a coffee and her laptop in front of her, continuing to write her reports. I watched slyly, her eyes tracking my every movement around the kitchen. I removed the roast that had been cooked earlier by my chef, serving up dinner for us both. As I told her, she would never be weak.

"It's the night before our wedding. Shouldn't you be staying somewhere else for tradition's sake?" She leaned back in her chair, crossing her arms over her chest, a smug look on her face.

"Why would I want to spend a night alone when I get sneaky snuggles from you in the middle of the night?" I turned to place her plate in the microwave and felt an object hit my shoulder. A pen bounced to the floor, and a smile played over my face. Every night since staying here, in her sleep, she would roll over and meld herself to my body. Daniella wanted me. Her body knew it. I just needed her mind to catch up. It wouldn't be too much longer until I could fuck her on every surface in this house.

Chapter Fourteen

A Nice Day For a White Wedding

Daniella

Today was the day I was being forced to marry the High Mage—the arrogant and egotistical Drake. Marriages within the Coven were bound by magic, and there was no option for divorce. The only way to remove that bind was death.

I could hear voices outside the door. Drake had already snuck out this morning. He liked to snuggle and run his hands over my body, but I managed to avoid temptation for now, refusing to give in to him.

I sighed, remembering the day that my father excommunicated me. My chest felt lighter and I could breathe. I knew that I had every opportunity to be me without their stupid and restrictive rules. Life could be whatever I wanted, and for a brief moment, I expected to live with my child and be happy. At least I knew he was safe. Nobody would ever hurt him.

I looked up at my wedding dress, hanging in the corner of the room. In the Coven, you didn't wear white like tradition dictated. You were to wear your husband's family colour, which normally indicated the power that ran through them. With Drake being a Mage with Fire magic, it was red. The gown appeared more maroon than red, though. I knew he picked the dress for me to wear, stating it would highlight my curves and show off my ample assets. It was an off-the-shoulder gown with a corset bodice. Black lace covered the top half, with a flowing skirt, but the thigh-high split had me worried.

"That's what he picked," I mumbled to myself, throwing my head back into the pillows, wishing to be swallowed whole.

A light knock sounded against the door. "Come in," I grumbled, glancing towards the stunning dress hanging in the corner of my room once more.

A stunning blonde entered, a huge smile on her face. Her grey skirt was tight, and her boobs threatened to spill out of the revealing white tank top. Her heels clacked on my wooden flooring.

"Miss Romano, it's an honour to meet you." She bowed her perfectly styled head and body, a sign of respect. One I didn't deserve.

"Thank you. So, when does the shit show start?" I asked, moving to the edge of the bed.

"Par—Pardon?" she spluttered.

I cleared my throat, knowing it was better to pretend I wanted this to than to piss off the entire Coven and create animosity for Drake.

"I don't like to be the centre of attention."

"Oh." She laughed. "Everyone will be staring at him more than you. He gains more power today with your union. Drake is…incredible." Something in her eyes and the way her cheeks flushed unnerved me.

"Yeah…he sure is."

She was biting her lip, making our interaction even more awkward. "Hair and makeup are here, and the photographer will be here at twelve. We will begin the drive at two and arrive just before dusk. It'll be finished, not long after that. You'll return home, and Drake will stay behind for the reception, which you're *not* needed for."

I pushed the blankets back. Her words sounded cheerful but felt hollow and almost envious. I didn't like the girl. I paused at the bathroom door. "What was your name?"

"Melinda."

"Thanks."

The water washed away some of my anxiety over the fact that I was stuck here. Part of me thought it could be worse. Drake could be abusive, but at the moment, his biggest vice was control. I rinsed the soap from my hair, watching the bubbles rinse into the drain before stepping out and noticing the beautiful maroon gown had been switched to a deep blue.

I covered myself with the towel, exiting the room without a thought, more concerned with the insult toward Drake. It was tradition, and for as long as I have known, you *had* to wear your husband's colour.

"What happened to the dress?" I shouted to be heard over the people lingering in my home.

The peppy blonde popped into view, and I took a step backwards. Where the hell did she come from?

"Drake changed his mind." She whipped her ponytail behind her head. "He is our High Mage and has final say. I guess because you haven't transcended, you're not worthy of his colours." She shrugged like it didn't matter.

It was a backhanded remark. I knew then that we'd never be friends. Drake didn't seem to mind that I hadn't transcended. He only wanted to understand why I never spoke about it. I glanced over my shoulder at the blue gown. It was stunning, but certainly couldn't compare to the original. I smiled and re-entered my room, reaching for the phone that Drake had left for me. It barely rang before he answered.

"Yes, Daniella." His deep voice caused me to shiver.

I cleared my throat. "Did you change the dress?"

The line went quiet for a moment. "I don't understand what you mean," he said slowly, the uncertainty in his tone impossible to miss, even over the phone.

"A navy blue dress has replaced the beautiful maroon one that you left here last night. Isn't it customary to wear your colour?" I asked hesitantly. Part of me feared being rejected. This whole situation made me uneasy.

He laughed, but it wasn't sincere. It sounded evil. "I certainly didn't." He paused for a moment. "Wear that dress. I have a feeling someone is playing a game. We will flush them out. I'll have a spare dress for you at the dinner tonight."

"The dinner? I was told I *wasn't* needed. That it was just the council."

"I think I have the answer to who our duplicitous individual is. Put on your game face, Daniella. The sneakiness of witches has begun. Text me updates on everything and I mean *everything*."

"Sure will," I quipped.

I hung up before anything else could be said, tapping the phone to my chin. This was another reason I hated this place. The underhanded shit. My father always partook in dirty deals, and now someone had decided to play games with me. It was clear who this individual was, but why Melinda had decided to dislike me, I had no idea. I was sure she would reveal her true colours soon enough.

◆

I stood in the bathroom, staring at the person before me. I barely recognised her. This wasn't me. The tight bun my hair was twisted into didn't suit my oval-shaped face, and the makeup was thick around my eyes. I took a photo, sending it to Drake.

> Drake: You look like a clown

> Daniella: Right?

> Drake: Wipe that shit off your face. That dress is hideous but your breasts look amazing.

> Daniella: Keep dreaming.

> Drake: You have 15 mins before the car arrives, do whatever you wish. I don't care as long as you are at the end of the aisle.

With his permission, I pulled out a cloth to remove the eye make-up. This wasn't me. My eyes were dull, but I knew how to make them stand out. The rest of the makeup appeared acceptable, but my eyes were just a disaster. I couldn't be more grateful for Drake's response. I smudged a soft bronze over the lid and left off the eyeliner. Simpler, sophisticated, and more Daniella. I pulled out the clips, letting my hair fall flat and fluffed it out. I wanted it to be more natural. If this were to be my life, I wouldn't let them take my spirit.

Melinda pursed her lips upon seeing me, and I felt better within myself. I flicked my hair over my shoulder and headed toward the black BMW SUV with blacked-out windows. I slammed the door closed and relaxed into the warmed leather seats. Drake certainly had a luxurious lifestyle, but when you ran an entire coven and had multiple businesses and had a finger in everything, it made sense. They would make donations to the government to avoid being discovered, a continual cover-up, so to speak. I sighed, playing with my navy gown, and watched the trees change to buildings before skyrises came into view.

The Church of Eve was located within Melbourne, hidden underground, because why would Mages have their existence known on the surface? We pulled into the undercover car park, and the driver I had barely paid attention to opened the door and bowed his head. A sign of respect for my new title, the wife of the High Mage. A position that demanded respect when your husband was known as a murderous, arrogant arsehole. He held out his hand, and I slid mine in, slipping out of the car. He gestured toward the bronze door. From memory, the church had an affinity for metal. Regular humans used gold, but we preferred bronze for its symbol of strength and stability. Its earthy tone represented where our magic came from.

The door creaked open to reveal a face that I didn't wish to see in this moment.

"Ah, Daniella, my *beautiful* daughter." The man who had haunted my dreams for decades stood with his arms outstretched. I shivered at the sight of him and his use of the word beautiful.

"What the hell are you doing here?" I snapped at him, frozen in place. This couldn't be happening. This man shouldn't be allowed at my wedding.

"I'm your father, and it's tradition to walk you down the aisle. I'm glad to see that you are wearing our family's colour. It suits you and brings out the depth of the red in your hair."

"You can fuck off. I refuse to be tied to you, to be near you on this day. If I have any say as the wife of the High Mage, it is this. I'll ensure that you are never near me again. You'll never be allowed within five metres of me." I turned toward the driver. "Find Drake, NOW!"

I stayed close to the car, refusing to enter the church or get closer to the piece of shit before me. The man who killed the father of my child because I dared to question this way of life. John was innocent, and I lived with that guilt daily. Time seemed to stand still as I waited patiently for Drake to arrive.

The door burst open. "What the fuck is this?" he bellowed through the parking garage. His hands were alight with flames in preparation.

"I've come to escort my daughter down the aisle, as per tradition."

Drake's hands extinguished, and he pulled upon his lapels, a charming smile plastered on his face.

"Giuseppe." He strolled over, holding out his hand. "I'm honoured to be considered your son-in-law." I watched as he crushed my father's hand. Giuseppe faltered, his face turning white. "I'll give you this warning. If you ever come near my wife in the future, I'll ensure that all your assets are taken away. She is no longer your property. She was mine the moment you signed the dowry. Your life is in her hands from now on. If she asks for your removal, it *will* be done. Is that understood?"

I smiled at the knowledge that his life was in my hands. Drake would protect me and side with me. For once, I felt safe, even if it wasn't with a person that I picked. Giuseppe scampered away, the door slamming behind him. Drake walked over, whistling for his men to leave. He took my hands in his, giving them a brief kiss before touching my face.

"You will tell me what happened one day." Not a question, but a demand. The truth I never wanted to reveal.

"You wish." I moved to walk around him, but his hand clasped around mine.

"Daniella, that isn't a request. You forget it's my duty to protect you, as is yours within this union. We spill our blood for one another, a union forged in blood. I cannot protect you unless I know the truth."

"I'm aware, Drake, and some *things* are better left in the past. Can we get this over with, please?"

I stepped toward my new chains, each link a reflection of the choice I was never given. This blood union wasn't love, but rather a life sentence, carved in flesh and sealed in magic. Eternal and inescapable. From this moment on, my life no longer belonged to me. It was his to command. And his? Bound to mine. A union forged for security, power, and offspring, not for love.

CHAPTER FIFTEEN

THE VOWS

DRAKE

I rubbed the scar on my brow while watching *my inferno* walk away. I salivated thinking about finally being able to own her. I followed behind, knowing that Giuseppe would be cowering at the back of the church. I hoped that would be the last of the drama for the day, but I knew that to be short-lived, especially with Melinda deciding to sabotage Daniella's dress. She may be a woman, but she acted like a child. I hoped for some antics at dinner, mainly to remind any who dared cross me of what the consequences would be.

Daniella stood in place at the entry to the church. I stepped cautiously toward her, taking a position beside her, seeing her hands fidgeting and her teeth biting those luscious lips.

"What is it?" I questioned, following her line of sight. Her father stood with the remainder of her family. "Ahh, I see. When was the last time you saw your siblings?"

"Don't pretend to care, Drake. It really undoes that whole 'I'm the fearless leader' act."

I chuckled, holding my chest and moving to block her view. "Daniella, you can drop the strong feminist act. I know deep down that you just want me to bend you over and fuck you so hard that you'll be screaming my name." I watched her throat bob, her eyes looking past me.

"They are part of the council, but if you desire, I can ask them to leave." She shook her head. "Then wrap your arm around mine. We will enter with our heads held high, say our vows, and have minimal contact."

Her grey eyes began to water. "I just hope she's safe." Her voice was barely a whisper before she glanced at the ground.

Her arm interlinked with my own, and the music proceeded to echo through the church. I'd avoided coming since the death of my mother. I found it hard to believe that Eve, the beginning of the magical line, would leave us in a situation where we constantly had to fight to survive. My mother was devout and would strike me if I ever spoke ill of her. I learnt to keep my thoughts about Eve to myself, and since her passing, I never felt the need to return.

The church was covered in bronze, the symbols of the powers displayed in each corner—flame for Fire, a droplet for Water, wavy lines for Air, and a green spiral for Earth. The centre contained a four-pointed star with a purplish tinge. That was the representation of Eve, the first Witch, ordained with magic since biting that apple and being cast out. Adam became the first hunter, and so began the rivalry that had lasted thousands of years.

We arrived at the altar. The High Ember wore his robes with a symbol of each magic represented. He smiled, taking our hands and placing them on the star, our fingers linked. We had to wait until dusk settled before we could begin.

"Welcome, beloved parishioners, kindred spirits, and weavers of magic. We gather here in the sacred presence of the Goddess Eve, Mother of Magic and our silent Guardian. In this enchanted hour, we will witness the union of two souls who have chosen to walk the path of life, hand in hand as one."

He picked up the silver dagger, raising it to the sky and muttering a few words before turning toward the altar behind him. A sliver of each magic was evident upon the table, and he waved the dagger over them before stopping and kissing it.

"By the flame, we summon transformation and the spark of creation." He dropped the tip in the fire, and I watched it begin to glow. "By Water, we invoke depth and the flow of love." He paused again, dipping it into the water, and the glow extinguished within seconds. "By Air, we call forth clarity and the whispers of hope." He moved about the table, and Daniella proceeded to shake beside me. I clutched her hand tighter. "Lastly, by Earth, we grow devotion, strength, and encourage fertility."

I wondered if she remembered what came next—the blood union. He tilted the knife toward me, and I took it, pressing my lips to the dagger before taking Daniella's hand in my own.

I exhaled, closing my eyes for a moment to steady myself before the vows I was about to speak.

"Under the watchful eye of our creator Eve, I call upon the

power that created the world— Earth, steady and brave,

to root our bond.

Air, sharp and unseen, to whisper our names in time.

Water, deep and unyielding, to drown all doubts.

Flame, fierce and consuming, to forge our fate in ash.

Let the blood in our veins be the river, our bones become

stone, Our breath a tornado, and our hearts the fire.

Bound not in love alone, but in the raw truth of magic.

Now I vow, with our hands to be cut and joined,

Let the Goddess Eve bear witness—

We are one, and we are forever, from today until our last."

I drew the blade slowly, its edge catching the light that shone over us. Her hand trembled, just barely, while I guided the tip across her palm—a thin line blossoming red. She hissed quietly, so as not to alert others. Her eyes drifted to mine, showing no fear, unlike those that surrounded me. I saw the same fire in her eyes, a passion to match my own. Her voice was steady as she echoed my words, her gaze locked on mine, unflinching before she took the dagger. The cold steel pressed against my skin, and her eyebrow quirked. A swift slice with no hesitation. Blood surged, warm and fast, dripping from my hand in heavy droplets that splattered against the stone floor. A sly, knowing smile tugged at her lips. Her act of defiance was a sign of what was to come in our marriage. A constant fight between us until our deaths.

I laughed under my breath, rough and low, and dragged my bleeding hand slowly across her cheek. The smear of red stood stark against her skin, claiming her as mine on another level. She took my hand, joining our wounds as one, while the High Ember wound bronze string around our flesh—binding blood to blood, fate to fate. The copper thread shone in the shadows, and with every loop, the ancient rite was spoken for the entire coven to hear. Our veins pulsed in unison, the elements stirring in silent witness: Earth trembled, Air thickened, Water stilled, and Flame curled closer. In that moment, we were no longer two. We were bound, from now till forever.

We turned to the witnesses, and raising our hands, I shouted, "Sanguis cum sanguine ligatur." *Blood is bound with blood.* I turned back to Daniella, pressing my lips against hers. Her body arched away before relaxing into my tight embrace. "Now you are *mine*," I whispered against her lips.

"Keep thinking that, Drake. We might be wed, but I'll never fuck you."

I threw my head back in laughter, gripping her hand tighter and pulling her down the aisle toward the back of the church. The ceremony was finished, and our hands would be bound until dinner, when the High Ember would remove them. We weren't to wash our hands until midnight to ensure that the blood union had solidified. The treachery would begin at dinner, cloaked in wine and false smiles.

Chapter Sixteen

Reunited

Daniella

The car ride was eerily quiet with little spoken, even between Drake and his driver. My hand felt wet and sticky where I was forced to be bound to him for another few hours, to solidify the union between us. It was the part I had always disliked, even as a child, when I had to witness ceremonies in the past. Drake pulled my arm, a sharp sensation shooting through my hand where the string lingered.

I glanced up at him. "Yes?" I batted my eyes with a sweet voice.

"I found your original gown. I had to make a small alteration, and I've secured space for you to change. Make sure you listen to *all* my instructions tonight. The treachery of witches will begin."

"Drake, I'll be faithful and loyal as per the vows that I spoke, but *don't* expect blind devotion."

"Daniella, this world has changed since your departure." He didn't like to utter my excommunication and preferred to use any other word to describe it. "There's more underhanded behaviour, more scheming." He tugged at his tie, frustration evident in his tone.

"I'm aware. I saw what my father would do, even to those he considered friends."

"That isn't a surprise, but when I ask you to be quiet, I expect silence," he stated, ignoring the comment about my father.

I rolled my eyes, staring out the window at a freedom that no longer existed. A simpler world without the magic, power, and the threat of the Morteferi. The city of Melbourne was considered one of the most liveable in the world, but all I saw were its secrets—the world hidden from human eyes, the symbols that had meaning beyond their comprehension. The car rolled into another parking garage where Drake's door opened. He slid out, gently pulling me along before offering his other hand. The doors were opened by others, without Drake ever needing to touch a thing.

We stopped when his men approached, whispering in his ear. Drake nodded and tapped their shoulders. They had blind devotion to him, a loyalty that many dreamt of. He had fear and respect all around him. We entered a room, and I noticed the gown in the corner before realisation hit me.

"Wait." I peered down at my hand, fastened to Drake's. Looking back up, I was faced with his eyes, dark with desire. "Oh, come on. You planned this."

He shrugged. "I believe we're wed, and I'll see this eventually. Plus, you'll need a hand with that zip."

I spun, showing him my back so he could help remove my current dress. The faint scuff of his boots shifted closer. His fingers brushed the nape of my neck, light, with no hesitation. He swept my hair aside. Drake's skin was rough and hot, but the touch was careful. Unexpected. Warm breath ghosted across my spine. He moved closer, tugging on the zipper—slow, deliberate. Cool air brushed against the exposed skin. Then, his lips. The press of them trailed along my neck, lingering just long enough to ignite heat beneath my skin. Teeth grazed my ear, a teasing bite that made my breath catch. My eyes fluttered, threatening to close. My head tilted back on instinct, the tension in my body unravelling beneath his touch. It shouldn't have felt so good.

"I often think of that day, in that pub, and how soft your skin felt. How tight you were. You'll only be able to fight for so long, Daniella. You can't deny the way your body responds to me. The way your breath hitches, the bumps that appear over your skin"—his hand snaked around my waist and up to my breast—"and how hard your nipples are. I bet if I touched you right now, I could slip right in."

I cleared my throat. I couldn't let him know that he was telling the truth. My body did crave him.

"We can't be late." I pretended to be totally unfazed by his contact, but I heard his chuckle behind me. He knew what he did to me. I wished I could hate it, but it truly felt amazing to be caressed in such a sensual way.

I stepped out of the navy gown before stepping into the maroon one from earlier. Having Drake's hand in mine made it easier not to trip or fall. I did notice his eyes on my near-naked body, and his hand travelled down to re-adjust himself on a few occasions.

I slid into the dress before Drake zipped it up. I smoothed it down with my free hand, pulling Drake to the closest mirror.

Drake fake coughed, his eyes darting to the side where a black box sat. He nodded before I reached toward it, my fingers grasping around the cool object.

"I know that you were given a ring and it held significance to your family. You are my wife from today, my partner and my bonded consort. I wanted something to signify our union from this moment on." I flicked open the lid and stared at the rose gold ring before me. The thick band was layered with black diamonds, with a two-carat princess-cut ruby. It was unique and unlike anything I had ever seen. The matching wedding band had the same black diamonds, matching the eternity ring.

"The eternity ring is optional for you to wear now, after a year of marriage, or you could use it as a push present."

My eyes met his serious gaze. The truth of this union was a child. He knew about my child and allowed him to stay on the outside, living amongst the humans, even though this was generally not permitted. They were to wait to see if they had been blessed with powers.

He walked over tentatively, taking the ring from the box. He slid the original off my finger and replaced it with the new one before pressing his lips to my hand.

"Now, let's enjoy the festivities." He beamed and pulled on his lapels, my wrist aching from the strange angle.

Drake opened the door, our hands still firmly clasped together. I hesitated, knowing that walking into that room would bring back memories from the past. A past I had been trying to run from, a past filled with pain. The last time I had been here, it was for the wedding of Giuseppe and stepmother. I had been pushed aside, deemed unworthy of being part of it because of my lack of power.

Drake dragged me along gently before stopping and searching my face. His hand stroked my cheek.

"I take my vows seriously. You are *mine*. Nobody will dare hurt you from this moment on. One day, Daniella. One day, you will come to trust me." His Arcanum opened the doors to reveal an arch covered in perennials. Drake flicked his wrist, and it exploded into flames. It had no warmth to it, though. "Don't worry, it won't burn you." Drake leaned in to whisper in my ear.

I smiled and continued walking. I heard a chorus of violins playing softly in the ballroom. Everyone stood, bowing their heads, and Drake led me over to the bridal table draped in a black tablecloth and red roses woven into the fabric. The symbol of Eve sat behind us on the wall, large, and a reminder from Drake that despite our powers, we were all equal. He pulled out my chair, and I glanced up at him suspiciously. Where had this chivalry come from?

"I can be charming, but behind closed doors, I'll be fucking you like the devil I am."

I gulped, my legs clenching from the memory of his harsh touch on my skin. Why did he make me feel things that I didn't want to feel?

The servers arrived, placing oysters in front of us. I peered at Drake over my shoulder, and he shrugged calmly, a sly smile on his face. Of course, he decided on an aphrodisiac. I picked it up, letting it fall into my mouth. It tasted divine. Drake certainly had style and taste. He finished and leaned back in his chair, twirling the golden liquid in his wavy whiskey glass. Our joined hands were strategically placed on the table while his eyes scanned the room. The High Ember returned, and all bowed their heads as he did the same for Drake and I. We lifted our hands toward him. He unwound the bronze string, bowing his head before handing it to us. The string was a symbol of our union, and would be displayed in our wedding photo.

I stretched out my hand, still sticky, but no longer wet, the mixture of our blood dry on my palm. The cut was barely visible. He placed his hand on the back of my chair—a power move, a reminder that I was his. A message to all that I wasn't to be touched. His Arcanum, Jackson, moved in, whispering in his ear. Drake nodded. I watched the two men stand, Drake fastening the button on his suit.

"I'll return shortly. I have a present for you." He kissed the top of my head, leaving all eyes staring at me.

I wanted to shrink or slide down the chair and hide under the table. I hated being the centre of attention. I kept my eyes focused on the table, playing with my fingers and hoping that nobody would notice me. The music continued to echo through the ballroom, a soft elegant tune with an almost ethereal tone to it.

"I never thought I'd see you again." Despite not having heard her voice for so long, she still sounded the same.

I looked up to see my baby sister, Willow, standing before me. We didn't share the same mother, and even then, she inherited more of her looks from *him*. We stared at each other awkwardly.

It had been years. The last time I saw her, she hadn't even started school, so innocent, and here she stood before me a teenager, wearing makeup, heels, and looking almost like an adult with her brown hair swept into a tight bun.

"I'm sorry," I whispered, my eyes beginning to water, my arms itching to hold her. My heart beat faster, filled with apprehension over her reaction.

Her hand gripped mine and squeezed it tight. "You never needed to say sorry to me. Bracken knew, and told me the truth." I peered over her shoulder to see Giuseppe – the man I called my father, who had raised me though we shared no blood. My *stepfather* watched our conversation intently. I wanted to ask which part, but feared any retribution against her. "He never hurt me."

Willow reached up, wiping the tear that I hadn't felt fall, a tear of relief that she hadn't received the same fate that I had. I stood, reaching over the table and pulling her into my arms. Feeling her against my body brought all the emotions to the surface, a comfort that I needed.

"It's okay, Dani, it's okay." She kissed my cheek, reciprocating the embrace.

"Do I get one?" My brother's voice was clear, and I extended my arm, not looking at him before pulling him into the same cuddle. He had the same brown features as his sister. "I missed you, Sissy," he said, using the cute pet name from when he couldn't speak properly. I chuckled hearing it, all my anxieties gone. They were *safe.*

"This is cosy." Drake's voice cut through the tender moment I shared with my siblings. They let go, bowing their heads in respect or submission, I wasn't sure with this man. "Run along. I require a moment with my wife."

My heart sank. "We will see you soon, Sissy," Bracken said with his usual cheek and a wink.

I waved before turning back to my *husband.* "Yes, darling?"

He chuckled, gesturing to the pretty brunette beside me. Her hair was swept from her face into an elegant bun with not a wisp of hair out of place. Her dress was respectable and not so tight that things were falling out of it. Her hazel eyes shone against the simple makeup painted on her face.

"This is your *Aurelia.*" Drake had organised for my own second. "Her name is Penelope Percy, and she'll help you to assimilate into Coven life once more."

She extended her perfectly polished hand, a bright smile on her face. "It's a pleasure to meet you. I'm honoured to have been selected as your Aurelia. I look forward to our journey together."

I slid my hand into hers, still suspicious. Her overly eager attitude and the intensity within those hazel eyes filled me with unease. Drake had selected her, so surely that meant she could be trusted, but her eyes looked like they were harbouring a deadly secret.

"Lovely to meet you." I placed a bright smile on my face, returning the handshake and making eyes at Drake.

He moved, wrapping his arm around my waist, pulling me close to his body. I noticed the servers returning to place down the Caprese salad for the next course. *Would this night never end?*

Chapter Seventeen

Dinner and a Show

Drake

Jackson had selected the perfect choice in Penelope. She stayed away from the bullshit and had no bravado to her. Exactly what Daniella needed to assimilate back into Coven life. I returned to my seat, digging into the pathetic excuse of a salad that had been placed at my table. Fuck me, I wanted this night over. I knew the possibility of sinking deep inside Daniella was slim, but that didn't mean it was impossible. I might be an arsehole, but I'd never force myself upon a woman. My mother taught me to respect women. Daniella had a voice, one that I would endeavour to never silence.

I was thankful that our hands were no longer fastened to one another, the blood still sticky on my palm. The wound would take a while to heal after her knife play.

I tapped Jackson's shoulder. "Where is the piano?"

"Why?" His brow creased, and he looked beyond me at my wife.

"Because I asked where the fucking piano is, find it!" I snapped at him for questioning me in such a manner.

Daniella seemed to be conversing well with Penelope. Rubbing my chin, I reached for my glass and leaned back in the chair, gazing out at the coven. A harmonious environment had been created—something my father could never achieve. He ruled with an iron fist, demanding obedience but without the respect. My rule was no less firm, yet the people's loyalty was genuine. If only *she* were here to see it. My mother's absence weighed heavily; her death had been both premature and unnecessary.

Jackson came into view, pushing a piano into the centre of the dance floor. I snorted, placing my hand on Daniella's back. Her head turned.

She pointed to the floor. "What's *that?*" The disdain in her voice was clear. She wasn't impressed with my decision for her to sing.

"It's either a dance together, which I doubt you would enjoy. Being so close to me and the temptation to take it further, it would be too much for you. I opted for a piano for us to sing a song that will define our relationship."

"You're so full of yourself. I know the perfect song, what's it called again?" She tapped her chin. "Oh, that's right. 'She Hates Me'."

I laughed out loud, standing and placing my hand on her chair and leaning in close. "Hold onto that hate, Daniella. It will only make your cum on my face taste like a fucking rainbow." I moved away, buttoning my jacket and pulling out her seat.

"Drake, wait, I…I haven't played in years. I don't really remember any songs. I…I can't do this." Her voice was pitchy and uneven, her eyes wild with fear. I touched her face before taking her hand and leading her to the piano.

"Whichever song you remember is the song that we shall sing. You will begin, and I shall recite the next verse before we join in the chorus together."

The Coven erupted in applause as Daniella took her seat at the piano, her fingers poised just above the keys, trembling slightly with anticipation. Her eyes flicked to mine, that familiar grey now laced with something fragile. Beneath the fear was that same quiet strength. She was extraordinary. Even before we met, just from a photo, I'd sensed it; we were mirrors of one another, shaped with the same darkness.

"'Wicked Game'."

"By that Chris guy?" I asked quietly. She nodded, a small, unreadable smile ghosting across her lips.

I laughed softly, recognising the weight of her choice. It was a song drenched in longing, a confession of a desire so fierce it eclipsed reason. A warning about needing someone so completely, it hurt. About a love that tasted like destruction. I knew her well enough to understand what she'd cling to: not the craving, but the resistance. The refusal to fall. The denial. To her, our love would be a challenge, a dance on the edge of reason. And somehow, I already knew that I would lose this game.

She touched the keys like she was summoning something sacred, her hands moving with grace and restraint. Then came her voice, soft and achingly clear, drifting through the room like she was casting a spell. The Coven stilled, as if held in place by the sheer vulnerability in her tone. Her eyes closed. She let go, and I felt every note like it was meant for me alone.

I joined in, my voice anchoring hers, a deeper, heavier tone, but in perfect harmony. Drawn to her like a tide to the shore, I brushed my fingers across the back of her neck. Fleeting contact, the kind you remembered, that lingered on your skin long after it ended. I pulled away too quickly, afraid they'd see it, the crack she was making in my armour. A weakness I couldn't afford, *not now*.

Yet, as our voices merged in the chorus, something raw and beautiful filled the air, unspoken words hanging between each note. When the final chord fell into silence, she didn't move. The Coven rose to their feet, but I couldn't look away.

She was still at the piano, still half-lost in the music. I took a step toward her, an odd sensation rushing through my system while I closed the gap, the space between us getting smaller. Lines that were never meant to be crossed, now blurred and filled with promise.

Chapter Eighteen

Too Much Tension

Daniella

It had been a week since our wedding, and it could only be described as torture. Drake hadn't been pressing sex, but he certainly knew how to tease a girl. He had purposely been wearing grey sweatpants and a tank top, or no top at all. Drake's physique, for his age, showed that he looked after himself. His abs were so well defined, and his arms were strong enough to throw me over his shoulder and spank my arse. Fuck, my body ached with need for him. The smell of his cologne permeated in my tiny house, a strong, bold scent that was deliberate, with sharp notes of smoked cedar, leather, and a hint of expensive whiskey, like a power suit in perfume form. I wish it would fade. It would make living here easier.

It didn't change the fact that I had no desire to cross that line. Lying down on the couch, his scent clung to the pillow, a reminder of the encounter in the bathroom. Legs were clenched at the memory of that night. A glance at the time showed Drake would be gone for a while, caught up in another ridiculous Coven meeting. One would've expected to be brought to one of them by now, yet he had spoken of another attack before the wedding.

The clock chimed just after eight. The last time he had a meeting this late, he didn't return until after ten.

"Fuck it."

I flicked off the lights and went to my room. I searched my drawers for my trusty vibrator, and a smile spread over my face. I didn't need a man. These toys were invented for exactly that reason.

"I told you I don't need you, Drake." I brought the toy to life, ready to ease the excess tension within my body.

I climbed into bed, finding that perfect position before sliding the device inside easily, already wet from the pent-up tension. Hitting the right spot, I closed my eyes and flicked the switch, bringing it to life. I moaned at the intensity, moving it in and out, feeling myself growing even wetter by the second.

"Oh, yeah," I shouted on a gasp, opening my eyes briefly to ensure I was still alone.

Eyes fluttered closed as warmth spread through my every nerve. I increased the setting, but found it hard to reach that peak, so I started to picture Drake – imagining teeth grazing a nipple, lips and tongue tracing a slow path down the body before settling between the thighs. Every touch and thought stoked the fire, making the heart pound and breath hitch. The rhythm quickened, need pulsing with relentless insistence, every inch of my body trembling on the brink of release.

"Fuck, Drake," I groaned, knowing that perfect euphoria was within my grasp.

The door burst open, and I froze in an incredibly vulnerable position. Drake crossed his arms before leaning against the door. A smirk played over his arrogant face as he rubbed the scar on his lip. He looked incredibly sexy wearing a black suit and white shirt with enough buttons undone to show off his tattoos. The man knew how to dress, to make himself appear larger and intimidating.

"Such a pity. You sounded so close." He dropped his bottom lip with a pout-like expression. I glared at him. "Please don't stop on my account." He removed his suit jacket and rolled up his sleeves before climbing onto the bed to lie beside me. "Just one question, Daniella. Were you thinking of me?" he asked.

I rolled my eyes. I was so close, and I refused to let him ruin my euphoria.

"Bit full of yourself there." I pushed it in harder, avoiding his gaze. He wasn't going to stop this from happening. I needed it.

"I'm not the one with a vibrator in my cunt, moaning my name." His hand moved over my breast, groping it before slowly walking his fingers down my body. He gripped my leg, pulling it closer to him before grabbing the vibrator and pressing the button to increase the vibrations. I groaned, feeling that familiar feeling again.

"See, Daniella, I think it's healthy to give yourself an orgasm. Remove that tension." He slid it out and thrust it in again. He leaned over me slightly, and I grabbed his muscular arms, digging my nails into his inked skin. I bit my lip, and he rolled it over my clit, my body aching with need. The absence of the sensation caused my body to crave more.

"Oh, God," I muttered. Drake knew exactly what to do. His simple breath on my neck made goosebumps explode on my sensitive skin.

"Not God, just Drake. The only man to ever give you mind-blowing orgasms for the rest of your days. Do you understand?" His voice was rough and filled with warning. His pupils darkened and locked onto mine, licking his lips, and his breathing shallowed.

"Yes…yes…yes." My voice grew louder. He pulled it out, teasing me by slowly pressing it back inside. "Drake," I moaned, shocked to hear his name roll so easily off my tongue in this moment.

"Fuck, that sounds good. You're close, aren't you?" He raised an eyebrow at me, and I could feel his own erection poking me in the leg.

I nodded. He slid it out and stood up, twirling it in his fingers.

"What the fuck?" I shouted at him, sitting up.

"Weren't you listening? Only I'm allowed to make you come."

"You can't do that," I squealed, launching myself at him to grab my toy.

"Oh, I can and I have. You only need to say two, three, no wait, four words." He winked, running his fingers through his hair. He paused and tapped the vibrator against his jaw, taunting me into saying the words he wanted to hear.

"What are they?" I gritted my teeth. I was so frustrated, I didn't care. I wanted a release. I needed one.

"*Eat my cunt, Drake.*" He carefully enunciated each word to ensure that I heard it perfectly. "Say those words, and I'll gladly devour those juices seeping from you right now." His eyes focused on my bare pussy before him. I closed my legs, rubbing them together slightly for a little bit of relief.

He licked his lips.

"I hate you," I grumbled, rolling over and covering myself with the blanket. I slid my hand down slowly to finish myself before Drake yanked the blankets back.

"Nope, it's me or nothing." I couldn't take the torture. I needed a release.

"Fine…" I threw my hands in the air. "Eat me."

"I didn't hear you." He placed his hand behind his ear, a seductive smile playing over his lips.

"Eat my pussy, Drake." I refused to say the word he wanted, my own form of rebellion. His eyes flamed with lust. He dropped to his knees, and his hands clasped around my ankles, pulling me toward him. His breath on my pussy, the simplest sensation, caused my body to erupt with need.

"Oh, trust me, I will, and I'll enjoy every last drop." His voice was hoarse as he licked my inner thigh. I relaxed into the pillow, hating myself a little for needing him to give me this, but my body craved his touch.

Chapter Nineteen

She's Mine Now

Drake

My mouth salivated at the scent of her wet cunt. I had been dying for a taste, dying to feel her under me, hearing my name come from those luscious lips. After she moaned with the vibrator, I couldn't take it. I had to hear it again, except this time, it would be from me and nothing else. I ran my finger over her sensitive clit, a groan escaping her, and she lifted herself to my mouth. She was dying for a release. She wasn't the only one. Masturbation didn't give me any relief after I felt her that day. I had to have her again. She was so fucking tight.

I blew cold air onto her sensitive clit, and her body erupted in goosebumps. It was a sight. She shuffled closer.

"Eager are we, Daniella?" I asked, my mouth ready to devour what I had desired for so long. I needed to taste her, eat her up, and claim her as mine. She was never going to escape me now. I would ruin her for all others. Her body and pussy would be *mine*.

"Mhmm," she muttered. My eyes drifted over her sexy body, taking in the swell of her breasts as she covered her face with a pillow.

"Remove the pillow. I want you to watch as you come on my tongue," I demanded, desperate to watch those eyes roll into the back of her head.

"Fucking hell, do you have to be so fu—" I didn't want to hear words, only sexy sounds coming from her. I plunged a finger inside. It slipped in so easily, her walls tightening around me. My thumb circling her clit, I pulled them out, licking the juices from them.

"Mmm, you taste good. Now be a good girl, lie back and try not to enjoy yourself too much." I chuckled.

I licked up slowly, watching her body twitch and writhe. Another slow lick. She tasted fucking phenomenal, a sweetness I didn't know I needed. A taste I was ready to feast on. I sucked on her clit, pulling it into my mouth and letting it go. She groaned, my cock hardening further at that delicious sound. I quickened my pace as her body moved away. I growled, pulling her back to me. This one wouldn't be allowed to escape. Her stomach was held down, tongue moving faster as her wetness grew with every passing second. The taste begged to be savored, devoured. Moans grew louder, body writhing, begging for more, until she rode the face like that fucking toy. A chuckle escaped when her hand found the head, pressing it back down.

"Yes, like that…fucking perfect. Oh, oh, oh, Drake."

That sound was music to fucking ears. Her hand was shaken off, arse lifted for a better angle as a squeal escaped. Her body trembled with the orgasm coursing through her. The play wasn't over yet – whimpers of need were sought, begging for my inevitable cock. I lowered back onto the bed and thrust two fingers inside her before sucking on her throbbing clit. Eyes met – filled with a passionate hate, no doubt over the pleasure being unleashed. They rolled between glare and euphoria as cunt tightened around the fingers. Another finger pushed inside, thumb circling once more, stoking the fire brewing inside her.

"Who's a good fucking girl for me? Do you like the way I make your body feel? Did you enjoy coming on my face?"

She mewled while her body grew closer.

"I want to hear you say it," I demanded.

"Say what?" Her words came out breathless as her body moved, chasing her orgasm. She was so close.

"I'm the only man to make you come."

"Yes, you are." Her voice was strangled.

"Say it, Daniella."

"You're the oooonly man to make me come," she exclaimed as the orgasm tore through her like a fucking tornado. I stood up, unzipping my pants, stroking myself while staring at the sight of the beauty before me, who had come undone twice. Once by my tongue and the other by my fingers.

"What are you doing?" Her eyes watched my cock spring free.

"It's time for your dessert." I licked my lips, tasting her on my tongue once more. My hand pumped my cock, rubbing that tiny drop of precum over the top. Her eyes were laser-focused on my hand moving up and down.

CHAPTER TWENTY

I Shouldn't Want This

Daniella

He was insane if he thought I would be sucking his dick. Not a chance. I didn't care if I just let him eat me like a bloody meal and give me the best orgasms I'd ever had. My eyes bulged in my head, looking at how thick he was. Not long, thick. I felt like he would tear me in half. Precum beaded at the end of his shaft, and some sick part of me wanted to lick it off. *No, Dani, bad Dani. He doesn't get to fuck your mouth.*

Why did I want this so badly? I was sick in the head.

He bent down, grabbed the vibrator as he climbed onto the bed, kneeling beside my head. He stroked the hair from my face, moving closer.

"Try not to enjoy this, Daniella." The way my name rolled off his tongue should've been illegal. My trusty device slid inside, and he brought it back to life. "Look into my eyes," he ordered. He exuded power, and I was under his spell. "Good girl."

The way he said that made me melt inside, and I wanted to do whatever he asked of me. My issues were undeniable – official even – psychological help might be needed. Lips around him, rolling my tongue over his knob. I felt invincible and in control of this powerful man. He was pushed deeper, each groan from his mouth fueling the need for more. *That's right motherfucker, I can bring you to your knees as well. Don't forget it.* I smiled as I tickled his balls, and the toy intensified.

"You're going to come one more time before you swallow my load. Do you understand me, Daniella?" I didn't answer as I focused on just how fucking horny I was. He threaded his fingers into my hair, forcing me up without stopping my movement.

"I asked you a question." His gritted teeth showed me just how much he was struggling to hold it together. I ran my hand over his dick, synchronised with the movements of my mouth. "Fucking hell." His hand pushed me deeper, and I gagged on the size of his monster in my mouth. I wanted more. I needed therapy. He worked the vibrator to different angles, hitting my G-spot, and I moaned, my legs shaking from another orgasm. Drake roared as his warm seed spilled down my throat. He held my head in place for a moment before letting me go. I licked the final beads from his knob, enjoying his salty but sweet taste.

I smiled as I sat up, moving toward the bathroom to clean myself up.

"What are you smiling about?" he asked as he sat on the edge of the bed to catch his breath.

"The fact that I had you on your knees. The great and powerful High Mage at the mercy of a woman's mouth. It's almost poetic."

He chuckled as he grabbed his pants. "You loved every moment of it. Don't deny just how much you enjoyed having my cock in your mouth. I saw the way your eyes lit up like a fucking Christmas tree."

I rolled my eyes and pulled on a nightie to go to bed. "The couch is ready for you."

"Oh, Daniella, we've been over this. We are married, and I will never sleep on that couch. Plus, your sleepy self loves to snuggle." He strolled into the bathroom, and I heard the taps squeak from being turned on.

"Fucking arsehole," I mumbled.

"I heard that," he called back.

"Good, I meant it." I went to get some water and some fresh air. The question that plagued me was the pleasure I took in making Drake come. Why did I want it so badly?

Chapter Twenty-One

Back to the Routine

Daniella

Drake had allowed my return to work, but under certain stipulations to ensure my protection. He had his guards stationed at every exit, a constant supervision which I hated and only Sam knew about. I dressed in a checkered black and grey skirt with a jade green blouse, grabbed a cardigan, and swiped the coffee off the counter when I noticed that Drake was nowhere to be seen.

"Drake?" I called out, unsure of where he might be. I walked to the spare bedroom, which he had claimed as his office. The space was empty. It wasn't like him to leave without saying goodbye and some sarcastic line about being his wife. "Drake?" I tried once more, and the front door opened.

Drake entered wearing a pair of black shorts and a black tank top, his hair dripping with sweat, his skin glistening. I glanced over his physique, seeing the bulge in his pants and remembering the feeling of his dick in my mouth. My eyes roamed back up and over his arms. I hadn't been able to inspect all aspects of his tattoos, but I wanted to know more about what they signified. I only knew his lust for power after burning his father alive. Drake was elusive in revealing any part of himself to me, but expected me to open up to him.

He removed his tank top and stretched out his arms.

"Enjoying the sight, Daniella?" He winked and stretched them up, flexing his biceps and his abs.

"Not much to enjoy with such an egotistical arsehole. I'm off to work."

"Try to concentrate on teaching when all you can think about is how damn sexy I look and how good my cock tasted inside your mouth."

"You're disgusting." I slammed the door on the way out. I slid into his ridiculous blacked-out SUV, checking my emails and knowing he was right. My mind drifted back to his impressive physique for a man of his age. It infuriated me how good he looked, and with an ego to match it.

✦

The year nine geography double was enough to make any person question their sanity. Biomes would never be an exciting topic for students. They knew what they were, but putting them into the appropriate categories and analysing them made it downright boring. Back in my office, I put my bag down and dropped my head onto my desk.

"Was it Chase or Clay?" Sam asked, knowing that those two boys in my class were utter nightmares. They weren't dangerous, just mischievous fifteen-year-old boys who thought it was still funny to make fart noises with their mouths. I just ignored it as they were better in class, at least semi-learning, than removing them and dealing with angry parents who didn't understand just how naughty their children were.

"Both, but just being silly boys. I get a break until period five now. I can relax and do some marking and lesson planning. How's your day?"

"Another stupid leadership meeting where we all sit there and nod our heads like robots and comply with others who only care about what makes it easier for them and not for the rest of the staff."

"So, good so far?" I winked at her.

"I'm going for a coffee, do you want to come?"

"No, I really need to do this marking, but here…" I took money from my purse. "My shout, or rather *his* shout." Sam took the money eagerly. She knew my coffee order, and at least this gave me some peace and quiet for the next thirty minutes before she returned.

I pulled out my marking and connected my headphones to focus on the task at hand. It truly was the bane of my existence, this time of the year. I bopped to the music and smashed through one class before entering the results into my laptop.

A hand landed on my shoulder, which elicited a scream that echoed in the tiny office.

"Whoa, I'm sorry. I didn't mean to startle you. I just needed to ask you how to work the printer. It doesn't want to connect for me."

My hand stayed on my chest to calm my racing heart, taking a moment to catch my breath. I nodded and walked over to the printer, showing Kris which button to press. He stood awfully close, and his forest scent enveloped my senses. I found it rather refreshing.

"Tell me more about Dani." He leaned on the printer, brushing his hair from his face. My eyes drifted to his bicep, the muscle taut beneath his rolled-up sleeve. There was something about him, something almost raw—he had rough edges and a relaxed posture. Completely opposite to Drake, who lived his life in suits tailored perfectly to his muscular physique, every aspect showing his attention to detail and control.

Kris snapped his fingers before my face. "Is it normal for you to zone out?" The back of his hand rested on my forehead, concern covering his wrinkled brow. I swatted him away.

"No, I'm just tired." My thoughts drifted to Drake and the warmth I experienced in his embrace, but also the temptation of his touch. I vowed that nothing would happen between us again after that night. I couldn't. I didn't want to be his wife. I didn't want to be a baby-making machine. I wanted my life without the expectation of power woven into it. *Freedom.*

"Kids?"

"No." I laughed awkwardly, my eyes glued to my feet.

"Did I pry too much?"

"No, no, it's fine." I sighed. "You know I'm married. It was arranged. I know they don't happen often, but in my family, they do, and it's new. It's not exactly something I wanted. He's older than me and rather set in his obnoxious and possessive ways. He just…infuriates me. I'm not the person that I used to be, and I've worked hard for everything in my life. I don't want to go back to the girl I was. I don't want to be scared to move, scared to breathe, scared to sleep because of the man who would sneak into my room at night." I shook my head, recognising the conversation had taken a turn away from Drake. "Sorry, I shouldn't have unloaded on you. I barely know you."

He shrugged. "I have that effect on people. Don't worry about it. Do you ever question why he's that way? I'm sure he has his own damage. Maybe try to get to know him better."

"Alright, Mr. Know It All." I rolled my eyes and chuckled, returning to my desk.

Kris and I continued to talk for the rest of the afternoon until the final lesson of the day. We got along really well. He made me feel comfortable when he spoke in his soft tones. Drake had allowed my phone to be returned and had been blowing it up ever since the other day.

Drake: I can't stop thinking about how good your cunt tasted. Shall we go another round tonight?

Daniella: Do you have to be so crude? I told you it is never happening again.

Drake: The sooner you accept that you are mine, the better it will be for both of us.

Daniella: Keep dreaming.

Drake: I will, the taste and feel of you is like fucking heaven.

My cheeks flushed. I put the phone away as Sam entered, snatching it from me and gasping at what she read.

"Oh, he's a poet!" She fluttered her eyes and held my phone to her chest.

"Stop it, Sam, it's not funny. I told you why it isn't." I reached for it, grabbing it away from her.

"I'm sure there is, but you're keeping quiet."

It was something I had to do for her safety. I'd told Sam too much already, and the thought of her getting hurt would destroy me.

Chapter Twenty-Two

Council Meetings

Daniella

I lay on the couch with my fluffy purple blanket, and something trashy was playing on the television. With my pen and notebook in hand, I wrote down more lyrics to the words that kept floating through my mind.

A fog so thick, I search for clarity. A musk that causes more confusion

Drake moved to stand before me. Ignoring him, I continued to think of what was next when a dress dropped onto my book.

"Put it on. We have a council meeting."

"Please. Manners matter, Drake," I quipped back at him.

"Pardon me, darling wifey, would you please dress in my family's colours so we can attend this redundant council meeting and not piss off the other members of the council?"

I snorted and laid the garnet-coloured wrap dress on the bed, pulling my hair from my face and picking a pair of eggplant heels to go with it. I waved my hair and put on minimal makeup. From what my mother told me, these meetings were used to measure dicks. Drake bringing me was sending a message to the other families that he'd no plans to give up his title as High Mage. I could hear loud voices outside the door. I zipped up the dress, stepped into my shoes, and left the room.

"Jackson, you're out of order," Drake warned his Arcanum. It wasn't the norm for these men to fight. They were bonded to one another in a similar way that Drake and I had to bond with blood and string. Jackson and Drake were more like brothers than friends.

"You know I'm right. She's not an acceptable choice. She hasn't transcended to her power. She's weak and will project that weakness onto you."

The warmth within the room increased in seconds, and my arms itched. I shook it off and walked over to Drake, laying my hand on his chest. I wasn't sure what compelled me to go over there, but it just felt right. He broke his gaze with Jackson and locked eyes with me. Heat radiated from his body, his fists clenching and releasing before he took my hand and kissed it. A simple nod, and I took a step backwards.

"Maybe it's best that I don't attend." I looked between the two men. I knew Drake's decision would have caused waves within the council, but I never thought that his second would question him. That showed more disharmony than I think even Drake expected.

"Out of the question. I don't give a flying fuck if they see you as appropriate or not. I've selected you to be my wife. You come from a strong family line. The fact that you haven't transcended means nothing and can be organised when the timing is right. My Arcanum needs to remember his place and that I have no issue removing him from his post if he so much as utters another word about your removal again." He paused, rolling his shoulders. "Are you ready?"

"Yes." I nodded, and he moved forward and kissed my cheek.

"You look fantastic. Jackson, take another car and think about your allegiance."

I slid into the blackened-out SUV, knowing the drive would be long. They held their underground meetings in the city, and Trafalgar wasn't exactly close by. Drake seemed to have no issue living in my tiny house, at least for now. He cleared his throat and fixed his cuffs.

"Daniella, it's important that you do *not* speak during this meeting. You're to sit beside me and smile. That's all that I expect from you. You haven't transcended to your power and therefore have no standing within that room. You'll be treated as second class, but you know this. Do not, and I repeat, *do not* disobey me during this meeting. It reflects poorly on me. I've built a reputation, and I'll have no problem issuing you a punishment that I see fit. Understood?"

I rolled my eyes, crossing my arms over my chest. "Yep, perfectly. Sit there and look pretty." The words made me ill. I'd worked almost a decade to erase the rules that had been instilled in me as a child, and here I was, back where I started, back to the beginning. Feeling like a pathetic, lower-class individual. I glanced out the window, tears welling in my eyes. I knew my father would be there, and the thought caused my skin to crawl. I hated the man, the harm he caused me, and his lack of remorse. These were the moments where I wished I had power, so I could drown him or suffocate him with a lack of oxygen, or wrap him up in vines.

"We're here," Drake grumbled, exiting the car, then walking around and holding open my door.

He offered his hand, and I slid mine inside. This was one of the few occasions where he seemed like a gentleman and not a complete and utter egotistical arsehole. I observed his black suit with a shirt matching the colour of my dress, a small tattoo threatening to reveal itself under his collar, and the eagle on his left wrist. It seemed a little cliché, but…

"Admiring the view?" A low chuckle erupted from his chest, and I snorted.

"You're not that important."

"Oh, Daniella, your denial makes it that much better. See, right now, all I'm thinking about is wanting to taste you, licking you up and down nice and slow, my tongue diving deep in your tight cunt. I want to feel your legs squeeze around me like you never want to let me go."

Heat rose to my cheeks, my mouth dropped open, and I stumbled on my footing.

"Yeah, I thought that might set you off a little bit. I bet you're already soaked – fuck, I'm hard at the thought of how good you tasted."

"Drake the Cinder King." A man bowed before him, lower than the expectation. Cinder King – a name bestowed on him by the council as a tribute to his reign, burning bright and leading fiercely.

"Ah, Travis, it's good to see you. How's your wife? The babe must be due soon, no?" He slapped his hand on his back, leaving me to follow two steps behind him as per our custom. The men were more important, especially a High Mage.

"Glad to know that you can follow the rules," Jackson muttered beside me.

"I can. I just don't make a habit out of it. Maybe you should remember some of those rules. You work for me as well now. Don't forget that." My voice sounded foreign, and that unfamiliar fog returned.

Drake peered over his shoulder and gave me a small wink, smirking as he turned his attention back toward this Travis. They were deep in conversation.

I followed them into the hotel, entering the elevator and standing in front of Drake. I could feel his eyes burning into the back of me, so I flicked my hair over my shoulder, giving him a sly look. He licked his lips. He wasn't wrong. I was soaked and horny as fucking hell. *Nope, you are sick in the head. There will be no sex with this man. You are simply biding time until you can escape, that is all, just biding your time.*

The elevator beeped open. The hallway was black and lit by a few circular sconces on the wall. I stepped out and moved to the side. Drake squeezed my arse on the way past, pausing for a moment.

"That's a good girl," he whispered in my ear, and my knees almost buckled at the sensual tone in his voice.

The door opened, and Drake entered, the remaining families bowing their heads. Drake pulled out my chair, and I took my seat beside him with my hand on the table. A sign of our union, he laced his fingers with my own, his thumb placed underneath, making small circles on my palm. I noticed Penelope in the corner, a small smile on her face as she took her seat.

"Gentlemen, I believe my bonded consort needs no introduction." He lifted his hand, placing a gentle kiss upon it. Another gesture to signify our vows to one another. It was antiquated, but part of me liked belonging to someone when I never had that growing up.

My eyes locked with my father's, and he sneered. I tore my eyes away. It hurt to look at him more than I needed to.

"Is something the matter, Giuseppe?" Drake queried, and I snapped my head in his direction. His eyes flared red for a small moment. A projection of his Fire power, lingering just under the surface. I scratched at my neck.

"No, I just don't understand why she's here when her opinion isn't needed."

"Yet here I sit, living rent-free in your head, it appears," I chimed in without thinking.

"You always were so full of yourself, Daniella."

"Better than being full of insecurities and projecting them onto your children," I snapped back at him, standing so fast that the chair fell backward. My hand was shaking with an all-consuming rage that I'd never experienced before.

"That's enough." Drake slammed his fist onto the table. "I will not have disorder in my chambers. If you dare to question my bonded consort, Giuseppe, you may do that in private and not within these sacred walls. She's *my selection.*"

"She hasn't transcended," Travis quipped.

I sank into my chair, wanting to disappear, but I couldn't be meek. I had to show them strength. I was the consort of the High Mage. I had to speak up. *Fuck his rules.*

"Ask Giuseppe about that. I wished to, but I was never given the chance because of him." I pointed toward him.

"You insolent child! You always were a little brat," he hissed in response.

"A brat? A brat? A *fucking* brat? You piece of shit. You don't deserve to live. You don't deserve to breathe the same air as me. You're worth nothing but the dirt that lingers under my shoe, pure utter trash. If the men here knew what you did, I doubt they would have your respect." My eyes grew fuzzy, my body shook. I wanted to kill him, to stand over his body and –

"DANIELLA!" Drake yelled, standing and towering over me, breaking the dark thoughts.

"No, he doesn't get to insult me when he –"

"ENOUGH! Out. Now!" he bellowed, his eyes intense and filled with emotions I couldn't read— anger, but it almost appeared that it wasn't directed at me.

"Drake, you ca –"

"I said out and I mean it." The room smouldered in heat, a small flame flickering from his fingertips.

Jackson walked over, offering his arm, but I ignored him. I left the room as instructed by our leader. I slammed the door closed and screamed. I made a promise the day I held my son in my arms that I would kill my father one day. I hoped that day would be soon.

Chapter Twenty-Three

A Messy Meeting

Drake

I watched Daniella be escorted from the room. Her relationship with Giuseppe certainly was complicated. Both spoke to one another with no respect. I could sympathise with having a fucking arsehole for a parent, but most daughters often loved their fathers. While she yelled, her eyes were wild, and there was something unusual about the way she spat at him.

I stroked the scar on my lip when Travis turned toward me.

"She isn't worthy of being your consort. We have a standard to uphold as Mages, and someone who hasn't transcended to their power goes against that. How can you consider her to produce heirs when she failed at the most basic of tasks?" Giuseppe smiled, clearly having whispered into Travis's ear, forming an alliance.

I cleared my throat, standing and moving to be opposite him. "Do you think I give a fuck what you think?" I leaned forward, the room warming from the intensity of my anger and my fire threatening to escape its containment. "Giuseppe hasn't mentioned the fact that his daughter is fertile and conceived a child before he excommunicated her for it. He never gave her the chance to receive her powers." I flicked flames between my fingers, snapping them. Small flames circled his head, and Travis clutched at his throat as they consumed the air around him. "If you ever speak of, about, or to my wife again, Travis, I will make sure that your entire family line is destroyed. Is that understood?" The flames grew brighter, his face paling at the realisation that I could kill him right now without hesitation. He nodded.

I snapped my fingers, watching the fire extinguish, before taking my seat once more and directing the discussion to the severity of the situation with these pesky Morteferi. They had attacked another family. It was only minor, but still, any attack on the coven weakened us. It seemed to be their aim at the moment. I may have contributed to this with my assault on them the other day. The meeting ended, thankfully, it was now time to discuss Daniella's behaviour.

"Giuseppe, a moment." It wasn't a request. He understood and waited.

"What's the history of the relationship between you and your daughter?" I queried, tapping my fingers together. It had been obvious since our first discussion and her behaviour on the day of our wedding, and today, that there were skeletons in the closet.

"She's no child of mine. I raised her with her fool of a mother. I told her from the start she was trouble. Unable to follow simple requests, she would stay out late at night despite the warnings of the dangers. She did what she wanted, whenever she wanted. She's a menace." His words irritated me. Something in them seemed almost hollow despite sounding fierce. He opened his mouth to speak once more.

I raised my hand. "That's all. You're dismissed."

I sighed, rubbing my forehead. I did question whether she was worth this trouble. She deliberately ignored my instruction to sit there and shut the fuck up. But the moment she spotted her father, her entire demeanour changed. Both were cryptic about why they despised one another. Jackson took a seat beside me, pushing a glass of scotch toward me.

"Don't say a word. I really don't need it right now, Jackson. You've made your point, and I don't agree. Yes, she hasn't transcended, but I can feel her power. It's dormant, but I can feel it when I'm around her. She's powerful, but has never been given the chance to actually use it."

"Her father said that she never really declared."

"Honestly, the man is a scumbag and always has been. Do you seriously believe anything out of his mouth?" I questioned, taking a sip. Jackson raised his glass before we clinked them together. "If you will excuse me, I must deal with my bonded consort and her disobedience. Head home, Jackson. It's about to get loud, no doubt."

I entered the office, my rage palpable after Daniella's outburst. She embarrassed me, even after I told her the expectations. She stood instantly, waiting for the inevitable fight. I did enjoy her passion.

A candle narrowly missed my head. "You had no right –" I raised my hand, informing her to stop.

"I had *every* fucking right. You're my wife."

"You don't get to tell me what to do." She threw a porcelain figure at me.

"Can you stop throwing shit like a fucking child and listen?" She lowered her arm. "You're not part of the council in any titled position. I told you not to speak. I warned you. All you had to do was sit there and look fucking pretty. It wasn't hard. You're aware of our rules and customs. You were raised with them."

"Giuseppe is a fucking arsehole. He shouldn't have even opened his mouth." She crossed her arms over her chest, pushing up those perky breasts. My eyes were drawn to them for a moment. She wasn't angry if her nipples were that hard.

"He's part of the inner sanctum; it doesn't matter how he spoke to you as a child. You're nothing in there. You're to be seen and not heard. You have *not* transcended. When you prove that you are worthy, you may speak. Until then, you sit down and shut the fuck up. Is that so hard for you to understand?"

"Fuck you, Drake," she snapped before she turned her back toward me, shaking her head.

"Oh, I fucking wish you would. Trust me. But instead, you fight me every fucking day. I know you are looking for a way out. There isn't one. Stop denying the chemistry we have. You're downright sexy, and I know just how good I look. Give in to that temptation and spread those fucking legs for me."

"You fucking wish," she spat at me, looking back, her grey eyes filled with passion. I grabbed her arm, spinning her into my body and kissing her harshly. She pushed against my chest, slapping my cheek.

"How dare you?" Her words were in anger, but her eyes showed desire. She wanted this.

I smiled at her. "I enjoy your fight. I know you're already dripping for me, Daniella, as you were in that elevator." My voice purred. I took a step closer, but she didn't move. "Stop denying what we have."

"What, contempt? Hatred?"

"No. Passion. You want to feel my cock inside you. You know how good it felt that day at the bar. How your cunt clenched around him, wanting him deeper. You want to ride him like you did my face the other day. Fucking perfection."

She stared hard at the door before looking back at me. Her brow creasing, she glanced at the floor and back at me and around the room once more. She bit her lip, and my cock hardened, knowing she was close to throwing down on this.

"Fuck it," she mumbled, unzipping her gown, pushing it down her curvy body. She stood before me wearing nothing but a bra. She'd been commando, her cunt just sitting there, waiting for me to reach over and touch it. The thought drove me wild with need.

"This means nothing." She walked over, pushing me onto the couch.

"Absolutely. I'm just a toy for you to fuck." I raised my hands in submission. I'd take whatever she would give me in this moment. I wanted to feel her.

She kissed me, and I grabbed her head and waist, bringing her closer. There had been so much tension, so much need for this one woman. I didn't care, I just wanted to fuck her so fucking hard until she screamed my name.

Her fingers fumbled with my shirt buttons. I ripped it open, pulling it off as her eyes sparkled at the sight before her. My body had been trained since I was young and moulded to perfection. Her finger traced a tattoo. My own finger trailed its way down her skin, hooking my fingers into her bra. Her body was flawless, her curves on full display, the rush of blood to my hard cock almost like a drug. If only she knew how sexy she was. I kissed her as she pushed back against me for control. I ran my fingers over her slit, her wetness seeping through.

"Fucking hell." I groaned as I slid my tongue into her mouth. She moaned against me, her body moving to the rhythm of my fingers. My thumb circled her clit as my finger found her entrance. I wanted to pick her up, but right now, I needed to be inside her. She rode my hand like a fucking dildo, chasing her release, and the noises she made were like music to my fucking ears. I quickened my pace, adding another finger into her tightness.

"Harder," she moaned, and I plunged deeper and harder.

"That's it, come on my hand." I flicked her clit.

"Yes!" she screamed, her eyes finding mine. She kissed me with a fierceness I didn't expect. I rushed to unfasten my pants, and she grabbed my face and kissed me. My hands ran up her back, unclasping her bra and grasping the hair at the back of her neck, forcing it back. I wanted to see her face as she lowered herself onto me.

It was a sight. Her eyes rolled slightly as she slowly took each fucking inch. I groaned, her walls already wanting to milk me, the idea of filling her making my balls want to explode inside her.

"Fuck me," I mumbled while I watched her ride me. Her tits were bouncing perfectly, her face showing the pleasure she was savouring. I wanted to capture the moment my wife fucked me, her sexy body bouncing on me, taking all of me inside her. Her hands landed on my shoulders for stability, and I held her waist as I watched my cock disappear into her wetness. I groaned.

"You're so fucking tight, Daniella, and all fucking *mine*." My words were harsh as her eyes sparkled, and she increased her pace. I matched it, her pussy tightening on me, the sensations fucking exhilarating.

"Drake!" she screamed and rode me harder. My hand snaked around her.

"We're not done yet." My fingers tightened, and her eyes burned with fire. She wanted this. I pushed her deeper onto my cock, thrusting harder. I growled at the feeling of her clenching around me.

"That's it, come for me, Daniella." Her walls spasmed as my own release came. I groaned, feeling my seed shoot inside her, and it gave me a different high, a need I never realised I had until her. She stilled as we stared at each other, panting and dishevelled. She stood, and I watched my seed run down her leg, pleased I had claimed her as mine.

I put my arms over the back of the couch, watching her collect her dress, the sight of her bending over giving me more ideas. My cock twitched at the thought of having her again.

"Not happening again." She pointed at me, and I laughed.

"Sure, Daniella, sure." I stood, strolling over to her. My fingers collected the seed threatening to escape, rubbing it over her pussy. Her eyes closed as her breath hitched. I grabbed her chin, forcing her to look at me.

"You're fucking mine now. This cunt is all mine."

"Just because we fucked doesn't mean shit." She reached for her bra.

"Oh, Daniella, you're filled with me. It's fucking mine." My fingers found her neck, walking her back toward the wall. She gasped from the thud. "Don't you fucking forget it." My other hand ran over her curves. "I made you come, and I'll do it again and again and fucking again."

"I *hate* you." Her grey eyes sparkled with loathing, but her body leaned into mine.

"Not what your body said five minutes ago. Get dressed," I ordered, grabbing my pants while she ran into the bathroom, slamming the door behind her.

I found her behaviour odd. Her father stated that she never declared, but she had shown Water magic. I observed the plant behind her father move tonight, shuddering in support while she argued with him. I noticed that around her, my fire burned brighter. I was curious to know more about her, but I needed the wall between us to shatter. I'd opened her legs, but I wanted her to open her soul to me.

CHAPTER TWENTY-FOUR

WALLS AND FLOORS

DANIELLA

I had never been more grateful for the rod in my arm, the constant birth control. No babies were coming anytime soon, like he wanted. Sex after our argument was phenomenal. The man knew how to touch a woman, but fuck, I hated him. He enjoyed watching me bounce on his dick. My legs clenched together, remembering how he filled me. I literally fucked him on a couch. I sipped my coffee, trying to focus on the day. Thoughts of him couldn't be allowed – Drake would never become a husband. The only goal now was escape. Sam had said we needed a plan, and maybe it was time for this planning to occur. Sam entered with her usual swagger, throwing her bag onto the desk, bags under her eyes.

"Kids didn't sleep?" I questioned, spinning my chair in her direction while drinking my coffee.

"You would think, considering they didn't during the day, that they would at night. I hate these stupid *leaps,* as they call them. Stupid fucking name. Something is happening in the baby's brain; new synapses are forming, and they will learn a new skill. It has been six weeks, time for this new skill already."

I snorted, pushing her morning coffee toward her. Sam always sent a text in the morning telling me what type of night she had, and we now had this unspoken language. No sleep equalled coffee, tantrums equalled chocolate, and spousal fighting equalled cake. Sam pulled chocolate out of her bag. As I leaned over to grab it, she yanked it back.

"You had sex." She pulled her chair out and moved closer. I was grateful nobody else was in the office when she continued, "No, don't you dare deny it. I can tell. You're glowing. Did you actually finish this time? I thought we hated that Mage fucker."

I bobbed my hands in the air. "Quiet, Sam, please." I rubbed my temples. "Yes, we had sex, and yes, it was fucking amazing. The man knows what to do, but I guess he's older and more experienced. His hands..." I coughed. "Not the point. He's a prick who literally claimed my vagina. He stated something along the lines of 'my seed is in you and therefore you are mine,' and I hate him." It wasn't a lie, but was also not completely truthful. Knowing that I belonged to someone when my family had literally treated me like crap, I felt a little at peace.

"Yes, yes, I'm so happy. What happens now? More sex? Also, what's with the possessiveness? I hate it, but I can't help but also love it." She laughed.

"No, I'm never doing that again." At least I knew she understood my daily struggle with some of the things he said. They sounded so rude, but they did things to my body that I'd never experienced before.

"What are we never doing again?" Kris entered, opening the fridge. My eyes were drawn to his biceps on display. Did the man not know how to dress professionally? My god, they were massive. "Dani?"

My gaze locked with his. His brow was creased, waiting for the answer.

"She was just telling me about her sex life."

"SAM!" I shouted at her. "No, I just…I'm heading to class." I fumbled over my words and rushed from the office. Sometimes her unprofessional behaviour really irritated me, especially talking about my vagina in front of Kris. I glanced over my shoulder to see him watching me with a smirk, crossing his arms over his chest. I spun quickly, but darkness enveloped me.

I woke up suddenly, looking at the ceiling, with Sam and Kris leaning over me.

"Dani, are you alright? Dani, can you hear us?" Kris's voice was soft as my ears perked up and my body registered that I was on the ground. I sat up suddenly before falling backward. Something solid stopped me. I peered over my shoulder to see Kris behind me. I was leaning on his chest, his legs on either side of my body. "Shh, Dani, I've got you. Gather yourself before moving. You ran into the wall with quite a bit of force."

I watched Sam run off toward the main office. I allowed myself to fall onto his back, and his hand stroked my hair while I composed myself. The world stopped spinning when Denise ran over. Denise did first aid while Kris continued to stroke my hair. I had never known such relaxation in my life.

"I've called your husband; he requested an update ASAP," she said with a rather mocking tone. I chuckled.

"That sounds like him. I'm alright, just have a slight headache."

"I think it's best to rest for now and see if you're up for staying for the rest of the day," Denise stated, tapping my leg and standing.

"Do you feel like moving, or did you want to sit in my lap for the rest of the day?" I sat up. "Not that I was complaining about it," Kris mumbled.

Sam laughed, holding out her hand to help me to my feet. I didn't bother to turn round to see Kris, shirt huggin his torso, rugged waves falling to his ears.

I waved over my shoulder. "Thanks, Kris." I turned to Sam. "I need a coffee. Want to go for a drive?" I asked, eager to get some air out of the school after embarrassing myself enough in front of teachers and students.

"I have a class. Sorry, you're stuck here because you shouldn't drive for a little while." She clicked her tongue while we returned to our desk.

"I'm free," Kris piped in. The hairs on my arms raised, and I stopped walking. Time seemed to slow down.

"She would love that." I rolled my eyes at Sam's remark. Kris strolled over with his keys in hand.

The car ride was awkward; neither of us spoke. I stared out the window at the old-style weatherboard homes with white picket fences and various colours of rose bushes. We saw students out and about when they should've been in school. We had a legal obligation to tell them to return to the school, but most teachers knew that they often returned home to collect food for lunch. They always came back. Kris gestured toward the one group who were renowned for wagging school.

"Should we?" Kris queried.

I sighed. "Yes. Did you want to call the office or speak to the girls?"

"I'll call the office," he deadpanned, pulling the car over.

I opened the door. "Girls, we know where we need to be. Turn around and go back to school, please. Mr. Fields has already called the office to let them know. Make the smarter choice and return, thank you."

"You're such a bitch," one of the girls replied with pure snark.

"Yep, but at least I'm an educated one. Bye now." I waved at them sarcastically, shaking my head and biting my tongue. I worried about the girls' future, being in the same position as them once upon a time. I hoped they would find their feet.

I returned to the car, my head splitting in half before noticing that Kris was laughing. I nudged him playfully. He pulled away from the kerb before parking about two hundred metres up the road. He ran around to open the car door, offering his hand, which I accepted. We entered the café, and I sat down while he grabbed some menus. He slid it over the table, and I opened it, avoiding eye contact for now.

"What would you like to order?" he asked, breaking the silence between us.

"I think an iced mocha with extra cream. I feel like indulging my sweet tooth. It isn't every day that you run into a fucking wall in front of what, about fifty people?"

He stroked his chin. "I think it was about sixty, actually. I'll order it now."

I put my phone in my purse, deciding not to respond to any more messages. I was allowed to have a life. Kris returned with a number.

"So, Dani, I know about your husband and your complicated life, but what else makes you tick?"

"No, you're the mysterious new teacher in the area. Tell me about Kris."

"Ah, yeah, I'm sure there are plenty of rumours." I nodded. "I moved out here to get away from the city. I hate the busyness. I prefer the quiet atmosphere. The school offered extra payment for being rural, and I thought it was a great opportunity. More money and more greenery."

"That tells me…absolutely nothing. Are you purposely trying to be cryptic?" I sniggered.

"How about you tell me about this so-called husband, and I'll tell you more. Quid pro quo." He chuckled as the drinks were delivered. He had a relaxed nature, but I noticed his eyes were constantly moving about the room.

"Drake. His name is Drake." My heart fluttered for a moment. "We have an arranged marriage. He's a good guy. He looks out for me, but we're still getting to know one another. It's hard to form a relationship with someone you've just met. We're very different. I'm only twenty-eight and he's forty-eight, so there's a big age gap, and of course, he wants children."

"What, you don't?"

"I honestly don't know if I want any more."

"Any more?" I closed my eyes. I'd never slipped up before. "Your secret is safe with me. I'm sorry for your loss."

I would take that. It was easier to explain than the truth, that I had to give him up to avoid any repercussions from the *organisation.*

"Your turn now." I motioned for him to speak.

"I lost my girlfriend late last year. We had an electrical fire, and she perished. I was away at camp and…" I noticed tears welling in his eyes, and I reached over for his hand. His eyes drifted, a small smile spreading over his face. We were still for what seemed like ages, just frozen in the moment together. Not looking away, my hand still on his for comfort.

"Glad to see you're feeling better." A deep voice echoed through my body. I let go of Kris's hand, quickly taking a sip of my drink, the fog disappearing. *What just happened?*

"Oh, you must be Drake?" Kris stood, offering his hand, and I watched Drake grip it tightly.

"Thanks for looking after my wife. I'll take over now. I've made a doctor's appointment to get a scan to ensure that everything is alright. Are you ready to go?" He posed his question toward me, but never broke eye contact with Kris. I couldn't believe he was marking his territory, but I giggled a little at Kris never breaking his focus on the man who towered over him in every manner of the word. There wasn't much competition between them. Drake would be able to snap his fingers and end him in seconds. I held my drink and stood, making my way toward the door.

Chapter Twenty-Five

A Fiery Encounter

Drake

My fists clenched while Daniella slid into the car. I slammed the door closed, adjusting my collar before taking my position in the front seat. I needed a little bit of space. When security informed me of her leaving the school—and with a male—I became enraged. I had to make my statement to the man. He crossed a boundary.

Daniella was naïve with her beauty. Her father had mistreated her, but she shone wherever she went. No need for makeup, she had natural beauty and those curves. I bit my thumb to contain the growing erection tenting in my pants.

"Are you just going to ignore me the entire drive?" she asked, shuffling in her seat.

"You're being checked out by a Mage expert. I have organised for other tests to be run while checking for any brain bleeds or concussion. What do you wish to discuss?"

She scoffed. "Maybe your attitude toward Kris. It was certainly not needed."

"Is he aware that you're married?" I queried, knowing the answer already from inspecting his file. I investigated all of her work colleagues.

"Yes."

"Then the attitude is warranted. A respectable man doesn't meet with a beautiful woman who is married to another unless he's a man of lesser morals."

"He's a work colleague. Don't you think you're being a little bit overprotective?"

"Did I not make myself clear the other night? I fucked you, I came inside you, I own you. That ring and that cunt are mine, and if any man dares to look at you in that manner, then I will be marking my fucking territory. Is that understood?"

"Yep, totally understood that you're an insecure arse. He's a work colleague. Get over yourself, Drake."

"Do you find him attractive?"

"I…argh…don't."

"Exactly, a man who wears tight shirts like that is a peacock. Stay away from him, Daniella. He's nothing but trouble, and it has nothing to do with insecurity, but more to do with keeping you safe. You seem to have forgotten how dangerous the world can be. Living amongst these humans has made you weak. He could be hexed by the Morteferi to lure you to them."

"Drake, you're paranoid. If the Morteferi knew about me living amongst the humans, don't you think they would have attacked me by now? I'm literally powerless." She scoffed. I looked in the mirror at her. She leaned back in her seat, crossing her arms.

"I wish, Daniella, I wish," I mumbled as the car entered the parking garage.

I always had to be alert and with Daniella close, and that had only amplified. Her safety was my priority. The area was quickly scanned before the door swung open for her. My hand reached out, steady and waiting, and she slipped hers into it without hesitation. She saw nothing but an arse but I'd always protect her.

The doctor checked her over; she had a mild concussion and had to be watched for twenty-four hours with no screens or phones. Her brain needed to rest. She grumbled, but complied. He gave her some stronger painkillers for the headache. He drew some blood; there was a marker within a Mage's blood that would inform Mages or Morteferi if they had been blessed with power. Something was missing from Daniella's past; I needed information to protect her from the unrest within the council about her lack of magic. I honestly found no reason to be misguided by her; she came from a Mage and would pass on those genes to our children. I didn't care for any other nonsense.

"Hand over your phone." I put my hand before her, waiting patiently.

"You can't be serious, Drake. Do you honestly believe that this will make much difference?"

"Do you think that I don't take your health seriously? Hand it over. You can have it back once you've rested."

She grumbled and handed it over before opening and slamming the car door. I laughed and sat beside her.

"Where are you dragging me now?" she snarked at me.

"You do realise that you act like a teen on occasion. I think you've been around them for too long."

"That doesn't answer my question."

I pinched the bridge of my nose and exhaled. "The doctor said you are to be monitored. The Morteferi attacked another family. I'm going to visit them and see if they need anything. You'll be coming along, and luckily, you're dressed appropriately. It's a win-win."

More silence enveloped the car. The family lived on the other side of the city. Craig had survived the attack, but his wife had grown rather anxious and paranoid.

"I didn't realise that you cared so much for the people in the Coven," she muttered.

I glanced over, watching her fidget with her skirt. She had become shyer, more guarded than usual. I watched her for a moment. This wasn't like my fiery little red head.

"Daniella." My voice was soft to match hers, and her gaze locked onto mine. "I care about more than you could ever imagine. Every person within my Coven, I consider them family, and I will protect and care for them as such. Why do you think I've grown one of the strongest in Australia?"

"I heard…" She stopped.

I twisted in my seat. "You heard that I murdered my father for power. I took control of this coven and wanted all to live in fear and killed any who dared question me."

"Not quite, but I did hear that you murdered your father. It happened before I was excommunicated, and I remember Giuseppe was terrified because of his close relationship with him. You apparently came around a couple of nights after that, but we never met."

"Yes, your father said you were out drinking."

She scoffed. "I wish. He locked me in my room so I wouldn't embarrass him."

"He did what?" My voice rose. He locked her away, for what?

"It's nothing, Drake. He was ashamed of me, but I think it was his own shame that he attempted to hide." She rested her elbow on the window and watched the scenery. I opened my mouth to speak.

"Drake, we are here." The driver's voice irked me. I wished to discuss this further with Daniella, wanting to know why he tried to hide his shame. She was slowly opening up more about their complex relationship, and I didn't want the interruption.

"Am I allowed to speak here?" She raised her brows and bit her lip. I wanted to sink my own teeth into them. She was so sexy. I adjusted my pants and nodded. This wasn't a typical council meeting, and her presence might aid Craig's wife's anxiety. Her eyes sparkled while I fixed my semi. I winked at her, and she shook her head. I knew she wouldn't be able to resist my charms. I had an enviable body. I worked hard at it, and I played that against her.

We entered the house to see Craig sitting on the couch. His arm was in a sling with bruises all over his face, and his wife, Adrianne, bit her nails while she waited for the kettle to boil. Daniella made her way over to his wife and pulled her into a tight embrace. Soft sobs echoed in the small space. I moved closer to Craig, needing answers more than anything.

"I need you to tell me what happened and why she's so upset. You've been attacked in the past, so what's different this time?" I queried, putting my hand on his leg.

"They were our neighbours. We were close. They babysat our son. They just attacked with no warning, and we weren't prepared." The house was eerily quiet. Something was off. I could feel a shift in energy.

Daniella strolled back into the room, her eyes locking with my own. They were intense, trying to convey a message. She glanced at her hand, pointing her thumb toward the ground. A pulse surged through the house, and I jolted to my feet, reaching for Daniella, my hands clasping around hers.

"We need to get out of here now," I muttered to her.

"Drake, I apologise, but I think the concussion is starting to have an effect. My headache is more like a migraine now." A perfect excuse to make our leave.

"Of course, I apologise, Craig and Adrianne, but I'd best take Daniella home to rest. She tripped over and ran into a wall, silly little thing. I'll be back to check on you tomorrow." I squeezed Daniella's hand tightly; she understood, moving toward the door.

"Do you honestly think we're going to let the powerful Drake leave?" Craig stood, his face contorted, and the room shook before as their hex was removed, revealing the dead bodies of the entire family. I pushed Daniella behind me, fire licking my fingers and ready to attack.

I stared at my opponent, his dark hair pulled back into a tail, wearing dark pants and a white shirt. He cracked his wrists and his fingers. I could see the gold of his Air magic moving between them. I could take him, but I had to be quick.

"Drake." Daniella's voice was soft and weak, terror evident in her words. She was powerless in this moment, and we were against two Morteferi. I held up my finger to my opponent, turning toward my bonded consort. I didn't fear an attack while my back was turned—they liked to fight like face-to-face.

"I need you to trust me. Turn around and stare at the door. Don't turn around until you feel my hand in yours. I won't let anything happen to you, I promise." I noticed the leaves of the fern move closer to her, despite there being no draft in the house. She nodded and did what I asked.

I spun back around. "Let's dance."

He pushed his magic toward me, trying to suffocate the air around me. The problem with this naïve move was that I could use it to my advantage. I flicked one flame toward the magic and watched it ignite, forcing it toward the arsehole. I would enjoy listening to his screams. I hated the Morteferi, and I would relish the day I destroyed them all for what they had done to all of us Mages.

Fire engulfed the room, and he attempted to put it out, which only fuelled the flames to burn brighter. I took a step closer, forcing the fire to surround him and his accomplice. I had to focus on one at a time, but having them trapped made it easier.

"Now tell me, what's your next move?"

"Go to hell."

"I'll see you there one day, you fuck, but right now, it all depends on the answer you give and the type of death you shall receive."

"I'm loyal to our Lord God, the unyielding and all-powerful."

"If he were all-powerful, he wouldn't be worried about a few Mages and slowly wiping their existence from the history books since the beginning of time. Now, spill or prepare for a fiery death." I chuckled at my pun.

"Fuck you."

"As you wish." I grabbed him by the throat, forcing a fireball into his mouth, holding his nose until he gasped for breath. I watched the fireball make its way down his throat, glowing as it burned his insides. He proceeded to cough, dark smoke escaping from his mouth. I punched him in the gut, and he fell to the floor, choking on what air he could manage around the flames slowly consuming his life.

I moved toward the second Morteferi, ready to attack, when I paused. I wanted to send a message to the leader. I waved my hand, extinguishing the flames in a second.

"You're the lucky one tonight. I want you to return to your cesspool with this message. Leave my Coven alone, or I will start hunting each and every one of you. I'll make it my personal mission to track down each of your houses and murder your families before drawing out your death in the worst possible fashion. Do you think you can remember that, or do you need me to write it down?" He nodded and ran out the back door.

"Drake!" Daniella shrieked, and I spun to see her surrounded by fire. I watched for a moment. The flames weren't harming her; only her fear was causing this panic. I snapped my fingers, and the flames disappeared in a second. She fell to her knees, sobs leaving her chest, her arms wrapped around herself. I picked her up, wrapping her legs around me and holding her for a moment. I reached for the door, and the handle burned my skin.

"Those fuckers."

"What is it?" she asked, lifting her head from my shoulder. I put her down, touching the door once more and feeling the same burning sensation.

We were trapped. They hexed the entire house. My only solution would be burning the entire house down, but I couldn't with Daniella inside. I paced the corridor. They planned this, and I had walked into their trap. They played on my nature to care for my Coven. *Those motherfuckers.*

Daniella was quiet, which was unlike her. She stood staring at the door, standing a little too close. The fern moved ever so slightly, and the temperature in the room increased.

"What are you doing?" I asked, moving closer to her.

"They hexed the door because they knew you would come. What if the hex only applies to you? They obviously have been watching you, so it would be the smart play. You would be too stubborn to call for help, or they would block the reception so you couldn't make a call."

"Your point, Daniella?" I exhaled, scratching my chin.

"What if I can touch the door? What if I was never part of their equation?"

"*DON'T* touch the fucking door!" I bellowed at her.

"Why not? I could be right. Think about it."

"I heal from burns; it's part of Fire magic. If you are burned, it will be a permanent scar on your skin."

"Drake, I have no magic. Hexes don't work on humans unless they are meant to do that. Just let me try, please." She placed her hands together. I didn't want to risk her, but what if she was right?

"Fine." I stood directly behind her, ready for anything.

Her hand shook, slowly reaching for the door handle. My heart thumped in my ears, my fire licking at my fingers, ready to explode at the idea of her being burned. I knew in my gut that she had power; it was either blocked or she never had the chance, but she was more than a mere powerless Mage. Her hand clasped around the handle. Silence. Nothing happened. My hand connected to her hip, and she pulled slightly on the handle. Intense buzzing echoed through my ears, and I let go, dropping to the floor, covering the noise that burned its way into my brain. Daniella's scream pierced through it. I wrapped my arms around her waist, lifting her over my shoulder and out of the house. She thrashed wildly on the ground, scratching at her entire body and her eyes as they glowed amethyst. I held her arms down, and her legs kicked wildly. She screamed incoherently. I tried everything to get her to stop or listen, but she was unresponsive.

I popped the trunk, hoping that the simple potion in the boot would stop the hex eating away at her soul. I rushed over, pressing the needle into her soft skin. I forced my body on top of hers, waiting for it to take effect, before there were only slight spasms and eventually nothing. I moved cautiously, pushing the hair from her face. She was unconscious. I shot flames at the house. There could be no evidence for the human world to see. I watched it take alight before lifting Daniella into the car. "Drive," I ordered, stroking her hair, and filled with guilt. But it was quickly souring into retribution. I would kill them all.

Chapter Twenty-Six

What Happened?

Daniella

The dark room was oddly silent. My eyes struggled to focus with the pounding in my head. My body ached in places that I wasn't aware it could. I took a moment before feeling somebody stroking my head. I smiled at the idea of being cared for with such tenderness.

"Drake," I murmured, leaning further into the hand.

"Who's Drake, sweetheart?" A soft, feminine chuckle filled the space. I hadn't heard the voice in so long, I'd almost forgotten who it was.

"Mum." My voice croaked, my eyes snapping open to see the woman who could pass as my twin.

"Hello, beautiful girl, you took quite a tumble. Take it slow." It took to moment to register. I was in my childhood bedroom. I glanced around, seeing the posters of fairies and unicorns. My legs were tiny. I was a child again.

"Mummy." I jumped from the bed, wrapping my arms around her tightly. She passed when I was five. I barely remembered her. I had a few photos, but Giuseppe had tried to remove all aspects of her from his life. I hated never having known her. My stepmother—who I considered another mother, had raised me, but I was always considered belligerent by my father, or rather *stepfather*. I never knew my biological father. I had been told that he wasn't worthy of being known, but part of me wished I had. "I miss you."

"I haven't gone anywhere, beautiful girl. I've been by your side as I always will be." She kissed the top of my head.

"Daniella…Daniella…Are you alright? Daniella." I could hear Drake's voice calling me, but I wanted to stay in my mother's arms. I never wanted to leave her.

"Don't make me leave. I want to stay with you."

"I love you, Daniella Irina Romano."

"MUM!" I shouted, my eyes opening to see my bedroom and Drake sitting beside me.

"Hey, hey, calm down." He pulled me into his arms, and I rested against him, gathering myself after having seen the woman I missed so much. "You saw your mum, I'm guessing. How was it?"

"Surreal."

"What I wouldn't give to see my own mother one more time." He sighed deeply, tightening his grip on my body, a small sniffle echoing between us.

"What happened to her? I heard it was the hunters."

"A little more complicated than that, but yes, ultimately the hunters took her life. It's why I'm determined to destroy them and want to focus on growing the strongest coven imaginable, in hopes of making them terrified to attack us. It isn't quite working for me." He paused before moving to fluff some pillows and handing me a coffee. I settled into them, smelling that delicious scent of comfort. "It was my father's doing. They attacked our house, determined to kill any Fire Mages. They spoke of ancient stories of them being the undoing of magic. I remember it vividly. Father was a Fire user, and Mother was a Water user. I cowered in my mother's arms while my father tried to fight them off. We ran to the garage, managed to escape into the car, and waited."

He stroked the scar on his lip, moving about the room. "My father entered, stating the coast was clear, but when we re-entered the house, we found one of the hunters still alive. My father fell to his knees, gasping for breath. My mother used her water to surround the hunter, and he became distracted, dropping his attack on my father, who…" He clenched his fists. "He used this as an opportunity to push my mother toward the hunter. He grabbed me and ran. He threw me into the car, and we drove away. That cowardly act cost me my mother. He killed her for his own selfishness. I lost—"

He stopped. I understood his cold demeanour now. He lost the positive influence in his life for a selfish reason. I pushed away the blankets, walking over and rubbing his back. He tensed for a moment before relaxing, then he spun, wrapping me in his strong embrace.

"I promise, Daniella, I will never do that to you. I'm not the man my father wanted me to be. I'm the man my mother wished for me to be. I—"

"You're the best of both worlds; you're ruthless like your father, but your heart is bigger than you let people see. I understand, Drake. There's no need to say anymore. I'm sorry for your loss."

"As am I, Daniella, as am I." We stood holding one another, not moving, before a knock broke the focus. Drake kissed my head and moved toward the door. His cold demeanour had returned in a second, and he flung the door open. "What?" he growled, his rash attitude back like he wasn't just showing he had a heart. I felt weak and needed to rest.

He turned back toward me. "Rest. We need to discuss what happened at that house later. I have to tend to something. Sorry, Daniella."

I waved him off, already about to fall asleep.

Chapter Twenty-Seven

The Buried Truth

Drake

I needed to discuss this attack with the rest of the Coven and called an emergency meeting. The Morteferi were increasing their attacks. It made no sense to lure me into a trap and harm my wife. I paused in the doorway, glancing over my shoulder at my wife, recovering from being hexed. I had never seen amethyst-coloured eyes before. They caused her harm, but it would never happen again. I couldn't lose another woman in my life; one was enough. Those fuckers.

I drove myself, needing time to settle my rage. A rage that palpated through my entire body, wanting to explode, wanting to tear every single one of those motherfuckers to pieces. My hands flickered with flames while I banged my hand against the steering wheel. I tore into the car park and rushed toward our conference room. A safe place, a place to fix this shit. I pushed the double door open, the bang bringing their focus to me.

"What's the meaning of this, Drake?" Zane yelled, clutching his chest at my dramatic entrance.

"The meaning of this…" Flame exploded from my hands, my anger taking control. "They set a fucking trap. They have an insider in our Coven, and I want to know who the fuck it is. My bonded consort almost died. Who knew about Craig's death?" I asked, watching each of their faces intently for any clues. They would be fools to betray me, especially knowing what I did to my father.

I watched as every man bent the knee and bowed their head. A sign of respect, a sign of loyalty, a sign that they knew nothing of this.

Giuseppe looked up. "How's Daniella?" he asked curiously about the daughter that he didn't seem to care for.

"She will live. The hex caused her body to have a visceral reaction. Unlike anything I've ever seen, almost as if"—I offered my hand to him—"the hex didn't know what to do with her. Normally it attacks, but her body fought in a way that…" I closed my eyes, remembering the way her body shook and twitched, trying to rid it from her. My thoughts drifted to the fern that seemed to respond to her. "I think a trip to The Keepers may help with answers on that hex placed upon that house."

I planted myself at the head of the table. We spoke of our game plan for future attacks and how we'd to have protections in place. Even going as far as to converse about restrictions on movements. My people had to be safe.

I arrived home shortly after midnight, washing away the stress and energy that lingered under my skin. I slid into bed beside Daniella, her soft snores filling her tiny room. I rolled over, pulling her into my arms. Her body melded to mine and brought a relief I didn't know I needed.

"Drake." Her croaky voice cut through the darkness.

"Shhh, back to sleep, Daniella." I kissed the back of her shoulder, the room filling with her sounds once more. I held her tight, realising how much this woman had slowly been infecting my soul.

✦

I woke the next morning, the bed devoid of Daniella. I heard her laughter. I rubbed my eyes, opening the door to see two of my men sitting at her tiny dining table, eating breakfast while Daniella sipped on her coffee. Her gaze met mine, and a brief moment of tenderness flickered in those grey eyes, replaced with a passion-fuelled hate.

"Give us the room," I ordered my men, wanting to discuss an issue she needed to know about. They collected their plates and headed outside to finish their meal.

"You could've given them time to finish." She poured the rest of her coffee into a thermos before moving about and placing a plate on the table for me. I sniggered at the routine that had been developing between us.

"They know their place. We must discuss the new restrictions placed upon Mages going forward." She took a seat beside me, stealing a piece of bacon from my plate. "Mages must be home before sunset and must be accompanied by another person at all times. This is mandatory to ensure that no further attacks occur."

"I understand. It makes sense."

My knee bounced, anxiety filling my body at the words I wanted to say, words that would explain many things about me. Her hand reached over, squeezing mine tightly, the tenderness returning with the tiniest smile on her beautiful face, framed by her fiery red locks. My throat burned, and my mouth opened to utter a truth that nobody knew except my Arcanum.

"Dr—" I shook my head; it had to be said.

"I killed him because I lost control." The heaviness was gone within seconds. My breathing slowly stabilised as her hand caressed my cheek. I placed mine over the top of it. "After my mother's murder," I chuckled uncomfortably, "my father turned to drugs. Not the standard, but the magical type. The ones that cause Mages to lose themselves. Every night, he would dose himself to forget the pain, to remove the guilt of leaving his wife behind to die for his own selfishness. Every night, I had to carry him to bed after he passed out. The longer he used, the more dangerous he became. His powers grew erratic, and he would burn random objects in the house by mistake."

I stood up to put space between us, my hands leaning on the counter, my back turned to her. I could feel my fire tingling in my fingers, my nails glowing in preparation. Her cold touch soothed the demons infecting my brain with the memories I had buried for so long.

"He became violent after a while, the drug no longer taking away the pain. He used my face as a punching bag to process the emotions he'd buried." I tapped the scar on my brow and lip. "One night, it got worse. He lost control of his fire, and the use of it triggered my own as a defence. My father had always been in control, while I had always walked that line of control and chaos and…I lost it. The man who sacrificed my mother, the man who should have taught me better, but instead became a dangerous monster. The house began to burn around us, and he threw fire at me. I caught it; my anger seethed that he had intended to harm me in such a manner. I tossed it back, and the flame consumed him. He barely screamed. He knew it was his time, and he appeared almost at peace. I killed him."

She pulled me into her arms, holding me tight. "It's alright."

I could feel an invisible wall around my heart shatter, a small insight into the monster I'd become. The pain that ate away at me for years, the pain that didn't feel so bad after telling her.

"I suppose we have more in common than we realise." I chuckled, and attempt to hide the ache growing in my chest.

"It wasn't your fault." Four words that chipped away at my frozen heart, letting *my inferno* in to bring me back to life.

Chapter Twenty-Eight

Emotions, what are they?

Daniella

I returned to work two days later under the guise of a concussion, determined to tell Sam the truth when we were alone. I sat at my desk, getting myself organised for the day by printing out worksheets on the importance of having renewable resources, such as water. It was an incredibly boring topic, but one mandated by the government. I typed the lessons into the learning program we used before finishing my coffee and heading to the main staffroom to make another. I kept to myself. It was awkward now that my colleagues knew I was married to a mystery man I had never mentioned. I tried to avoid bringing up my personal life in general.

I checked my pigeon hole before opening up the coffee sachet and adding my sugar. I wanted to get in and out quickly.

"Ah, there she is." I glanced up, seeing Kris with an elbow leaning on the bench, his legs crossed, and sipping his coffee. My eyes were drawn to his thick forearms, the muscles twitching as a smirk played over his lips.

"H-hey, Kris." My hands shook; the man always made me feel a little off-centre. I couldn't stop looking at him. Something about his relaxed nature intrigued me. I was the girl who always had to be put together, but he was the complete opposite.

"How's your head feeling?" he questioned, pushing himself off the bench and strolling over toward me. The smell of his earthy cologne ignited my senses. I cleared my throat and shuffled away, wanting to add space between us.

"Yeah, I feel better. I pretty much slept all day yesterday. It just felt like my body had been split in half, my head wouldn't stop spinning, and the nausea was next level. I feel more alive today. How has work been?"

"Oh, you know, the usual. Worrying about my work colleague after her husband"—I wanted to roll my eyes, but I lifted my coffee to my lips instead—"went full alpha dick on me." My coffee spurted from my mouth all over his shirt.

"Fuck, I'm so sorry." I grabbed the napkins, patting his hard chest. He unbuttoned the top two buttons, pulling it over his head. My hand instinctively reached for the shirt, his semi-wet chest on display with his incredibly defined abs drifting toward that delicious—

"Dani?" I glanced up, my cheeks flushing at realising the perve I was having on my coworker's naked body.

"Sorry, I got—"

"You got a good look. Can I have my shirt back? I'll dry it in the bathroom. Lucky it's black, and I'll smell like delicious coffee for the day." I handed the shirt over to him, and he glanced over his shoulder before entering the bathroom. I grabbed my coffee and left the main staff area promptly.

I packed my bag with everything I needed for the day, so I could hide in my classroom with my embarrassment. I flicked on the lights and started to write up the lesson on the board.

> Drake: Enjoy your day at work. I'm sorry I wasn't here this morning.

> Daniella: It's all good. I will see you for dinner.

> Drake: I'll be late, but I have plans to cook for you.

I sniggered at the thought of his impossibly large frame moving about in my tiny kitchen. Despite the fact that I never wanted this, Drake was trying to be as accommodating as he could.

I returned to the office at the end of the day, grabbing my notepad and heading to the cafeteria for our nightly meeting. I sat at the back of the room, hoping to hide from those pesky questions. A few staff came up and asked to see my ring (which I never wore) and how the wedding was. I gave them all the same response—that I was focused on work right now, or that I didn't have my phone to show them any pictures. Everyone had taken their seats, and I breathed out in relief at being alone at the table.

The chair squeaked beside me and flipped around before Kris sat down beside me, backwards on the chair.

"How's the coffee shirt?" I asked smugly.

"I didn't feel the cold for the first half of the morning." A smile played over his lips, while I chuckled and glanced back down at my piece of paper.

I needed to draw to focus on what was being discussed during the meeting. I started with small circles in the corner when Kris stole my pen to draw a grid for knots and crosses. He handed my pen over, and I drew an X in the middle box, nudging him to have his turn. He moved closer, causing his elbow to brush against mine.

"You don't have any liquid with you now."

"Oh, you're funny."

"Dani! Kris! Are you two paying attention back there?" our principal asked.

"Yeah, you were talking about the NAPLAN results being better than the previous year and the increase in literacy, but a small decrease in comprehension. We heard it all. Please continue."

I stared at Kris, dumbfounded. I was too focused on kicking his arse to listen to the presentation.

"One of us has to pay attention, especially with you dead set on beating me at this game."

"I hate to lose," I whispered, letting him fall into the basic trap. I placed my X in the top right corner. He was essentially at checkmate; he just didn't know it yet.

"I find it comical, the way you bite your lip and your tongue comes out slightly when you concentrate. I could be letting you win."

"I doubt that."

"Why? I never mind when a woman wins. They should always be on top."

I swallowed hard, pushing the paper away after beating him at this game.

"Round two?"

He drew another grid, and by the end of the meeting, we were giggling like teenagers. Sam waltzed over, a smug look on her face, kicking the back of my chair. The meeting had finished, and we barely noticed. I scrunched up the paper, throwing it into the bin and returning to my office with Kris walking beside me. I packed up for the night and left. I paused for a moment.

"Were you waiting for me?" he asked while he batted his eyes; he was a little flirt.

"Don't be so full of yourself. I was trying to remember if I had everything." We exited the building. When I dropped my sunglasses, Kris bent down to grab them before placing them on my face.

"There we are."

I snorted, pushing him out of the way playfully. When I looked ahead, it was to see Drake leaning against the blackened-out SUV, his arms crossed, the seams of his suit threatening to explode at the size of him. He had a scowl on his face.

"You're in trouble now. I'll see you tomorrow, Dani." He snuck off to his car while I waited for Drake to berate me about my naïvety. I held my head high, and he stared over my shoulder, presumably at Kris. He put out his hand, taking the strap of my bag from my shoulder and pulling me flush against his body. His lips crashed mine, a demanding and possessive kiss, claiming me in front of my work colleagues. His grip tightened on my arms, and I could feel his need harden, poking me. A small groan rumbled through his chest. I leaned into him further; he was setting me on fire, whether literal or figurative.

"In the car, Mrs. Vatras," he ordered, opening the door and giving my behind a small tap. Hearing a different last name had no effect on me. I'd changed my name after running away. As long as Daniella never changed, I didn't care what my last name was.

"Yes, sir." I raised my brows and slid inside. He climbed in not long after. "Did you enjoy staking your claim…again?" I mumbled, noticing my phone beep with a message from Kris. I put it away, not wanting to check it.

"Yes, I did, and you taste amazing. The best part is, you also enjoyed it…" I opened my mouth. "Don't try to deny it. You started to grind into me. You wanted to feel my cock deep inside. It's been a few days, and I must say, I'm itching to be inside your tight cunt once more. It felt euphoric to know that I filled that little hole with me." He looked down. "Look, I'm already rock hard thinking about it."

"Oh, go away, Drake. I told you it isn't happening again," I responded, quickly avoiding eye contact.

"Why? Because you're waiting for that weak man to give you a sign. I saw the way you smiled at him. Do you want to fuck him?" he snarled, his tone unlike any I had heard before. He was jealous.

"Drake, just stop, seriously." I glanced out the window, done with this conversation.

He slammed his hand against the car door. "Answer the fucking question."

"No, I won't because it's absurd."

"Turn the car around!" he shouted at his driver.

"What are you doing?"

"Let's go and visit this Mr. Kris Fields and ask him the question."

"Drake, just stop. This is when I fucking hate you. You don't own me, and I have every right not to answer your messed-up questions."

"You almost died, Daniella!" he shouted, his hand igniting with flames. My body warmed, and I felt tingles rush through me

"Is that what this is about?" The car went quiet, and he didn't say another word.

✦

I sat in my room, staring at the ceiling. I knew Drake cared about me, but could I cross that line with him? I had so many secrets. I felt sick thinking of actually saying them aloud. What would happen if I did? What judgement would I receive? Would he be able to forgive me for my mistakes? I sighed, my fingers running through the tangles in my hair.

There was a soft knock at the door. "Daniella?" His voice was meek and croaky.

"Yes," I answered, unsure of what else to say since the car ride, when he showed some form of emotion toward me — emotions I hadn't thought him capable of, revealed in his temper as he mentioned me almost dying. He projected strength, but his heart was larger than either of us realised.

He entered, his gaze locked onto mine. I noticed his hands, his fingers fixing the cuff of his shirt.

"I would still like to take you to dinner. I have reservations at eight. If you would like—no, I'm not asking. You will be dressed within the next ten minutes. I'll wait for you in the car." He turned on his heel and left.

I sat for a moment, sighing, before I stood and flicked through my robe to find a dress. My fingers settled on a beautiful, tight black piece that clung like a second skin. Hair was fluffed quickly, then pinned off my face, leaving my face makeup free. Pink heels were chosen with a matching clutch, and with that, I was ready. Drake was nowhere to be seen. One of his guards pointed toward the car outside, and I ventured out, seeing him standing at the letterbox.

His back was turned, shoulders stiff as he stared out at the open road stretching endlessly before him. The silence hung between us. The clack of my heels echoed against the concrete. I was ready. He glanced over his shoulder, slow and deliberate. I wondered if he was afraid that I would run if he turned too fast.

I watched his muscular frame move, rotating with a kind of solemn grace. His eyes dropped to my feet first, travelling upward, slowly taking in every curve, like he was memorising me one inch at a time. The serious look on his face began to soften, his eyes alight with sparks. Almost like he was seeing me in a new way—me, dressed up and elegant—for *him*. A version of myself I hadn't given him yet. Seeing him this way, the vast distance between us seemed to grow smaller, almost close enough to touch the barrier that kept us from connecting. The barrier I was terrified to lower, but maybe tonight, that would change.

He moved to the car, opening the door and extending his hand. I slid mine inside his warmth, squeezing slightly. Drake sat beside me, a little closer than usual, that gap shrinking that little bit more. His hand sat in the empty space between us instead of in his lap, placing my own hand beside his. I watched my small town disappear, moving impossibly fast. I'd been focusing on running away, but in this moment, I was beginning to question whether or not that was even a choice. Drake appeared beside me, offering everything I had ever wanted from life, the one thing I had been chasing since my father kicked me out over ten years ago. I closed my eyes. I had to break the metaphorical wall. I had to tell him the truth.

Tonight, I would tell him everything.

Chapter Twenty-Nine

The Pain of the Past

Daniella

The conversation flowed between us, filled with small questions about likes and dislikes. I took a deep breath, and Drake reached over, almost like he could sense what was coming. He smiled, and it was one of the few times that it reached his eyes. The man who had threatened and killed people was displaying a tenderness that almost seemed impossible.

I exhaled deeply. "Drake, I need you to promise me that once I open this door to you that you won't act on it. You'll take this information and lock it in a box, and you'll leave this past in the actual past. I'm not telling you to start anything, but I want you to understand me."

He squeezed my hand. "You're aware of my mother's death—the one commonality between us is losing our mothers at such a young age. It leaves a mark on your soul, and it causes more harm than you ever thought possible. The strength in the family is torn away in seconds. Giuseppe, as you're aware, isn't my biological father. My mother married him while pregnant, and when I was born, he was a kind and caring father. He taught me how to ride a bike, taught me how to swim, and he did all the things that a considerate man does. He remarried my stepmother, whom I love, and I don't blame her. I never have and never will. I doubt she is aware of how sick the man she married was. They conceived my siblings, and despite being no blood relation, I'll always see them as my brother and sister. After she gave birth, my stepmother struggled with her mental health and turned to the bottle to placate her illness. She became a shell, so I took care of my siblings, getting them dressed, fed, and anything they needed."

My heart thumped faster in my chest, sweat beading on my forehead. I'd only told one other person about this, and he was now dead. I swallowed hard, pushing aside the fear threatening to shut me up.

"One night, Giuseppe came home drunk, and my stepmother was passed out on the couch. I'd just covered her with a blanket before getting ready to sleep myself. My father entered and said, 'I need a cuddle. I want you to join me. Come and have some cuddles with your father.' I was thirteen at the time, and it started with cuddles, but I'm sure you are aware of what it progressed to." I took a moment, taking a deep breath. My hands shook, and bile rose in my throat. "He manipulated me and messed with my head, making me believe that I had caused this, that I had seduced him. It was all my fault. He would call me his *little slut* and *his plaything*, among other names." Drake stiffened, registering why I ran that first night we had been intimate.

"I did what I could to stay out past curfew to avoid being at home. I encouraged my stepmother to get help and got her into programs, but that only infuriated him further. I couldn't stay in that house, in that family. My friend, John, and I devised a plan. He knew about all of it. I had confided in him on multiple occasions. We met at the park one night while out past curfew. He was human, and I never told him the truth about this world. I craved normality, and it was something John unknowingly offered. We slept together. Without protection. I knew what this would do, and I didn't care. I could escape. I know it was stupid, but I was young and all I cared about was escaping. Not long after that night, I saw the light at the end of the tunnel. I told Giuseppe I was pregnant, and he lost it. I think his fear that the child could be his is what caused my excommunication. I was finally free. I cried so hard, feeling that tether to the coven snap. *I was free.* I was allowed to live the life I wanted."

Tears were running down my cheeks. "I cried for days. Not out of fear, but the possibility, the future that stood within my grasp. Then he killed John. I wasn't going to risk my life and that of my unborn child. I ran, and I kept running until I found safety and security." I glanced down at my hands. The next words stuck in my throat, dying to come out but unable to move. My body was shaking at showing this vulnerable side, showing the hurt I'd held in for so long.

"You ached for warmth—not just the kind that comes from clothes, but the kind that touches your soul. You wanted to be loved and truly wanted. You longed for a steady hand, a soft place to lay your head. A life where love didn't come with bruises, apologies, or manipulation. A chance to feel safe. Whole. Happy. Free from the wounds that were opened daily."

More tears fell, tears that had been hidden for so long. Drake grabbed my chair, pulling it toward him and lifting me onto his lap.

"I have you, Daniella. I will protect every single part of you and never let it go, but I'm afraid that I must go against your wishes." I knew what he was about to say. I honestly couldn't blame him. "A man that harmed a child, a man that harmed my wife, shouldn't be allowed to live. He deserves to be desecrated back to the earth." I should care more. He meant so much to me as a little girl, and now I didn't care about his impending death.

Chapter Thirty

Vitae Helix

Drake

It took time for Daniella to compose her emotions. The hurt she had endured as a child made the walls placed around her heart make sense. It would live with her forever. I would visit Giuseppe to discuss the removal of his position on the Coven council. He didn't deserve any position of power. I knew that in doing this, it would cause ripples within my position of power, but a message had to be sent. I scratched my chin. She opened up about her damage, but I still had no answers about her power.

I placed my spoon upon the table, unable to stomach dessert until I knew more. "Daniella, I have to know. What about your power?"

She froze, the spoon centimetres from her mouth. Locking her eyes onto mine, she lowered her hand, sighing.

"I don't know. I showed the ability to use Water, Earth, and even Air at one stage, but I never had the chance to declare, plus my lack of transcending."

I reflected on the call earlier today with the doctor. Mages had a marker within their blood that signified power. It was called the Vitae Helix. Humans weren't aware of it, but Mages knew about this hidden aspect within our DNA.

I cleared my throat. "Daniella, you have the Vitae Helix within your blood. I made them test it after your concussion the other day. You have power, but after the trauma you endured, I'm wondering if it's dormant, hidden somewhere, and waiting to be unlocked."

"That thought terrifies me a little. Almost like I'm a ticking time bomb, ready to explode once the fuse is lit."

I laughed, throwing my head back and holding my chest. "Oh, *my inferno.* You light the fire in my cock, but I doubt you could ever harm a person. I'm meeting with The Keepers tomorrow to get an insight into this, I hope."

Daniella went quiet and played with the cheesecake on her plate. Her frustration was obvious from the scowl on her face.

"Are you upset that I tested your blood?"

"No, it's not that. It's more about how"—she scratched her forehead, her brow creasing and her focus flicking around the room—"I always thought I was normal, and now discovering that I'm the same is…It makes me feel weird. I have more questions than answers now. What would or could possibly trigger these supposed powers to come forth, and what are they? Fire, Earth, Air, or Water?"

"I honestly believe it is Earth. I've noticed on two occasions that plants seem to pull in your direction. The question I have for you, Daniella, is do you want to have access? Do you want to transcend, or would you prefer to stay as you are? I have no qualms with you in your current state, even with the council's grumblings. You're my bonded consort, my wife in all manner of the word, and I don't care about powers. You know what my expectation is." Daniella rolled her eyes, and I grabbed her hand. "I want to—"

"No, I'm aware this is more of a business transaction than anything else. I'm done. I'd like to go home." In a flash, darkness covered her features. She yanked her hand from my grasp and stood, making her way toward the door. I sat dumbfounded for a moment at the swift change in her mood. I threw money onto the table and went to join her in the car.

Chapter Thirty-One

On Your Knees

Drake

Giuseppe had spoken of her childish behaviour, and after her confession about escaping home, this was clear in her inability to process emotions. She would rather run and hide than process what had happened. I noted that Daniella and the car were gone, and I sighed, ordering an Uber in the hopes that she would calm herself down before I arrived home. I tapped my fingers against the side of the car. My guard, Marcus, sent a text alerting me of their safe arrival. I cleared my throat when Jackson called.

"Why am I hearing that you were left alone? She better not have put you in danger, or I will—"

"You will what, Jackson? Please tell me how you'll handle my wife. I'm intrigued by this sudden need to question my every decision." My fist clenched, my anger rising at the way he spoke about her.

The line went quiet. He knew he'd overstepped. We had been friends since we were young, so he knew about my father and the trauma I suffered, yet he dared to question Daniella in such a way. She was allowed to be emotional. I had turned her life upside down, and she'd never been taught how to express her emotions in a healthy manner. Her father abused her in the worst way possible, she was abandoned, and she ran from her problems. It was safe to say she had issues. Patience was important, and despite her testing mine, I knew this had a chance of working. She had fire and certainly lit the fire in my fucking pants.

"No, Drake, I'm sorry. I…I overstepped. I didn't enjoy hearing that you were alone without any men. What if you were attacked?"

I sighed. "I appreciate the concern, but it's important to remember that I can look after myself. I want you to start the process of removing Giuseppe from the council. Proceed with the paperwork to remove him from the Coven and cut off his funding. I won't have a rapist within my council."

"Yes, sir, I'll start it immediately." I hung up, throwing the phone onto the seat beside me.

The men's faces showed their fear at having left me in the restaurant. I found it odd how she managed to convince them to drive her without me. I paused in the doorway, removing my suit jacket in preparation for the fight that would no doubt ensue as soon as I crossed the threshold. I rolled up my sleeves before unbuttoning the top couple on my shirt, knowing it would distract her slightly. I predicted this would end up in the bedroom, at least that was my hope.

I entered to see Daniella sitting on the couch, watching something trashy. Why some famous people were even allowed a television show blew my mind, but humans had been proven to be fucking stupid on the odd occasion.

I lifted her legs, sitting down beside her before placing them gently on my lap. I turned to see her face focused solely on the TV, not even a glance in my direction.

"I'm waiting, Daniella." My voice was clear, cutting through the silence that lingered between us. I impatiently tapped the back of the couch, but was met with more silence.

Her bare legs were a temptation, and my hard cock was straining against the zipper of my pants. My hand slowly inched toward her, and I lay it softly on the smoothness of her skin. I rubbed my hand up and down her calf, and her body shifted slightly. I smirked, knowing it wasn't a rejection, but more that Daniella refused to admit that she wanted more. My hand steadily moved from her calf to her thigh, making small circular motions. Her eyes glanced in my direction. She swung her legs off me and moved toward the kitchen, scratching at her arms and legs. I squinted, noticing the pattern.

"What's the matter, *my inferno?*"

"Just don't, Drake. We had a moment, we connected, we opened up to one another, and then you just turned around and became a dick. Why even bring up children?"

"Daniella, you've lost me. When the fuck did I even say that? I had no—" I reflected on the dinner conversation and how she shut down and left the table.

I laughed at the immaturity of her reaction, but again, it was clear that she was never taught how to react or speak. Everything she had in her taught her to be reactive. I'd seen this many times in my life, and knowing her age and trauma, it made sense.

"Daniella, just stop and listen." She crossed her arms over her body, causing her breasts to almost spill out of her dress. I closed my eyes to focus, my cock already hard and dying to fuck the sexy woman before me, making it very fucking difficult right now. "I was speaking about your powers. I wanted to know if you would like to transcend. I'd like to give you the option without any pressure."

I watched her face, at the realisation that she screwed up, that she was wrong. Her arms relaxed, her breathing evened out. She scratched her nose before shaking her head.

"I'm sorry, I just—"

"You thought I meant an heir. Oh, that will happen, but we both know that Eve will bless us when it is our time. For now, get on your knees."

"Excuse me?" Her brow raised, and her eyes widened. Her lips parted slightly. Perfect to wrap them around my thick cock.

"You heard me. As an apology"—I pulled my belt through the loops, hearing the leather crack as I whipped it in the air. I took a step forward, she looked anywhere but at me—"you should get on your knees and wrap those lips around my cock. Show me just how sorry you are for taking my car and leaving me behind in the restaurant."

I took another step, removing my pants, and standing before her in nothing more than my jocks, my cock pressing against the thin fabric. She turned her back toward me, leaning her hands on the counter. My hands reached for her, gripping her hip with one and brushing her hair from her neck with the other.

"You can fight me all you want, *my inferno*, but you can't resist how fucking wet I make you. I'm still your husband, and you should be on your knees, begging for my forgiveness because nobody, and I mean nobody, defies me."

I kissed the soft skin in the crook of her neck, her body relaxing with my cock pressed firmly against her arse. Fuck, I wanted her so bad. My hand slid over the dress and up toward her breast, groping it while I peppered her neck with small kisses before increasing it to a bite. She gasped, her legs rubbing together.

"I can fix that itch. You know what you have to do, Daniella," I whispered into her ear.

She turned in my arms, her eyes alight with fire and hatred. She placed her hands on my chest, running her fingers over some of the tattoos. My hand pressed onto her shoulder, showing her the way to the floor. Her eyes locked onto mine, never breaking contact as she pulled it free, licking off the precum beading at the tip.

Her lips wrapped around it, her tongue swirling along the shaft. "That's my good girl," I mumbled, closing my eyes and enjoying the feeling of her mouth. I grabbed her head, forcing it further in. Her moan vibrated against my knob, and I groaned. Her hand travelled down to touch herself. She was so fucking sexy. Daniella relaxed, allowing me to fuck her face, her throat tightening against me. I was about to lose all my resolve.

"Stand up," I ordered, and she licked her lips, standing slowly. Her hands pushed her straps from her shoulders, allowing the dress to fall to the floor. "Fucking hell." Her body was a fucking vision before me, and if it were possible, I could've hardened further. That perfect hourglass figure, with those curves, could make any man drop to their knees and worship that fucking body. I grabbed her hand, pulling her toward the couch and bending her over, her arse in full view. A perfect fucking sight. Now, it was time for her to be taught a lesson.

Chapter Thirty-Two

Pleasure or Pain, Worth it Again?

Daniella

I knew it the first time I sucked his dick that I needed help, but this was next level. He ordered me onto my knees, and I did it, and my god, the way he spoke, it should be against the fucking law. Why, when he called me a *good girl*, did it make me hornier? My underwear had never been wetter, and I craved more of it. My body was bent over the couch, his hand slowly caressing my butt cheek.

"Are you going to take my car and run away again?" he asked, his voice hoarse. His erection poked at me.

"No." His hand collided with my bottom, a sting of pain causing me to jolt, wanting more. I needed to be spanked. I was a bad girl. I shook my head. No, yes, no, yes.

"What was that?" he asked, breaking my thoughts and moving closer, his cock pressing between my cheeks. Why did I want him inside me now? This was utter torture, and I was totally here for it.

"No." Another spank. I didn't think I could get any wetter, but I could feel it pooling between my thighs.

"No, what?" he asked.

"No, Drake," I said, loud and clear for him.

"What will happen if you disobey me again?" His fingers trailed my spine, a simple touch causing a need I hadn't experienced before.

"Maybe I'll do it on purpose." I chuckled, feeling mischievous and wanting to see how far he would go. He slid his hand over my cheeks, hitting them once more.

"Oh, you little minx." His fingers wrapped around my hair, pulling my head up slightly. His cock rubbing in my wetness, I pushed myself back to feel him even for a moment. "If you want it, you know what you have to say."

I groaned. I hated this, but I loved the way it made my body feel.

"Drake, fuck me, please."

"With pleasure, wife." There was a slight cheek to his words.

He lined himself up, thrusting inside and filling me instantly. It was euphoric, causing my eyes to roll into the back of my head. My legs shook at the sensation, wanting more with every single penetration from him. His movements were harsh but gentle, and with another smack to my arse, I squealed.

"You're a fiery, kinky one, aren't you, Daniella? I bet you're just waiting to be filled up by me, aren't you? I can feel you tightening, wanting to milk me fucking dry."

"Yes." I moaned, feeling so close. So fucking close. "Drake, harder." The sound of his skin slapping against mine filled the room, along with his ragged breathing. "I'm coming…I'm coming!" I screamed.

Drake stilled, small groans coming from him, before pulling out and rubbing my behind. "Are you alright?" he asked with so much tenderness, it took me by surprise. I blinked rapidly.

"I might fuck hard, Daniella, and take what I want in life, but I'll always make sure you're never hurt." He moved toward the bathroom, and he stopped in the doorway, glancing over his shoulder. "Never do that again, Daniella, or next time, I'll fuck your face a lot harder."

I heard the taps squeak from the bathroom and made the snap decision to join him. He certainly knew how to fuck like the devil, and I loved it.

Chapter Thirty-Three

A Triangle of Sorts

Daniella

The next day at work, I walked with a bounce in my step, entering the office with a big smile on my face. I looked around and noticed the bags under Sam's eyes—evidence of another sleepless night. The others were too busy staring at their computers.

"Good morning, everyone." I beamed with happiness.

"Someone got laid last night," Sam muttered, and I rolled my eyes, moving closer to her.

"I think the appropriate term is fucked…hard," I whispered close to her.

Her eyes sparkled, wanting the gossip. So quick that I couldn't stop her if I tried, she stood, grabbed my hand, and dragged me into the spare classroom.

I gave her every single explicit detail about last night. My bottom still stung a little, but it was more a reminder of the fucking amazing night than the actual punishment for stealing his car.

"Wait, have you told him you've got the implant?"

"No, that's suicide. You know he'll make me take it out. This is my protection, at least for now. It's complicated. Mages are crafty." Sam giggled. "We scheme and plan. Knowing that Drake is aware of the truth about Giuseppe, I do worry about what could happen next. My stepfather is an arsehole and has done some questionable things in the past. I worry about what he would do when his livelihood is threatened."

"I kind of understand all of that, Dani, but you can't lie to your husband."

"No, it isn't a wise idea." Kris's voice echoed through the room. "It might be arranged, but lying this early will only create cracks within your marriage. Honesty is the best policy." He walked further into the room, and Sam disappeared without any further words.

"How long were you eavesdropping?" I asked, curious to know what he had heard.

He took a step closer. "I think nearly every sordid detail. I couldn't not listen to it."

"Why?" His earthy smell filled my senses and caused my brain to fill with fog.

"I might've been a little jealous. I wish I'd moved here sooner"—he brushed the hair from my face, his touch sparking a yearning inside—"then I wouldn't feel so guilty about doing this."

His lips crashed against mine, his strong arms wrapping around my waist. I leaned into his frame, his tongue licking my lips, eliciting a small moan, and making them part so he could massage my tongue. My arms involuntarily moved around his neck, interlinking my fingers. I never wanted it to end. His hands slid up and down my back, his very touch filling me with desire. I pulled back, realisation hitting me.

"No, I can't." He ran his fingers through his hair, noticing the hard lines of his muscles underneath. "Fuck it." I grabbed his collar, pulling him closer to kiss him once more, his warm arms embracing me. His mouth took control, pulling me harder against him, and I could feel his erection. My hands twitched to reach down when I heard Drake's voice in my head. '*You are naive.*'

This was wrong. I pushed my hand against his hard chest, taking a step back. "I-I-I'm married." I fumbled over my words before walking away, the guilt following in my wake.

"It's not a real relationship, and you know it. We could have something special, Dani. Just because he knows how to fuck you doesn't make him a good husband. I wouldn't fuck you, I'd treasure your body, worship it to show you just how you make me feel."

I raised my hand. "That's enough, Kris. Never again."

It felt so good to be wanted in that way, but I made vows, and I couldn't break them. The consequences for cheating on your bonded consort within Mage law were dire. This wasn't me.

The rest of the day was a blur. My thoughts were muddled, I constantly fiddled, and my heart continued to race. I couldn't wait to get home, but I knew one thing—I had to tell Drake the truth. I didn't want to live with this secret. Was it considered cheating? I pushed him away, but I pulled him back again.

Chapter Thirty-Four

Kiss the Girl

Drake

When Daniella returned home, she appeared pale and withdrawn. The usual spark or fire within her grey eyes was gone. She sat down on the couch, staring at the floor intently. I waited patiently for her to speak, knowing not to pressure her. She would speak soon enough. Her head fell into her hands, and she hid her face.

"I kissed someone." She may have whispered, but I heard it clearly enough. I waited for more despite wanting to bend her over the couch and spank the answers out of her. My temper was rising, flames flicking out of my fingertips, itching to attack.

"Daniella, you are testing my patience. Unless you would like to see me lose my shit, I would appreciate information *now*." My tone was impatient and forceful.

She cleared her throat. "I didn't mean it, it—"

"WHO?" I bellowed at her, my hands alighting in flames.

"Kr-Kris." I saw red. I fucking knew it.

I stormed from the house, hearing Daniella yelling behind me. I didn't care. I'd knock that fucker out for touching what was mine. I would fucking destroy him. I grabbed my leather jacket and helmet, opened the garage, and rode my motorbike to his house. I'd destroy him, the piece of fucking shit. How dare he? I pulled over, slamming on the brake, and unease shot through my system. A nausea unlike anything I had felt before.

The slime bag opened the door, leaning against the frame with his clothing that needed to be tailored correctly.

I grabbed his collar, pulling him toward my face. "If you ever, *ever,* go near my wife again, I'll fucking kill you." I dropped him to the floor once more.

"What hurts more, Drake?" he asked arrogantly, as if I wasn't a threat to him. "The fact that I kissed her, or that she came back for another?"

He found his feet, but not before I punched him hard. He stumbled backwards against the closed door, and I heard it crack under the weight of his body.

"She may have kissed you, but tonight, she will be begging me to fuck her." I quirked my brow, walking back toward the car before spinning around. "Mark my words, touch her again, and it'll be your last day."

I returned to my bike, speeding away and finding the sensation disappearing with the growing distance. I needed to work through this intensity, but I wasn't sure how.

I pressed the button on my watch. "Call Jackson." The call didn't take long to connect.

"Drake?"

"What projects do we have now? I need to do something. I need to smash, destroy."

"None, presently. Maybe the gym?"

"I'll go home. Keep the guards with Daniella." I hung up before any more words could be spoken. I knew hurt, I knew betrayal, but this emotion from her was something I hadn't registered. She kissed another. Why did I care so much? We were wed, we took vows, but we didn't have a real relationship just yet. It would develop, but she kissed someone else. Not just someone, but that scumbag I warned her about. The piece of shit who needed a fucking stylist, his youth and his cocky demeanour a fucking insult to someone like me.

I returned to my mansion, which had plenty of space for what I needed. The staff made themselves scarce after I pushed the glass double door open, causing the noise to echo through the large foyer. In the gym, I changed into some spare shorts and a tank top before beating the bag with a ferocity that proved the supernatural element within my blood. She was mine, fucking mine, and another touched her. My eyes clouded over with a dark red haze, hatred of the piece of shit pulsing through my veins. I knew she wasn't innocent, but fuck me, he took advantage.

I took a break, sitting on the bench, staring at the weights before me. I glanced down at my biceps, tracing my finger along the vine tattoo that led toward the scars on my back. The pain of my past always lingered in my mind, but I'd never let it overpower me. I pulled on my lifting gloves, stretching out the leather. I lay down, lifting the bar above my head for a set of twenty. My muscles ached, but I needed to feel the pain. I wanted to feel it.

Sitting up, I noticed Daniella leaning against the wall. The pain disappeared, her face reflecting the guilt that was eating her up. My heart softened, and I stood, walking over to her. My hands rubbed her bare arms, her skin soft under the small calluses on my hands.

"Drake, I'm sorry."

"Daniella, tell me about you and Kris." I needed to know, to understand why she would risk breaking our vows for that piece of shit.

"We met the same day that you and I did. We connected, we got along, we flirted, and I asked him to come to the bar that night. I stopped flirting once I knew that we were to be wed because I'm not that person. Then he overheard my conversation about last night and having sex. I had this weird magnetic pull inside, and we kissed, but I couldn't stop myself. I kissed him again before I ran away. I stayed away from everyone and came straight home to you. I've felt sick all day. I don't know why, and I feel terrible. Why would I do that? You might be a controlling, possessive arsehole, but I know you care, and I know this relationship isn't conventional, but…"

She buried her head in her hands, and I took them away to peer into those hypnotising grey eyes. They stared back at me.

"Did you enjoy it?" I had to know the answer.

She didn't break her gaze, and an odd ethereal glow flickered through her eyes. She stepped back, running her fingers through her wavy red hair.

"Drake, you can't ask me that question. I feel sick."

"You feel sick because you liked it, admit it."

"I don't know, maybe? But I barely remember it. I forced it out of my head. I took vows with you, we shared blood, we are bonded consorts. That's sacred in Mage law."

"TELL ME!" I bellowed, and she trembled, her stare revealing a glimpse of fire behind her eyes.

"No! But I don't know why I went back, it—"

I crushed my mouth to hers, a violent outburst of need and fury. My hands bunched the fabric at her waist, pinning her against me, every step backward a silent command until her back hit the wall. A muffled gasp left those luscious lips. She was caged in my arms—and I wanted her closer.

I needed her to feel this. To have the memory of my mouth burnt against her like a mark. To breathe, and think only of me. *Mine.* I'd claim every inch of her as mine. The thought of another man's hands on her—I kissed harder, as if I could erase him from her skin.

"Drake." My name was a whisper, a silent pleading for more. I would give this woman my soul. She had become my addiction, consuming my every thought, my every need.

I dropped to my knees, lifting her dress and sliding down her silky black underwear, wet from the passion of our kiss. I groaned, knowing I could make her feel this way, knowing the effect I'd on her body. The temperature of the room increased, her skin like fire.

"Drake." She whimpered, as if desiring my touch in more ways than one.

I lifted her leg over my shoulder, her bare cunt in my view. I would remove the memory of another man from her mind. One slow, long lick of her wetness, and my cock hardened instantly. The sweet taste was one I'd forever crave. I would always want more from her. I held her in place, eating her up, her body gyrating on my face, covering me in her juices.

"Drake, please." She wanted my cock, but this would be her punishment. She could beg for it, but I would leave her tight cunt empty for now. Her fingers were in my hair, pulling it slightly, almost like she was pulling something else out of me. Her breathing was shallow, her legs shaking. Her orgasm was moments away, and her cries of pleasure filled the air. I stood, licking my lips.

She reached for me. "Drake, please." I shook my head, taking a step back. "Are you serious?" Her eyes flickered. I missed what it was, but I had never seen them do that.

"Your punishment"—my hand found her throat, forcing her against the wall once more—"for now. Never forget that I own and will claim every single part of you, Daniella."

I left her in the room alone. I knew, from the way her eyes changed, that the answers I sought could only come from The Keepers. The fire inside me faltered, no longer that roar within my ears but a dying spark. The magic dragged sluggishly through my veins, pushing against an invisible force. My arms and hands ached with a heaviness, almost like an empty feeling. *What was this?*

Chapter Thirty-Five

The Keepers

Drake

I called Jackson, needing my second. I was fierce and powerful, but even The Keepers terrified me. I ordered Daniella and my bike to be returned to her house. He slid into the car, and we didn't speak, silence enveloping the vehicle. My fingers tapped on the edge of the door.

"Drake, why are we seeing The Keepers? You know their opinion of you," Jackson asked, turning in his seat to look at me.

"I'm aware. I tested Daniella's blood, and it contains the Vitae Helix, plenty of it, but she still presents with no power. Earlier today, though, something flickered in her eyes. It screamed danger, but elicited an odd reaction from my Fire magic."

Jackson cleared his throat. "Could she be a hunter?"

"No, we would know by now." I paused, thinking it over.

"Would we? The Morteferi are getting craftier in their attacks. We might need to up our protections against them. I've discovered some of our wards are disappearing."

"How? Are you still infusing them with my blood?"

He rolled his eyes. "Drake, I'll pretend you didn't just ask that question."

"I'm the High Mage. Unless they are using dark magic, they shouldn't be able to scrub the wards."

"Unless your power was diminishing, unless you had a block placed upon you."

I shifted in my seat. "Don't, Jackson."

"You need to think of this, Drake. I say it with love, but could it be Daniella? Is it so hard to accept that—" I raised my hand to silence him as the car pulled into the parking lot.

I licked my lips, the taste of Daniella lingering. Giuseppe was a useless fucker who really had no purpose in this world, other than to be a leech.

A brief memory lingered of our wedding day, the moment we sang together, when I knew I would lose it all for her. I exited the car, buttoning my suit jacket and heading to the basement.

I dreaded the descent below, the space barren, a room of black, soulless entities, unyielding and ancient. The cold sank deep into your bones, threatening to break them with the slightest movement. I'd only ever entered this room once before, after the death of my mother.

"Hello, Drake, we've been expecting you." The voice hissed like it had a forked-shaped tongue, which was entirely possible. I snapped my fingers, a single flame flickering from the tip.

"Drake, one of the most powerful fire Mages to ever exist. The man who lives on the line of chaos, allowing his power almost full control, but pulling back at the brink. The use we have always frowned upon." A deeper voice echoed through the dark.

"I'm not here for me. Your bullshit tactics never worked on me. Always trying to scare us." My head spun to see the men behind the voices.

"Your bravado never did fool us. Beneath it has always been a scared little boy who missed his mummy." A third voice joined in.

"Fuck off," I growled at them. They had no right to bring my mother into this.

"There he is." I knew all Keepers to be present now. Each elder represented a power. They were joined in thought, formed to create our most sacred laws.

"What is it that you want, Drake?" the snake-like voice asked, causing bumps to rise over my skin.

"What would cause a Mage to have power within the blood, but present with no actual power?"

"Of whom do you speak?" The deep voice echoed throughout the darkened space, hiding in the shadows. Stories were always told of their deformed faces, caused by worshipping the darker elements of magic to see what we couldn't, to have the knowledge that we wanted.

I hesitated for a moment, unsure of what the repercussions were for revealing this. "My bonded consort, Daniella Romano, now Vatras." I bowed my head in submission, crossing my fingers that she wouldn't feel their wrath.

"Ah, yes, we have heard such a name before. The girl was excommunicated for bearing a child that didn't belong to one who is blessed. She never transcended, and her powers remain dormant. It's an intriguing tale. Are you aware of the start of our kind?"

"We were created from Eve, the first human, and Adam created the first hunters. That's all I know of our history." I scratched the back of my neck, unsure of where this would go.

"Eve was cast out after her bite of the apple, her inability to conform to what God wanted. As revenge, she created Mages, those who could make their own rules. She dug her hands into the ground and carved a piece of her into each power. Fire was blessed with rage, passion, destruction, and light. To another mage, Air, who had thought, freedom, swiftness, and voice. The third was given Earth, strength, stillness, growth, and memory. Lastly, Water, and with that they had change, feeling, healing, and depth."

"This is nothing new. I came for answers, not a story on what our powers represent," I impatiently announced over them, tiring of their stories.

"Yes, but are you aware of the last spirit that arose? The equaliser, the balance between creation and chaos. A spirit bound with no power, no flame, no wind, no stone, and no rain. They simply existed. They are a hunger that we all have, the desire for more. She never intended for this creation, but she feared an imbalance, and soon discovered they were anything but. A Syphon takes a Mage's power, their fears, their emotions, and they turn it into something else. If it isn't contained, it can be disastrous. Syphons in the past have always had problems. They become erratic and uncontrollable if they are not taught what they are. Eve wept upon this before discovering that it served as a reminder to God that even he is fallible."

"Wait, so she can take from all, but can she use it? Does this make her more powerful than an ordinary Mage?" I queried, wanting to know more about Syphons. They had always been whispers in the dark of night, creatures we were almost taught to fear.

"She will never be able to fully use her powers until she transcends. The longer it takes, the more unstable she may become. There is no telling if she could be more powerful than an ordinary Mage. The stories have only ever spoken about those who became so crazed, they lost control and took their own lives." The snake voice cut through the air, sending chills down my spine. "I fear, Drake, that you've stumbled onto a path of embers and ruin, a path that is not as simple as the old stories tell." His words were a warning, one I didn't understand, but one I was determined to discover.

It dawned on me then. Daniella had changed since we met, her strength replaced with a fiery side that seemed almost unlike her. The more she was around me and my men, the more she took from us. The more power seeped into her soul, her body and mind unsure of what it meant. The kiss, the hatred, it all made sense. Her brain was searching to feel whole, and it wouldn't happen until she transcended. I had to put some distance between us. The more time we spent together, the worse it would be for her.

I bowed my head. "Thank you for your guidance." I knew one thing: I couldn't return to her tonight. I had to discover more about her and these stories. I had to figure out how to save her.

Chapter Thirty-Six

The Morteferi

Daniella

I didn't expect Drake to avoid me, to hide the way that he did. I knew I had hurt him, but this seemed to be more than I thought possible. The bed was cold without him. This marriage wasn't planned, but I had come to enjoy his company, and since the kiss yesterday, my brain was overwhelmed with chaos, continual thoughts of anything and everything. I left the bed, showering and getting ready for work. No Drake to annoy me with his peppy attitude and cocky smirk, no text messages, and only one man stationed outside my house.

I avoided Sam, Kris, and basically my entire office. Sam had been texting me all night, but I didn't respond. Kris even tried texting, but I couldn't. I had betrayed my husband. Drake might be cruel with his mannerisms and his brutality, but he never lied about protecting me. A safety that I craved since my mother's death and my stepfather's abuse. Drake gave me clarity.

I sighed while I finished cleaning the whiteboard, before grabbing my keys and stepping out of the classroom. The air shifted. I could feel it. The temperature plummeted, and the wind picked up. I knew what was coming.

"Everyone inside now!" I shouted to the students below, my eyes scanning those still standing in confusion, before laughter erupted.

The speed of the wind increased, and the chill seeped into my bones. Drake warned me of this, a sign that they were close. The Morteferi were here. Two guards entered through the school gates, running towards me. They motioned for me to follow them, but I stared at the students still in the yard.

"No, I can't. I have to get these kids inside. Their safety is my priority."

"I'll create a mini tornado to scare them." Vince winked, looking up at the sky and waving his hands until a small tornado began to form.

I rushed over to students, edging them inside to safety and instructing them to pull down the blinds and hide under the tables. I locked the door, hoping to keep them trapped inside. An announcement sounded through the school's PA system.

Vince shouted, "You should stay indoors with them."

"I can't. It'll only increase their chances of getting hurt or seeing something they shouldn't. They are probably after me anyway."

Marcus chuckled. "You love making my job harder." He checked his phone quickly. "Drake's on his way." My heart beat faster knowing he would be here soon.

"Stay behind us," Vince ordered, and I nodded, hiding behind them, waiting for the hunters to make their appearance.

Marcus's hands twisted toward the ground, and small vines burst from the ground. The hunters appeared through a cloud of fog, their eyes glowing a bright yellow. Hunters had power over the air, making it easier to stop a Mage in their tracks. If you couldn't breathe, you couldn't escape them.

Marcus threw up a shield of vines for protection while Vince worked on covering their sight, making it hard for them to see us. My fingers tingled with anticipation. This was the part I hated. Being here and being powerless. I could hide, but I worried they would hurt the innocent students, and that brought on a wave of nausea. The area grew colder, and the wind speed became a gale. I struggled to remain upright on my feet. Vince moved beside me, standing like a rock. Marcus wrapped vines around my feet, locking me in place to avoid being blown away. I mouthed a quick thank you, and he winked. Drake wouldn't be happy about that.

The vines that protected us began to shake, a piercing sound from the wind whistling through the small gaps. I covered my ears.

The guards didn't care. They kept moving, trying to ensure the barrier held in place, a sphere of protection. We were cocooned in safety…for now.

My heart thumped in my chest, the anticipation of something about to happen. Small leaves started to flicker and fly away. I listened to the laughter outside, the Morteferi taunting us.

"That won't save you." The hunters cackled, the full force of cyclonic wind hitting the vines, the sphere shaking before it disappeared. My fingers tingled further, and I noticed flowers growing at my feet. Marcus tried to grow more, but the hunters moved closer, waving their hands toward him. Marcus grabbed his throat, gasping for air, and my arms prepared for his fall. I caught his body, which was heavier than I anticipated. His lips turned blue, his hazel eyes open and unresponsive.

"Drake, where the hell are you?" I whispered, placing my fingers on his lids, gently closing them.

Vince threw everything at them. He wasn't going down easy. The hunters pushed harder. I put my hand on him.

"Stop, I'll go with them. I won't have another death on my hands."

"Death?" he questioned before his eyes saw Marcus lying on the floor. He ran over, sobbing. I hadn't realised they were so close. Tears sprang from my eyes.

Vince stood once more. "They won't win. Stay behind me." He threw everything he had at the hunters, but they waved their hands like it was nothing. This wasn't a fair fight, and I knew Vince would follow Marcus to the grave. The air grew thicker, and I found it harder to breathe. They were taking away some of my oxygen. I held my chest, rubbing my arms to keep myself warm while my body filled with an overwhelming chill. One of the hunters had turned his full attention toward me.

"It's not my time," I mumbled, spreading out my fingers, ready for anything. The ground broke open, and one of the hunters teetered on the edge before vines pulled him under. I glanced back toward Marcus. Was he alive? Was he able to use his power, even unconscious? Even Vince glanced behind with his brow furrowed. The air grew thinner again, and I coughed at the lack of oxygen. Then, I heard his voice.

"DANIELLA!" Drake's voice cut through the surrounding noise. My eyes grew heavy. Vince fell to the ground. We were running out of energy and air. I peered into the distance, watching Drake throw fire at the hunters. He moved impossibly fast. I couldn't hold on any longer.

"DANI!" he shouted once more, and I smiled. He'd never called me that. The worry in his voice was clear. The coldness in the ground seeped into my skin while I lay on the floor. Warmth fought through the chill, rushing into my bones. Drake was trying his best to keep me awake, keep me alive.

Screams erupted, and the sky turned red, but my vision turned black. My chest heaved with the last of the oxygen that surrounded me.

"Daniella, no! Daniella, I'm here. Don't leave me. I'm sorry. This is all my fucking fault." His words fought their way through the haze, but I couldn't fight any longer.

Chapter Thirty-Seven

Beware the Crazed

Drake

The moment the message appeared on my phone, I saw red. My hands lit up with flames, and I fought the urge to destroy everyone. They attacked my fucking wife. I didn't care if they were human, Mage, or fucking hunter. Nobody touched her but me. I wanted to kill them, burn their bodies to ash before watching them float away in the fucking wind.

I arrived at the school, and seeing her collapse caused my fire to explode.

"DANIELLA!" I screamed while flames danced around the sky, turning it from blue to red. I noticed the crack in the ground, and a hunter's motionless body lying within it.

"Drake!" one of the pathetic Morteferi yelled, the other running away with their face hidden from sight.

I focused my attention back on the last man standing, one of the men who attacked my wife. He forced his Air magic toward me, and my throat tickled, but he didn't know that I knew the trick to overcoming it. I shot my flames to the ground, watching it take hold before consuming the air around it and growing, destroying the spell in a second. I cleared my throat before smiling. Despite the hunter's face being obscured, his mouth dropped open in shock.

I laughed, the sound echoing through the wind tunnel they had created. I watched his feet hesitantly step backwards and threw up a wall of fire, lighting up behind him. He was trapped. I stepped over the body of the hunter in the cracked road, vines still tightening around the corpse trapped in their grasp. With a flick of my wrist, the hunter ignited in flames, his screams bringing me joy. One less fucker to deal with. I reached Daniella, noticing that Marcus lay beside her, motionless.

I touched his head. "Thank you for your loyal service. May the Shadowmere open its gates within the veiled realm. May it accept you and shower you with all that is owed." My heart ached. Marcus had been loyal since I took the position of High Mage decades ago.

Vince was on his knees, panting. His hands were on the ground, and sweat dripped from his forehead. I touched his shoulder, a silent exchange of thanks. He saved her. Daniella lay unconscious on the ground. I stroked her hair, her body icy to the touch.

"Daniella, no! Daniella, I'm here. Don't leave me. I'm sorry. This is all my fucking fault." I scooped her into my arms, silently vowing that she would never return to this school, not after today. It wasn't possible. I waited for Vince to stand, and we walked toward the car. I slid in the back, keeping her within my arms the entire ride.

I called one of the guards stationed at her house. "Nate, organise people to pack up her house, all her clothes, and anything that seems of value. Bring it to the mansion. She will never return to that place after today." I kissed the top of her head, scared to let her go. Her breathing felt shallow against my chest. "Turn the heater up." I didn't care if I burned, only that she lived. I never should have left her alone. I closed my eyes, understanding my mistake, but realising it also meant that somebody had informed them of my absence. Despite suspecting for a while, this confirmed it—I had a traitor in my midst.

✦

The world stilled, my eyes focused on the woman before me. My leg was unable to sit still, thoughts coursing through my head. *When did they become so fucking brazen?* They attacked in the middle of the day, in front of fucking humans. How could this have happened? I'd become complacent, routine, forgetting to be as thorough in my checks. Daniella was my blind spot, a beautiful, chaotic fucking blind spot. I stood, kicking the chair back, fire dancing through my fingers. My anger radiated so powerfully through me, I could barely contain myself. Daniella moaned beside me; she would already be syphoning the power without realising.

"Fuck!" I shouted, leaving the room to put space between us. The more my power was used, the more she would absorb. There was no telling what she would be like when she woke.

It all made sense. The more she interacted with Mages, the more unpredictable she'd become. She never had a one-night stand, she ran away from her child, she uprooted her whole life to be near him, she stabbed me, she lost it at the council meeting, the hex on the house, and she kissed that fucking prick. Everything made sense, but I had no clue how to stop it. She had to transcend, but—I glanced over my shoulder at her door—how was she going to wake?

I hadn't felt fear like this before, and sitting on the couch, staring at the door, I began to sweat. Tiny droplets falling to the floor, fire licking my fingers. I listened intently; small groans could be heard. I waited for what seemed like hours, staying at her house until she woke. Nate moved about doing what I ordered, packing up her life.

Jackson entered, rubbing the back of his neck.

"What is it?" My eyes remained glued to the door.

"The—Marcus is dead, but his vines were still moving. The hunter was tied in them, barely living, but alive enough. We have taken him to the basement. Is that normal?"

My head fell back, staring at the ceiling. The conundrum that had become my fucking life. Here I thought she'd be the simplest choice, only to discover that she was slowly becoming my undoing.

I cleared my throat. "She's a Syphon." I stood, making my way to the alcohol in her tiny kitchen and pouring us a large glass of scotch. It burned my throat. "Yes, you heard me correctly. The stories are true. Eve screwed up and made another by accident. They were supposed to be the balance between humans and Mages. They take in strong emotions and powers, which shouldn't be an issue, but Daniella hasn't fucking transcended, which means it affects her more than usual. It explains her odd behaviour, even after we did a character profile on her. She has strength, but it's…The more she is around me, the worse my power makes her. Jackson, I don't know what to do. I mean, I do know, but fuck me, it's not that easy, and what if the behaviour stop when she transcends." Another groan echoed through her tiny house.

"You have two options before you, Drake: divorce her, which will bring about more issues, but at least she can cleanse herself. Or you begin her transcendence now. Which is it?"

The question lay heavy upon my shoulders. I could walk away, but the thought of it made my chest ache. I stared at her door, the beauty unconscious behind it, the woman I couldn't stop thinking about.

"You can't, can you? She's gotten under your skin."

I ran my hands over my face, smashing down the bitter liquor, the familiar burn a comfort in this moment. Her grey eyes haunted my dreams, her beautiful, wavy red hair sprawled over my chest. It was what I needed, the small comforts. I needed them more than I needed air to breathe. I shook my head; it hung low for a second. I was taught never to show weakness…

A crash echoed through the wooden door. She was awake. The room grew dark as it clouded over outside. *Fuck me.* The door burst open, her eyes wild, her hair dishevelled, and her breathing erratic.

"Jackson, leave."

"But Drake—"

I snapped my head at him, baring my teeth. "I ordered you to leave. Do as you're asked. Inform the men not to enter under any circumstances."

Daniella charged at me. She squealed, beating my chest with her tiny fists. I grabbed them and stared into her eyes, unable to see the brightness that normally shone through, completely devoid of who she was. The magic had poisoned her. She shouted at me incoherently, nothing making sense.

"Daniella, it's fine. You are safe. I'm here." She pushed me with a force I never thought possible. I stumbled backward. She charged through the house, running back at forth, rubbing her hands over her body, pulling at her hair, and speaking absolute nonsense. Every so often, an ear-piercing scream came from her throat before she clasped her hands over her ears. It wasn't making sense.

I charged over to her, wrapping my arms around her curvy frame and holding her tightly. She kicked her legs wildly, trying to move her arms. She even attempted to bite me. I walked into the bedroom, throwing her onto the bed, and she bounced. I had to get her to see reason; pull her out of this psychosis. I pined her down, holding her face in my hands and gazing into her eyes.

"I'm here, Daniella." Fire burst from her hands, the room warming instantly. She was syphoning power from me in this moment. I had to fight fire with fire. Her hands scratched at me to move, but I clasped my hand around her wrists, lifting them above her head. I pressed my lips against her forcefully, and her movement slowed slightly. I pulled back to look at her. "I'm here, Daniella. You're safe with me." I kissed along her jaw, nibbling her ear and down to the curve of her neck. A soft sigh escaped her lips.

"Drake." I glanced at her face. Her lips wobbled, and her eyes filled with unshed tears and fears that had come to light. I let go of her hands, stroking her face.

"I've got you," I whispered softly against her lips. The world grew quiet as I listened to her breathing slow.

"My head's going crazy. It's shouting at me. I can't understand what it's even saying. I'm scared. What happened?" Her voice filled the tiny room, and I leaned my forehead against hers, taking the moment in. She was alright, she was safe, and she was in my arms.

Chapter Thirty-Eight

The Danger in the Truth

Drake

Daniella broke the silence between us. "What is this?" she asked. I hadn't had the chance to tell her the truth about what she was, deciding to shy away from her instead of handling it.

"You're a Syphon. You're a Mage, but you'll never specialise in one element because you can channel from everything. You draw the power from those around you, whether it's their power or their emotions. You have more power than you realise."

"Weren't we taught that Syphons are dangerous?" Her eyes flicked around the room, and she picked at her fingers, biting her nails.

"That's what we're taught about anything we don't understand. You aren't dangerous. You cannot generate your own power; you absorb it from those around you. Have you never noticed?"

She slid off the bed, pacing the room, her fingers running through her hair. It was happening again, the power working its way through her. I could see the signs, the small movements slowly building to her explosions. I closed the space between us, taking her hands in mine. Her eyes darted in every direction.

"Daniella." I spoke softly, and in seconds, she snapped. Ripping her hands from my grasp, fire exploded from her fingers, and she threw it toward me. The force of it knocked me into the wall. The flames burnt my clothes, but my skin remained untouched. The inner circles of her eyes were glowing purple while the rest were flaring red from the fire coursing through her system. A small orb formed in her hand, and she threw it at me. I caught it, bouncing it in my palm before closing my fist and watching it extinguish. This only seemed to anger her further; she growled. She was a sight.

I took a deep breath, storming toward her. Pushing her against the wall, I took her wrists in one hand, forcing them above her head and pressing my body into hers. Kissing her harshly, I tried to distract her thoughts, stop her brain from overanalysing. She groaned before parting her lips. I kept her hands fastened in mine, my hand running down her body, lifting her leg to wrap around me.

"Drake," she moaned.

I let her go, lifting her and laying her on the bed. I tugged at her pants, pulling them off before ripping her top in half. "Holy fuck," she said, watching me remove my own shirt and pants.

"More like unholy, with what I'm about to do to you." I beamed at her, pulling her ankles and bringing her to the edge of the bed. I dragged her underwear down her silky legs, my touch causing her to shiver.

I groaned at the sight of her dripping cunt before me, my tongue sliding through her folds, her taste fucking magical. I circled her clit, and her gasps filled the air. This was just the beginning. I devoured her sweetness, her taste covering my face. I owned her. Her thighs closed slightly, and I growled, pushing them wider to delve my tongue deeper into her.

All fucking mine.

Her moans filled the room, and I sucked harder, my tongue circling her swollen bud, flicking and pressing into her hips, which started to move about.

"Drake," she whispered breathlessly. I bit her lightly, her hands coming down to my head.

"No." I looked up at her in warning, and she chuckled as I ran my hand up her body, grasping her breast and pulling her clit into my mouth once more.

"Don't stop," she pleaded, and I pulled her closer, enjoying the euphoric taste of her on my tongue. Her back arched, her legs began to tremble, and I paused, thrusting two fingers inside her. I wanted to watch the moment she came undone. I licked my lips, my cock aching to be deep inside her. She gripped the sheets, her cunt tightening against my fingers, clenching with need. She was so close.

Her body rose slightly, and she came hard, so fucking hard. It was fucking perfection. I stood, spreading those legs wider, running my aching cock through her wetness. Watching it coat me brought a different type of joy. Knowing that this was mine was otherworldly. I plunged inside, groaning at her tightness wanting to milk me of every last fucking drop. I grabbed her hands, forcing them above her head once more, sparks shooting out of her fingertips.

"Show me that flame, *my inferno.*"

Her hand lit up, covering my own with flames. If it were possible to harden further, I did. The fire wouldn't burn us; we could simply feel the warmth. I removed my hand, moving it down her body, her eyes alight with passion and need. I slowed, kneading her breasts, and she moved to touch me.

"Uh, nope. Hands above your head. I'm in charge here, and you'll take every single inch of my aching cock." She returned them above her head. "That's my good girl."

She moaned, the sound of my praise causing her walls to tighten. I glanced down, watching him disappear into fucking paradise. I couldn't take much more.

"Drake." She mewled with need. This was my undoing. My balls clenched as my release came, feeling my seed fill her up. I collapsed beside her, pulling her into my arms. Her breathing was erratic, but she was safe. I kissed the top of her head as she wrapped her arm around my body, but I had shit to do.

I rolled out of her embrace, grabbing my pants.

"Where are you going?"

I looked into her grey eyes, the lucidity back. "I have to sort out those fuckers. I'll be back shortly. Your teaching career is over. Get some rest."

"Drake, we need to talk about this Syphon stuff."

"We will, tomorrow. Sleep, now," I ordered, grabbing my shirt and pulling it on. I lifted my vibrating phone out of my pocket to answer my Arcanum.

"Where is that fucker?"

Chapter Thirty-Nine

Saying Goodbye

Daniella

I woke to a dark room. The sun had long set, and the bed was cold. Drake had yet to return, but for the first time in weeks, I felt more myself. A clarity that I had missed. I flung my legs over the edge of the bed. I needed to shower; the sticky feeling between my legs was unpleasant. I rubbed soap over the implant within my arm, a reminder that Drake's plan would never come to fruition. I would tell him the truth eventually. Maybe today. I should do it today. I dressed myself in a pair of shorts and a tank top. The heater was on. Drake had ensured my comfort. I truly had judged this man to be something that he wasn't. He was possessive and controlling, but that was him, the man who had to have control over every single aspect of his life.

I strolled into the kitchen, opening the fridge to see containers of food. Meal prepping had been a godsend for moments like this, when I was unwell or just couldn't be bothered to cook. I pulled out the spanakopita, warming it in the microwave before sitting down and putting on something trashy to watch and staring at the boxes piled up in the corner.

My phone buzzed, and I glanced over to see Sam's name. My hand shook. How was I going to explain this? It rang out, and I noticed the multiple missed calls from Sam and even Kris. As well as a message from Drake, telling me that he would probably be home in the early hours of the morning.

My finger hovered over Sam's name. What would I even say to her? I pressed call before selecting loudspeaker, knowing she would probably start screaming at me.

"Dani, what the fuck happened? Are you okay? There was a tornado?" I was right—her voice broke at the loud decibel she screamed from. "Sam, take a breath. I'm alright. I'm alive. You can't get rid of me that easily."

"Don't make jokes right now. I have no fucking clue what happened, and everything is all hush-hush. Is this witchy stuff?"

"Yes, I was attacked by the hunters, and Drake's men saved me. Not without consequence." My thoughts drifted to Marcus's lifeless body lying beside me.

"Why? What reason did they have to attack you?"

"I'm a Mage, the wife of the High Mage. I'll always be a target now. I'll probably come into work tomorrow to clean out my desk. Drake is right, I can't go back to work. It puts those kids in danger; it puts you in danger. It's selfish to stay."

"But…Fuck, I get it, but this sucks. You're making the best choice, and I understand, but fuck me. In a couple of weeks, your life has literally turned upside down."

I heard the keys in the door and turned just in time to see Drake step inside. His suit was soaked in blood and dusted with ash, his face carved with tension, his jaw clenched tight. The weight of what he'd done was written in the deep lines across his forehead. Sam kept talking, oblivious, but I couldn't tear my eyes away from the man who had become the centre of my world. I moved without thinking, rising to my feet, crossing the room, and wrapping myself around him. I pressed my face into the firmness of his chest. He exhaled a heavy breath and folded himself into me, his chin resting on my head. We stood there in silence, no words spoken, but they weren't needed. We both knew what it meant. Sam's shouting pulled me back. I raised the phone to my ear again, but my mind was still with him.

"Hey, I'm here. Sorry, what's up?"

"Can we do lunch tomorrow?" I glanced up at Drake, and he nodded, his face solemn. He kissed my forehead, moving toward the bedroom and an inevitable shower to wash away his sins.

✦

Drake's men pulled into the car park. I stared out the window at the students playing, and my heart ached. The life I worked so hard for was ending. Drake remained silent for the remainder of last night. He refused to speak, and I didn't have the heart to push him. He lost Marcus, a friend. He didn't need to be pushed. He would tell me the truth about Syphons when he was ready to do so. I'd have to fully commit to be a High Mage's wife and all that came with it. The constant support meetings, the wife meetings to discuss children, *ugh*, a life I never wanted thrust upon me.

"Miss Daniella." Vince's hand on my shoulder brought me back to the present.

"Sorry, Vince, can you wait here for me?" I asked, reaching for the door handle. He nodded, the cool, brisk air hitting my face, a stark reminder of the cold people I would soon be surrounding myself with. I pressed my key card to the door, pulling it open and entering my office. Sam's face was solemn. She stood, walking over and hugging me. I wanted to cry, but that wouldn't achieve anything.

I stood before my desk, where boxes had already been placed. A definitive sign from leadership that I should be leaving sooner rather than later.

"Our Prinny dropped them off this morning. Do you want some help?" Sam asked. Today, she only taught one class, which was period five, so she had time to spare. I nodded, holding back a world of emotions. They could wait until lunch.

We packed in silence, slowly erasing my existence from the space that had been mine for the last seven years. All of it fit neatly into three boxes. I picked up two, with Sam carrying the third. We exited, and Vince rushed over to grab them from me before doing the same with Sam. She hopped into the car to be driven to the local café, which was no more than a five-minute walk.

We took a seat, and I noticed Sam checking her phone continually, an odd behaviour from her. I reached over, squeezing her hand.

"What is it?"

"Kris is coming." My stomach dropped at the realisation that I hadn't told her. "He told me the truth, that you kissed. Thanks for holding out."

"Sam, you can't. Drake will lose his shit."

"I don't care!" she shouted before lowering her voice. "I'm losing my best friend thanks to this arsehole."

"There is no denying his arsehole tendencies, but he saved my life. He has protected me. Sam, on the day of our wedding, he told my father to get fucked. He knows the truth about everything, and still, he protects me. This union might be forced, but I think he…No, I know he genuinely cares for me."

The bell at the door jingled, and Kris slid into the seat beside me, his warm hazel eyes filling me with comfort. I wanted to lean on him, but I couldn't. My lips could almost feel the kiss that lingered between us.

"You shouldn't be here." I looked away, keeping my eyes trained on the menu before me.

"Dani, there is something between us. I can help, I can get you out. Let us help." He pointed to Sam, and I glanced between the two of them. She'd betrayed me.

"Sam…" I croaked. "Why?"

"I see the way you two look at each other, the wanting in your eyes. You could be great together."

"I'm married. I can't." I shook my head, not wanting to hear this. I was the wife of the High Mage.

"You don't have to settle for this, Dani. You deserve better." Kris placed his hand on my thigh. I peered down before feeling that strong pull once more, as his gaze locked onto my lips. He moved slightly, waiting for the invitation. He stroked my face, his thumb brushing slightly at the corner of my mouth. "I can help you. Let me protect you."

My hand started to shake, and I pushed away, scanning the room for an answer, noticing the plant behind Kris leaning toward me. I was channelling power again. Time to leave. I pushed the chair back, moving to the exit. This Syphon shit scared the hell out of me. The fresh air calmed the adrenaline pumping through me.

"Daniella, wait!"

The urgency in his voice caused me to stop in my tracks, spinning around to face him. His hands were in his pockets, each step closer causing my heart to pound harder. His hand touched my waist, gentle but hesitant. My body leaned closer, my brain hating this feeling. I was drawn to meet his gaze like I was the only thing left in this world. Not like Drake.

Drake looked at me like the possession I was. Kris looked at me like I was something sacred, untouched, unbroken.

His eyes filled with emotions that I didn't want to comprehend. My brain wanted this to end, but my heart wanted more. It wanted to be chosen, cherished, and seen. I should've moved his hand away, but his fingers brushed my cheek, leaving my skin tingling. I didn't stop him, but part of me didn't want to. I swayed between logic and lust. His lips crashed against mine, filled with fire and need. Everything that we'd buried and denied. I melted into his touch. I froze with the sudden realisation that this was happening. *Drake.* His name bounced around in my skull. His touch, his claim, his safety.

I pressed my hand into Kris's chest, taking a step backwards. My head shook before words found me. I couldn't look at him.

"I'm sorry," I whispered, though I didn't even know who I was apologising to. Him, myself, or…Drake.

I turned before he could say anything else, forcing my legs to move, waving a silent goodbye to Sam. Then I slipped into the car beside Vince, shutting the door behind me like I was sealing away the part of me that wanted too much.

"Not a word, Vince. Understand?"

"He doesn't need to know some things, and I saw the way you pushed him away. It speaks to your character more than that pig." I smiled softly, knowing that returning to my house meant I had to pack up the last of my life, and move away from the town I had grown to love.

Chapter Forty

Sweet Revenge

Drake

My phone beeped. Listening to the council bitch and moan about the most trivial things really pissed me off. I sighed, pulling it from my pocket to check the message.

Nate: Home and packing her clothes, anything else?

Drake: No. Alert me when you arrive at the mansion.

"Are we boring you, Drake?" Giuseppe's nasally voice irritated my ears. I cleared my throat, looking up at him. I was surprised by his bravado. The man raped my fucking wife and sat there like he was a fucking king. I cracked my knuckles, my fire wanting to burn the arsehole to ash.

"Considering the tedious nature of the conversation, yes, I do find myself to be rather bored. I convened this meeting to discuss the increase in attacks from the Morteferi, and you decided to steer that conversation toward a matter that you felt was more important. Forgive me for thinking that the death of our people is more important than the paper that lines your pockets."

"The same paper that keeps your pockets lined as well, is it not?" he quipped back with a sly smile on his piggish face.

I snorted and smirked. Part of the hope lingered that he might actually start something. Allowances had already been cut, to send a message, though perhaps he was too dumb to piece it together. After all, the house had already been paid off for him, leaving little else for him to care for.

"Ah, Giuseppe, I do believe my father helped to build your *tiny* empire. It'd be a shame if it were to"—I snapped my fingers with small sparks—"go up in flames."

"You have no right."

That was exactly what I wanted to hear. Let him fight – a reason to destroy him in more ways than one. Jackson stood, locked both entry doors, then resumed his seat. Rising, my neck was cracked and suit jacket straightened.

"Giuseppe, I thought we'd an agreement. You run the business, I take those few pennies that you make to keep your family safe, and we go about our time together. But now…tsk, tsk, tsk. Gentlemen of the council, I must ask for your vote on this matter. If you discovered that a man of this council had touched a minor in a sexual manner, taking away their innocence, destroying their reputation, and kicking them out of the Coven, what should their punishment be?" I queried, testing the loyalty of the other men sitting at this table.

Owen, a Water user, raised his hand. "What was the age of the child?"

"Thirteen when the grooming began, before the sexual act occurred. Although I don't see how that is relevant. A child is a fucking child." I snarled at Owen. The men exchanged glances. They knew. They fucking knew.

"I see. How many of you knew the truth? Speak now, and I'll show some leniency."

Two men raised their hands, and Giuseppe's face paled. He knew what was coming. I wanted him to fear me. I wanted him to be a puddle of sweat with what was coming his way. Jackson stood, motioning toward the door, and they followed like good little soldiers. The rest of the men cowered, moving their seats away from the wrath that was coming to my father-in-law.

My phone rang, and I slid it from my pocket, her name flashing across the screen.

"Ah, my lovely wife. I'm just here with your father, where he'll be receiving his punishment. Do you have any last words?" I was met with silence, waiting for her inevitable answer.

"Words seem to be alluding me at this moment. I'd say burn in hell, but even that doesn't quite hit right. I only wish I could see his demise and stand over him as he did to me when he took pieces of my soul."

"Daniella, I loved you." Giuseppe whimpered. "I never meant to hurt you. I didn't have a choice. I needed to feel love, and that pathetic bitch was too drunk to do her duties." He paused. "You shouldn't have been wearing those revealing clothes."

"You fucking pig." I hung up the phone, knowing this would hurt her. I snapped my fingers, and his body erupted in flames, his screams filling the air. The smell of his charring flesh consumed my senses, and I lavished it. He'd never hurt another again. I clapped my hands, the fire extinguishing in seconds.

Jackson brought in the other men. "Let this be a reminder. Keep your mouth shut about similar matters, and this could happen to you. Now, we must discuss what extra protections can be put into place to keep our people safe."

The drive home was no longer hours, now merely minutes. Finally having her within my home brought a sense of calm.

Chapter Forty-One

The Choice is Easy

Drake

The car pulled into the drive. I spotted the glowing eyes in the dark, hidden behind a tree. I stepped out, igniting my hands with flame, prepared to attack.

"Mr. Vatras, I mean you no harm." By the sensuality of his voice, I knew what he was.

"What could a vampire possibly be doing lurking outside my home?" My hands remained covered in flame. I wasn't about to test this creature. They were sly and manipulative. You could never trust a blood-sucker.

"I've heard the rumours." He smiled, flashing his fangs.

"What rumours?" I queried, unsure of where this conversation was going or what exactly he wanted.

He turned his head, gesturing towards the window, where Daniella was brushing her hair in the bedroom mirror. I would have to get tint put on the windows. I never realised that you could see inside the rooms at night.

"She's a Syphon." My ears pricked up. Only two people know about this.

"What's that? Why does it interest you?" I had to play the fool. I couldn't show my hand.

He cackled, the sound causing goosebumps to form over my skin. "Oh, Drake, do not fool yourself into thinking that you are the only one who knows things. Syphons have existed for many millennia. One of the fuck ups of Eve's masterful plan."

"Why do you care what she is?" I queried, weighing up what to do next—listen or destroy?

"Syphons are unique beings with the ability to nullify any supernatural's ability. She has only just discovered how powerful she can be. With the right training, she could walk into a room and render the entire room powerless, eliminating access to any aspect of what makes supernatural beings what they are. If I get too close, my strength would diminish, and my healing wouldn't exist. She is pure, raw…power. You are not ready for what she is capable of."

I extinguished my flames, crossing my arms over my body. "Let me guess, you'd like to take her off my hands and teach her."

"Well, of course. I know how to control their power. I can teach her."

"And it would have nothing to do with her blood tasting what I can only assume to be delectable?"

"Of course, consuming that blood would bring me even more power, but Mr. Vatras, you forget. You are bonded to her. I could not try to claim her even if I wanted to. This is a simple offer of help. We don't have to be enemies. A shift is coming, Drake, a shift you are not ready for. The prophecy is coming to light. Be careful who you trust." He slithered back into the darkness, his eyes glowing before disappearing into nothing.

I sighed, shaking my head. He was right. He wouldn't be able to touch her. The protections from Eve would always be in place, and no other supernatural would be able to take her away from me. I trudged inside, the weight of everything heavy on my shoulders. But one question did linger: what was this prophecy he spoke of?

I wished for a simple wife to placate the council on their need for me to produce a fucking heir. Daniella was anything but fucking simple. This woman was going to be the death of me.

I headed to my office, needing to email a few contacts in regards to overtaking Giuseppe's shares within the empire. Bracken was the obvious choice, but he wouldn't inherit all of them. Who would be the most trustworthy? I had to consider sending money to Bracken to cover the costs of the funeral arrangements. I smiled, thinking about Giuseppe's body within the council room. The smell permeating the air, a warning to any who dared commit despicable acts. I sent an email to Penelope, informing her that her role would now be fully operational. Daniella would do all that was expected of a High Mage's wife.

I ran my fingers over my face, glancing at the time. Two in the morning. I closed the laptop, leaning back in my chair, my fingers drumming against the leather. So much had happened in such a short amount of time. Jackson's words floated into my head. I had two choices, but the idea of leaving her now, knowing that she was desired by other supernaturals…it couldn't happen. I had to keep her safe.

My thoughts drifted to her soft skin and those curves, the plumpness of her breasts, and my cock ached to be inside her. I pushed back from my desk, walking up the stairs, my steps echoing through the space. The door opened, and the smell of lavender wafting into my senses was a comfort. She calmed my chaos, and I was slowly understanding just how important she was becoming to me. The truth would never leave my lips. Her hatred had been softening since our wedding, and the sex was fucking incredible. Her tight cunt was heaven, and the thought of burying myself inside her daily had only increased my need for her.

I washed away the filth from the day before climbing into bed, my arms wrapping around her waist. A sigh left those luscious lips. It was melodic. My finger drew circles up her bare legs, her body melding to mine. Her inability to resist my touch hardened my cock instantly. I reached around, grabbing her breast. No bra, no fucking bra, yes! I rolled her onto her back, my lips finding her neck, trailing a path to her jaw and her mouth. She groaned, waking from her slumber. I climbed over her body, her legs spreading. So fucking hot and all fucking mine.

I had to taste her wet cunt, to forget about my problems between those sweet legs. I pulled down her tank top, bringing those plump nipples into my mouth.

"Drake, I'm tired." Her voice croaked while her fingers played with my hair.

"You shouldn't have opened your legs then." She chuckled, my lips finding hers in the dark, her arms wrapping around my neck.

"I'll be back for those lips later, but right now I'm starved." I shifted down, running my hand over her soaking panties. The idea of her always being so wet for me after the simplest touch was almost enough to make me blow my load. I snapped my fingers, burning her underwear to reveal the object that I would worship daily. I pushed her legs wider, dragging my finger over her.

"I love how wet for me you are, *my inferno*. So fucking wet."

I plunged my tongue into her sweetness, lapping up the divine taste of her cunt. Her hand pushed my head further, her bravado causing me to moan, knowing she was getting more comfortable with our intimate relationship. My fingers dug into her thighs while I softly bit her throbbing clit.

"Fuck me, Drake." She groaned, covering her head with a pillow. I pushed two fingers inside with my thumb running small circles over her pulsating centre. I just needed to apply the right pressure, and she would come undone on my tongue.

"I will soon, don't you worry. I just want to hear you come first."

She squeezed my fingers, and I knew she was close. I picked up a steady rhythm as her body arched for more. It was close. Her walls tightened, threatening to break my fingers. I would let her. Fuck, I would die happy between these legs. I wasn't going to waste another second, ready to explode at the sounds she had been making. I rubbed myself through her wetness, using it to coat my cock.

"How badly do you want it, Daniella?" I asked the same question. Hearing her say those words was fucking magical. I relived the highlight of her begging for my cock daily.

"Drake, please, fuck me." I wasn't going to wait another second. I thrust inside, and her eyes snapped open.

"Hello, wife." I snorted, pressing a kiss to those lips, using the same ones that had just been feasting on her. She groaned, licking my lips, and I revelled in the fact that she was just as perverted as me.

"I hate you," she whispered in my ear. I pulled out before pushing myself deeper and feeling her tighten. She loved the way I made her feel. Her nails dragged down my back, and I lavished the feeling.

"Yes, but who's my good girl, begging for my cock? Whose cunt is strangling my cock with need, wanting to milk me of every fucking drop? You feel so fucking good, Daniella."

I grabbed her hands, forcing them above her head. She was a masterpiece beneath me, her tits bouncing, her lips parted, her eyes rolling from the pleasure of being fucked. It only drove me harder and faster. She mewled for more, the sounds enough to drive any sane person crazy. I grabbed the wooden head of the bed as her cunt tightened, and my balls begged for release. I wanted to feel her coated with more of her sweetness. I had to be patient…

"Fuck me!" she screamed. Letting go, her hands grabbed her breasts and her legs fastened around my waist, keeping me locked in position while she rode out her orgasm. I pulled out, spilling myself over her, claiming her cunt as mine. A perfect fucking sight to see—my cum all over her perfect fucking pussy. No man should ever dare to touch my wife. I lay back on the bed, pleased with the mess I had made. She rolled over, a sweet smile covered with darkness, but still visible. Pain shot through my chest, her hand slapping me hard.

"I was having a dream."

"I made those dreams come true, wifey."

"I'm not cleaning myself. I'm going to dirty your sheets."

I laughed. "Fine by me. I'll happily have my cum covering you all night long. It's only making me hard again for another round." I winked at her, and she rolled over, mumbling to herself.

Chapter Forty-Two

Kiss and Tell

Daniella

I didn't have the chance to explore Drake's ridiculous Toorak mansion yesterday. I arrived and unpacked my clothes into the massive robe before falling asleep. After the last two days, I was both physically and mentally exhausted. Drake snuck into bed last night, surprising me. I wouldn't deny that he knew how to please a girl, both with his mouth and his dick. I snuck out of bed, throwing on some leggings and a baggy T-shirt before heading down to breakfast. He had a staff member for everything here, but when you ran one of the most successful construction empires, you could certainly afford it. It still shocked me that humans hadn't discovered the existence of Mages or any other supernatural creatures. Maybe they were purposely blind to it.

I closed the bedroom door as quietly as I could before turning around toward the stairs, my hand reaching for the black balustrade, the metal cool to touch with a slight rough feel. The stairs were black and white marble, reaching the landing with a courtyard with a Japanese-style garden to the left and the main living quarters to the right.

I could hear the clatter of pots and pans, but the aroma filling my nose was something else. The smell of eggs and bacon. I entered the kitchen and living area, the void in the centre showcasing the large expanse of the house. The detailed wooden ceiling, the sandstone wall above a fake fireplace that managed to provide actual warmth to the room. The couches were an odd mustard colour that looked to have barely been sat on. No television, which I found intriguing.

The kitchen was another matter. It was larger than my entire home in Trafalgar. The table had enough seats for fourteen people. The island bench matched the wall behind it, with the same wooden architecture. Food was on display across the entire space—eggs, bacon, fresh fruits, and fresh pastries. I pulled out the black stool, taking a seat when a plate was placed before me.

"Good morning, Mrs. Vatras." The butler appeared to be around the same age as Drake, with more grey scattered through his hair, and definitely not the same build. He wore rather casual clothes. For some reason, I was expecting an old butler's uniform, but instead it was a pair of denim jeans and a black long-sleeve polo. He moved about the kitchen with ease.

"Please, call me Daniella. May I ask what your name is?" I queried, not wanting to be rude when I needed to ask for something later.

"It's Adam. Do you need anything else?"

"Can you point me toward the kettle or coffee machine?" My voice was soft. I felt strange in this large house. Even though Giuseppe had a lot of money, it was still odd being around these luxuries.

He chuckled, disappearing into the butler's pantry. I pushed off, wanting to see what was behind that wall. Just as large and ostentatious as the rest of the house, I was sure. There were walls of cupboards with the same benchtop as the kitchen. This house was incredible. I returned to my seat, picking at the fresh strawberries on my plate. I wasn't very hungry, still feeling rather nauseous after my encounter with Kris yesterday. It didn't sit right that we kissed, and I knew I would have to tell Drake.

I spent the next thirty minutes chatting away to Adam about how long he'd worked for Drake and what else I needed to know. He wasn't a Mage, but a simple human with a spell cast upon him to forget about the existence of the underground magical world. It intrigued me why Drake would keep a human around.

I finished eating only to venture further into the house, discovering another living space with electric blue carpet, a study where I could picture Drake slaving away with his mountain of work to complete. A theatre room, a gym, and an absolutely insane cellar. I ventured to the upstairs sitting area, lying on the couch to stare at the ceiling. What else could I do with my day? I wasn't exactly a gym girl.

"Making yourself comfortable?" Drake called out, leaning against the wall with a coffee in his hand.

"I'm not sure what else I should be doing? I was kind of fired or quit, whatever you want to call it."

"I never expected them to attack you in that environment, Daniella. I'm deeply apologetic for it."

I waved him off. "It's fine, Drake. It's fine." I bit my lip, knowing I had to tell him before I vomited everywhere.

"I know, Daniella. I know already."

"About?" My heart beat faster, waiting for the answer, and worried that Vince had already told him when I explicitly told him not to.

"Kris." He cleared his throat, taking another sip and avoiding looking me directly in the eyes.

"Yep, right. I suppose Vince has sworn loyalty, so it's normal to tell you everything. At least you know I'm an honest person." I shrugged, the tension slowly disappearing.

He put his mug down on the coffee table, sitting beside me, his hand resting on my knee.

"I have to know the answer to this question, and I would like the truth, Daniella, no lies. I think we've reached the point in our relationship where clarity between us is the best way forward." He paused, his other hand making a fist. "Why did you kiss him?" His voice was barely a whisper, as if he feared the words I was about to speak.

My stomach tightened, bile rising in my throat. The unspoken words on my tongue, the words I never wanted to utter aloud, knowing what they could mean. He told me he'd already attacked Kris with the warning to leave me alone. I bit my lip, blood pouring into my mouth, the metallic taste horrible on my tongue. Drake touched my face, a tender action that I hadn't experienced from him.

His eyes finally met mine. "It's okay, I promise."

"As I mentioned before, we flirted before you. I just got used to him being around, I suppose. Yesterday, he told me he wished I wasn't married and that he'd protect me. But…it's more the way he looks at me, almost like I consume his entire world, like I'm the only thing he sees. With you, it's different, and I know it. I wouldn't ask you to change. I don't expect that from you, but to have that safety and adoration from a person when…"

"When you've never had it before." His jaw clenched, and he stood, moving away.

I stared at his back. "I'm sorry."

"No, don't." He spun back around. "Don't be sorry. Daniella, the only male in your life took something from you. You never got to experience real love from a man. Instead, your idea of love was through a disgusting act, and then you were thrown away like you meant nothing. You never had somebody tell you just how incredible you are, just how special you are. Kris did that. I understand more than you think I do. I came in, forcing you into something you didn't want, the same way that—that fucker did. I've told you what the rules are, taken the life you worked hard for from you." He put his hands on his hips, shaking his head. "I'm no better than him." He waved his hand, leaving the space without another word. I stood, dumbfounded. He wasn't angry at me but rather himself.

CHAPTER FORTY-THREE

WHAT AM I?

DANIELLA

I moved about the house, investigating the mansion that I now lived in. Drake's words replayed in my head, *'I'm no better than h—'* There was no comparison between Drake and Giuseppe. Drake never mistreated me. He might have been controlling, but he never forced anything from me. I gave my body over to him willingly, and I would again. He made me feel things I never thought possible. Those words would never leave my mouth, but I knew, no matter what, that Drake would always be there for me.

I pushed open the door to Drake's study. The electric blue velvet-like carpet with the black shelves illuminated with LED stripes, and the same mustard-coloured couch against the wall. I sat down, letting my hands drop between my legs before looking up at him.

"You're nothing like him." He sighed, staring at the desk. "You've never been like him. He stole something from me, Drake. He stole my innocence, he stole my self-esteem. I never felt worthy. I never felt beautiful. I always felt like a burden, like trash. You—" My voice broke, and my cheeks were suddenly wet. "You've shown me what it's like to be taken care of. To have someone risk it all for me, and never question my antics. You—"

"Stop, Daniella." He shook his head. "Please stop. I can't hear anymore." He stood, making his way over to me, taking a seat, and grabbing my hands before wiping away a tear on my cheek.

"Jackson told me I had two choices the other day, after I discovered the truth about you being a Syphon. I could let you go, leave you, and never see you again, or we fight whatever is coming our way." I peered up at him, his eyes locking onto mine. They softened, and I knew what was coming.

I stood, moving away from him and shaking my head, feeling vulnerable and exposed.

"Don't, Drake. You—you can't say it. Please don't, because you can't take it back. I-I'm not."

"Daniella, NO! You're worth everything!" He reached for my hand, pulling me back to the couch and him. "The moment Jackson asked me, it all came crashing down. I knew the truth. I don't care what's coming for me or for you. I would destroy all of them if it meant we had more time together. You're the light to my dark, the calm to the chaos in my head, the ice to cool the fire in my blood. *My fucking everything*. I love you, Daniella Vatras. It's fucked up, I know."

He paused, his knee bopping, his hands running over his face. "We barely know each other, but when I heard you were being attacked, I didn't think. I ran. I don't do that. I plan, I calculate, I devise, but with you…with you, I jump. Right now, I'm jumping in with no protection, no way back from here. I'm yours, Daniella. From today until the day I die. My heart, my soul, they're yours. And no matter how hard I might try, letting you go would tear me to fucking pieces."

The confession hung in the air between us. I was afraid to move, afraid to speak. The man before me, with the tough and fierce exterior, had laid his heart out for me, exposing every single piece of himself. I didn't know if I loved him back. I wasn't sure what that felt like. I'd never received love to know if I was even capable of it.

He chuckled. "I don't expect you to return those words, Daniella. I just need you to know that I'll love, adore, and cherish you until the day I die." He stood, offering his hand, and I slid mine inside. "We need to discuss the situation with you being a Syphon. Let's get a coffee and take a seat outside in the garden." He changed the conversation to give me time to process. A benefit to being with an older man.

My hand stayed inside his, a warm comfort, safe within his grasp. He led the way to the kitchen, the massive space coming into view. It certainly was beautiful.

"Adam, two cappuccinos please." Drake nodded, pulling out the black barstool. I slid my backside onto it, waiting, an awkward silence hanging between us

"Are you excited to plan the winter solstice now that you have the official role of being the High Mage's wife?" Adam asked, glancing over his shoulder.

"Um, what?" I croaked out.

Drake chuckled. "Oh, you put me in that one, didn't you, Adam?" Drake turned to look at me. "It's the winter solstice, and it's the duty of the Mage's wife to plan the event. I wasn't planning on asking you because of your full-time teaching job, but now that…Would you like to plan the event? All covens across Australia attend."

"Who was going to plan it otherwise?"

He cleared his throat, and Adam delivered the coffee, raising his brow and ducking from the room with haste. "Melinda."

"Oh, fuck no, are you serious? That bitch who tried to undermine our fucking wedding? You can't be serious!"

"She's efficient at her job."

"Is she now?" I quirked my brow at him, and he sighed, shaking his head.

"Fine, her mouth is good at doing its job, too. I had to keep someone around to keep me entertained."

"That makes so much sense now. Have you—"

"Daniella." He growled in warning.

I put my hands up. "Fine, fine. I'll plan your bloody solstice."

"Excellent. I'll bring Penelope over tomorrow to help with the ins and outs and proper procedure, all that shit."

"Sounds perfect. You wanted to sit in the garden, right?"

I followed him into the garden, where two chairs sat around a pit. Drake placed some logs in before throwing his hands and igniting them. It warmed the space outside, with the cool air of winter settling in slowly.

"Are you aware of the story of Eve and the creation of all Mages?" Drake asked, taking his seat.

"Yes. She bit the apple and was cast out of the Garden of Eden, but she created Mages and other creatures as a fuck you to God."

"Correct. She never expected that with the creation of those with Fire, Water, Earth, and Air that another would arise. A Syphon, a balance to counteract the rest of us. You can channel power and even emotions, which is where the danger lies. The more you absorb from others around you, the more deadly and, for lack of a better word, crazy you will become. Are you aware of it?"

I took a sip of my coffee, glancing around the garden before scratching my temple.

"The hex on the house. I remember freaking out. My body was shaking, my mind racing a million miles an hour, but I saw shapes dancing across my vision. I felt scalding hot, but my blood almost cut like ice. The strangest feelings that didn't make sense."

Drake rubbed his chin. "You probably know that when you use mass amounts of power, your eyes change colour. For example, mine will burn red."

"What's your point, Drake?" I asked, taking another sip of the delicious coffee in my hands.

"They were purple."

"I'm not sure I understand. How? Purple isn't the colour of any power."

"That's the question, isn't it? Now, let's go back to the start. What powers were you able to control when you were a child and a teen?"

"Water and Earth, but neither really called to me. We were taught in school that it whispers to us in the night, in the dark, in our dreams. I never heard any of that."

"Did you ever suspect anything?"

"I never had anyone to ask what was normal. It was always: *It will come.*"

"After you were excommunicated, you had no powers, or you just never practised?"

"I think a bit of both. It wasn't until just after we met that I noticed something. I was deep in thought when Sam called out to me because I'd started to burn the paper. What happens now, Drake?"

"That's the question I truly don't know. I've pondered why the hunters attacked you at school. Was that to harm me, or do they know what you are?"

The question hit me hard, and the answer I feared more than anything. My heart raced with the thought of what they wanted. Could it be me, or was it simply to harm Drake? But that still posed the question of why they wanted Drake so much. Why had their attacks increased?

"What would they want with a Syphon?" The words left my lips before I even thought about them, but they were true.

"I don't know, Daniella, I really don't know. I've also heard about a prophecy, a darkness approaching. This worries me more. Is there a connection between Syphon's and this prophecy, or is it something else entirely? The world is shifting. I've noticed certain things, but..." Drake stopped speaking, both of us confused.

We knew the answer to what I was, but still had so many unanswered questions, the most important one that played in my mind was: Why would the Morteferi want a Syphon?

Chapter Forty-Four

Let the Planning Begin

Daniella

I dreaded sitting down with Penelope and planning this event, but I would take this shit that life had dealt me lately and flourish. I wasn't going to let all this bring me down. I had worked too hard on myself for so long. The only thing I hated was being away from my son, especially if his parents ever needed anything from me. He was safe. Nobody knew he existed but Drake, and that was only after some pillow talk. The bond between us grew, and for the first time in a while, I found myself singing and creating again. I had been working on a song for the last week, feeling inspired.

Magic all around, magic in every touch, how I crave that…

"Daniella." Penelope's peppy voice broke through the words floating around in my head.

I waved. "Morning, Penelope." I motioned for her to join me at the ridiculously large dining table. I knew the gist of a solstice, but I hoped she would fill in the gaps for me. She took her seat, dropping a booklet before me titled, *The How-to of a Solstice.*

"Ah, thank you," I mumbled, flicking it open to reveal all the information I would need to plan this event.

"We have two weeks to plan this, with every single coven around Australia to attend. For Drake, having the most powerful one, it must be perfect; otherwise, it will reflect poorly on his leadership. Luckily, Drake booked the venue last year when he'd been selected to plan the event." She flicked through her folders. "At least he's organised," she mumbled.

I ignored her, pulling the folder from her hands and flicking through before pushing it back. Her system was chaotic. I stood, moving to Drake's study, even though he was busy working and attending meetings. I grabbed a notepad from his drawer, and his hand snuck around for a quick grab. I shot him a look, which prompted a wink. I chuckled before returning to Penelope.

"Alright, what do we need to plan?" I held the pen ready.

"Flowers, guest list, food, decorations, theme, auction, attendance gifts…" She continued with her list while I hurriedly wrote them all down.

I knew I could do this. I buckled down with planning, knowing which decorations would be appropriate. I knew that the tables would each have an individual wreath created from holly, ivy, mistletoe, and pine. They were symbols of eternal life and protection. I researched the idea of attendance gifts, deciding on gift bags that were filled with candles, herbs, crystals, and a talisman made from oak—symbolising strength and wisdom.

I paced the kitchen, picking at the array of food that Adam had left on the bench.

A theme. It was a simple concept, but one that was proving to be difficult. I wanted something to reflect the rebirthing, but also Drake's power—with flames, fire, or even light. The words rekindle, rebirth, reflection, light, and fire continually standing out.

"I got it!" I shouted, causing Penelope to spill her water down her shirt. I snorted, throwing her a towel with a soft smile.

She snatched it. "What have you got?" she snapped, dabbing her wet top.

"Rekindling the light within. That's the theme. Do you like it?" I asked her, beaming with excitement and bouncing up and down. I was nailing this planning.

"I mean, it's a little childish."

"I think it's fantastic. It encompasses the ideology of the solstice, the shift in the Coven with my new wife, and the power that runs within my veins. It's perfect." Drake's voice cut through the awkward tension between Penelope and me. She was a unique character. She seemed helpful, but also rather reserved. My paranoid brain thought she wanted me to fail.

"Yes, of course." Penelope bowed her head, writing it down. "I'll work on the designs."

Drake rolled his eyes at her, his annoyance rather clear. I quirked my brow at him, but he waved his hand at me. It was obviously not important right now.

"How's the planning coming along?" he asked, tapping his fingers on the bench, waiting for Adam to make him a coffee. He glanced toward Penelope, and I suddenly clicked why.

I moved closer, reaching toward his ear. "I might need a list of all the women that you've been with."

"Why? A bit jealous?" He nibbled on my ear, and I pushed him away playfully.

"Planning is coming along really well," I said with a clear voice, so Penelope could hear after noticing her craning her neck to hear what we were saying to one another. "Penelope and I have been working very hard, and I think we've almost nutted out all the ins and outs of it all. I'm excited to see it come to light."

"Just don't forget the rules when it comes to the Mages, councils, and all that nonsense." He kissed my forehead, took his coffee, and left as swiftly as he came.

I sat back down, offering Penelope her oat milk flat white. She took a sip before drying her lips to avoid ruining her makeup. "That reminds me, we must discuss the rules of proper etiquette and entry. All that jazz."

"Yes, I'm a little rusty on that." I took out my notepad.

<u>*Proper Rules and Etiquette at Events*</u>

1. The High Mage must be greeted with a talisman of their power's colour.
2. Magic must not be cast in the presence of High Mages.
3. Only Arcanum and bonded consorts may address a High Mage without their proper title.
4. A High Mage may not be touched without consent.
5. When a High Mage enters a chamber, all must rise or bow.
6. In conflict, only a High Mage may challenge another High Mage.
7. Each High Mage is bound to carry a sigil.
8. During a Solstice, High Mages must cloak their faces until the moon/sun rises.

They were all relatively simple and easy to understand. Memorising them would be my homework for the next two weeks, but honestly, it excited me.

Chapter Forty-Five

Too Hot to Handle

Drake

"Daniella, hurry up. We're expected at the event before the others arrive, and at this rate, we won't be there until fucking midnight!" I shouted impatiently from the bottom of the stairs.

I heard her laughter wafting from above. We had grown closer in the last two weeks while she worked beside fellow bonded consorts and other important Mages. She was thriving, and I couldn't be prouder of her. Daniella had found her stride, and my heart ached for her in every single way. She still hadn't said those three little words. She knew how I felt, and as much as I desired to hear them, she wasn't ready. I heard heels clacking on the wooden floor above, and I looked up.

Her bright red hair was waved, flowing down across her soft skin. The black corseted waist showed her womanly curves. Her breasts were perky and on full display with the sweetheart neckline. Soft flowing sheer sleeves, and a maroon skirt, displaying the high leg split leading the path to heaven. I couldn't tear my eyes away from her. I adjusted my pants, which grew tighter with every passing second. So *fucking* sexy.

"Do you need a moment?" she said, reaching the bottom of the stairs, a sparkle in her eyes.

In the time we spent together, she slowly showed more of herself, as did I, and the sex…un-fucking-believable. She was perfect.

"When you have a wife as beautiful as you, it's hard not to admire."

"Come on, you said we were going to be late." I cleared my throat, contemplating whether I'd enough time to get on my knees for her. I checked my watch quickly, clicking my tongue before grabbing her hand and dragging her to the kitchen.

"Out now!" I shouted at Adam and the other kitchen staff. They quickly left as I lifted Daniella onto the bench, my mouth salivating at the idea of tasting her and having her wet for the entire night. I was so fucking hard thinking about it.

"Drake!" she screeched. "We don't have time for this."

"I'll make time because I want to watch you come undone and taste you for the entire night. It'll make my evening more enjoyable." I dragged my hand up her legs, my finger hooking into her underwear. "Either lift that sexy arse, or I'll rip them."

I dragged them down, putting them into my jacket pocket, pulling her to the edge, and getting on my knees.

"Drake—"

"Don't finish that sentence. For once, shut your fucking mouth and let me feast on you." Her mouth closed, and her eyes shone with desire.

She put her hand on my head. "Get to it, then." And she lowered me down.

I parted her legs, wrapping my arms around her thighs, kissing them slowly, licking her while maintaining eye contact before swiping my finger through her, coating it with her wetness. I sucked on the same finger, groaning at her sweet taste.

My tongue moved slowly from the bottom to the top, enjoying the sweet, candy-like taste of her cunt. Her moans filled the space, her body relaxing as I took my time to enjoy it. My tongue slowly increased its pace, delving deeper. Her legs closed the small gap, almost suffocating me while her orgasm grew, but I didn't care. I could die a happy man between these thighs.

"Oh, Drake…Drake…fuck me." Her frantic pants filled the kitchen, and her hand gripped my hair while she screamed in delight, her legs shaking, her chest heaving.

I licked my lips while standing, keeping my gaze locked solely on her. She reached over, grabbing my lapels and pulling me close. Her lips crashed against mine, her tongue flicking out to massage my own.

"How do you taste, *my inferno?*" I asked her, pulling back and moving away. "Come now, we'll be late."

"Oh no, drop those pants. We aren't done yet!"

I chuckled, glancing at my watch and knowing we would be late, but the thought of her lips around me was all-consuming.

"On. Your. Knees," I said slowly, enunciating each word while pointing to the floor.

Her eyebrow quirked as she slowly slid off the bench. My hands carefully unfastened my pants as I walked to the kitchen table, pulling out a chair to take a seat before removing the restrictions and letting my cock spring free, standing at attention and eagerly awaiting her.

She walked over, her eyes laser-focused, her tongue outlining her lips. Daniella dropped to her knees, her hand stroking my throbbing dick, and my patience wore thin.

"It's time to serve your High Mage." My voice was hoarse with need, dying to feel her mouth on me.

"Yes, sir." The words rolling off her tongue made me want to explode right this second.

She took a deep breath before putting the entire length in her mouth without gagging. My head fell back, her throat tightening against my knob.

"Oh, fuck. That's my good girl." I stroked her head, opening my legs wider, giving her more room and access. My phone vibrated in my pocket, Jackson's name flashing on my watch.

"Fuck." I lifted the phone. "Don't you dare stop."

"Yes, Jackson."

"Where the fuck are you?"

"We're five minutes out. Where's the fire?" I asked, watching her head bob up and down on my cock, her hands massaging my balls. They were slowly beginning to tighten, and I groaned.

"You're so funny sometimes. Hurry the fuck up. Your wife should be handling this, not me."

"Oh, she is definitely handling it." My cock throbbed harder. I was ready to blow. I pushed her head back down, feeling my cum shoot down her throat before relaxing.

"Hurry up."

She stood, wiping her mouth, which was sparkling with satisfaction, before she extended her hand.

"Underwear."

"Nope, I want you wet and open for when I decide to fuck you from behind in the bathroom later."

"Fine, I'll meet you in the car then. We're late."

"Yep, sure thing," I muttered, standing slowly with the stars clouding my vision, before hearing her yell from outside. "Coming…again." I laughed to myself before sliding into the limo beside her. I reached forward for a mint, handing it to her. "Don't need you smelling like my cock while greeting all these important people."

"Sometimes, you are charming and a dick."

"You can't say anybody else is like me—the dick-charm that all women want." She chewed the gum while hiding a smirk.

Chapter Forty-Six

Winter Solstice

Daniella

The event started without any issues. People arrived with High Mages, their masks representing different animals. Drake wore a rather obvious one— a dragon. I stayed at the door, greeting any who entered. Whenever the cool air wafted through, it sent shivers through me, especially with my lack of undergarments. Drake's refusal to hand them over after his feasting wasn't fair. The Everwood Coven arrived, their leader the second most powerful. I bowed my head. He wore a raven mask with his blond hair pulled back into a tail.

"Kayden, it's a pleasure to meet you. Drake thanks you for accepting the invitation to his solstice. Please note the seating chart. Upon your table will be a bag of gifted items. The auction will begin shortly. If you have any desire to add an item, please let

Penelope know." I pointed toward her, where she stood near the stage, busily writing down information from coven leaders.

"Is Drake too special to be here to say hello to his fellow coven leaders? Instead, he sends *you,* the disgraced, powerless Mage, unworthy of being a bonded consort. I can only assume you're a firecracker in the sheets. It'd be the only reason to keep you around."

I kept my composure, flashing a smile at the prick before me. "I suppose that's something you'll only be able to fantasise about. Please, if you wouldn't mind taking your seat, we're about to begin, and I won't wait for someone who speaks so disrespectfully of my husband."

He grunted before walking away. I didn't turn towards the guests, not wanting anyone to see the hurt on my face. I stared out the door, waiting to calm my racing heart, feeling that slight craziness beginning to build. Being in a room with so many powerful men and women wasn't helping these Syphon abilities.

"*My inferno.*" His voice was clear, bringing comfort. "What did he say?"

"Who?" I asked, spinning around. His hands landed on my waist while I put my own on his shoulder.

"Kayden. The fucker never can keep his mouth closed."

"It's fine, Drake. It's not about me tonight. It is a celebration for all." He moved a stray hair from my face, pressing a kiss to my forehead.

"I love you. Don't think I won't stand up for you against these fuckers."

"I know you will. That's the problem. Go! I have another coven leader to greet before Penelope and I host the auction."

He snorted, squeezing my behind before moving closer. "The bathroom is calling our name very soon."

No sooner than the words left his mouth, the next leader arrived.

"Drake! I feel important. The High Mage, greeting me himself." The leader chuckled, offering his hand while wearing a mask with a mane, his animal clear. He stood taller than Drake, but had a finer physique.

"Logan, how are you?" Drake took his hand and shook it with a smile before turning toward me. "Allow me to introduce my wife, Daniella Vatras."

I offered my hand, which he took, planting a small kiss on it. "Careful now, Logan."

"Oh, come on, Drake, you know my taste. Anytime you want to switch teams, you know my number. The good ones are always straight." He winked, and I stifled a laugh.

"You're at table six. Enjoy your night, Logan." I pointed toward his seat before turning back to Drake. "At least you had options if you never found a wife." I poked at him.

"I could do worse. I mean, he's not ugly." We exchanged a look before he offered his arm to escort me to the table. I slid my arm inside, locking it into his elbow.

Drake pulled out my chair, and I glanced around the room, ensuring that everyone was taking a seat, and noticed the waiters bring out the first of six courses. All candles on the tables were lit, and there were roughly two hundred people in the ballroom. I glanced up at the sheer fabric linked to the massive chandelier in the middle of the room with fairy lights hanging low over the people. It was stunning. I was proud of everything I'd achieved in two weeks.

"You have created an amazing night," Tyler, another leader, stated, his short mousey brown hair hidden beneath the elephant mask with two tusks coming out on either side.

"Thank you, Tyler, I appreciate it."

"Just don't forget to enjoy it," Drake whispered in my ear before pouring me a glass of wine, less than a standard. He knew I would have some, but I had to stay level-headed before starting the auction in ten minutes. Plus, remembering that I went crazy with too many powers around, this room was my ticking time bomb.

✦

Drake squeezed my hand under the table as Penelope took the stage, clearing her throat.

"Good evening, everyone, and welcome to the winter solstice, a magical night to symbolise new beginnings and rebirth, as is our theme for the night. Now, I won't sit here and talk your ear off. I'd rather our host for the night do that. Can the lovely Mrs. Daniella Vatras please join us on stage?"

The room exploded with applause, and I stood slowly, ensuring my gown wouldn't rip on my chair. I waved before my eyes remained glued to the floor, *'Don't trip, don't trip.'* I repeated this over and over again in my head. I paused at the foot of the stairs leading up to the stage, my heart racing, my hands sweating, and a million thoughts running through my mind. This was true fear. I could stand before a classroom of students with no issues, but a room full of adults? Nope. I was an anxious wreck.

"You can do this," I said to myself quietly. My hand grabbed the rail, pulling myself up the stairs and plastering a huge smile on my face. I scanned the crowd before seeing his face, feeling an instant calm at knowing that he would protect me despite whatever stupid thing came from my mouth.

"Evening, everyone. On behalf of my bonded consort, Drake Vatras, I would like to welcome you all here on this marvellous night, celebrating the rebirth of Mages. I'm sure you've had a little sneak peek into the goodie bags on your table. They have everything you require to complete the cleansing ritual, should you desire to do so. Coven leaders have a little something special, a talisman made from oak, to protect them from any friend or foe. As we know, tonight is about celebration and also giving back to our community. Thus, we have a wonderful auction to bid on before we enjoy our second course and then the call to head to the dancefloor."

I cleared my throat. "In the auction tonight is a wide range of herbs, crystals, candles, protective spells, among more exciting things." I rubbed my hands together. "Shall we start the bidding?"

The hands shot up. None of the High Mages presented a bid, which was to be expected. They all sat with stern-looking faces, eyeing those around them.

"Final bid for five hundred thousand, going once, going twice…sold!" I clapped my hands. "Thank you for participating. As you can see, the next course of food is coming out. You will hear from me soon."

I rushed to my seat, ready to hide while others proceeded to eat. Drake leaned in close, his hand on my thigh, rubbing circles on my skin.

"I'm hungry for something else. I think it's time for our bathroom trip." My cheeks flushed as he stood, offering his hand and leading the way.

He slammed the door behind him, his eyes dark with desire. He loosened his tie, proceeding to unbutton his black shirt. Wearing all black certainly worked for him and his darker features. I stepped backward, hitting the bench, and he quirked his brow before running his hands down my arm and body. He lifted me onto the bench, his fingers drawing small circles across my skin.

"The hardest part about tonight is knowing that your bare cunt is sitting there for me, ready and waiting. I've watched men lust after you, smile at you, all while trying not to fucking kill them, but I knew that this would happen." He unzipped his pants, his eyes never leaving mine. He thrust in. "I knew that I'd be buried deep inside you, and hearing you moan my name."

He kissed me, bringing my lower lip into his mouth and sucking on it.

"Oh, Drake," I moaned, putting my arms around his neck, letting my head fall back.

"That's right, take my cock like the good girl you are."

"Fuck yes." I groaned, hearing the sound of our flesh slapping. He pounded harder and harder, but I was here for it. He knew exactly what to do. His hand moved down, rubbing circles around my clit.

"Oh." I whimpered with need. "Harder, please."

"Careful what you ask for, *inferno*," he forced out, sweat beading on his brow, bracing his hands on the counter and pulling me closer. His hands on my thigh squeezed tightly, lifting me slightly to get a better angle before fucking me rough and hard.

The moans from my mouth increased in pitch and severity. Fuck, he felt so good.

"Drake, Drake, Drake. YES!" My legs and walls tightened against him, his eyes rolling before letting out a roar. He stopped, leaning his head against my own.

"You're going to be the death of me, Daniella," he panted out.

"Maybe that's the plan." I chuckled, tapping his shoulder to use the toilet.

"Were you holding that the whole time?"

"That, you'll never know, but no, you should always pee after. It stops you from getting a UTI."

Drake chuckled, the sound slowly becoming my favourite. It lifted the air between us. I watched him put his suit back together as if nothing had happened between us. He helped to fix my hair before we returned to the event and another course of food.

Chapter Forty-Seven

All are Pathetic

Drake

Daniella had planned an amazing event. I watched her with pride. The girl who had support ripped from her by those she was supposed to be able to trust. Here she stood with High Mages and Arcanums, speaking like she belonged. She always did, but we still had one final task to keep her protected. The words of that slimy fucker rang through my head, his offer of protection. I shook it off, stealing her away from Tyler. He simply smiled and bowed his head. His Coven, Aquamere, was only small, but known for their above-average abilities. He made every individual partake in defence training to know and understand their powers better.

I spun Daniella in my arms. She smiled and laughed, throwing her head back. I would never get enough of her. Even after having her less than ten minutes ago, my cock was already straining in my pants for another round. It would wait, I hoped, until we got home. We glided around the dancefloor, my hand firmly secured to her waist, never wanting to let her go. Spinning her out before bringing her back into my embrace. Who would have thought that my dread over finding a wife would lead me to such happiness?

"Drake." A hand slammed on my shoulder, and I spun to see who dared touch me in such a way.

"Kayden, how may I help you? It must be of high importance to interrupt a dance with my wife."

He glared at Daniella, a sign that she must move on. I brought her closer to me. He wouldn't bully her. Not here, not ever. I had the power. This was *my* solstice, and *my* Coven was larger, even if his was considered stronger. Those who surrendered to Earth power always gave me the fucking creeps. Who wanted to play with leaves and trees?

"We must speak. These attacks from the Morteferi have to stop."

"I agree, but this isn't the place to discuss it. You're welcome to come to my home tomorrow, and we can have an undisturbed conversation."

"Drake, I'll just leave you alone." She attempted to move away, but my grasp on her tightened. My eyes met hers, a silent warning that she was not to move.

"She knows her place," Kayden responded smugly with a sly smile, waving her away. My hands igniting in flames, the touch searing her skin slightly, her Syphon ability protecting her within seconds.

"You dare speak of my bonded consort in such a manner. She has equal right to be included in all matters that relate to our Coven." It was a gentle reminder to the dick before me.

She pressed a hand to my chest, her eyes losing their spark. The power was consuming her.

"Drake, it's fine. I need some air." She stepped further away, touching my elbow. Time slowed as I watched her hand do the same to Kayden.

He gasped. "You dare touch me. You dare break our sacred rules."

"What? Wait, I was told that only High Mages, Arcanums, and bonded consorts were able to touch."

"You fool!" he shouted, bringing the attention of the entire room to us. "You poison me with your disgraced hands."

"Drake." Her lip wobbled. "Penelope told me."

I raised my hand at her. "Leave now." This mess wouldn't be easily cleaned up. I knew what Kayden would request, and it would cost me dearly. Daniella ran from the area. I watched her leave through the front and into the waiting limo.

"Now, Kayden, I've tolerated you for a while with your entitled attitude and holier-than-thou beliefs. The fact that you think you deserve anything at the celebration I'm hosting is beyond anything. You're a fucking maggot, an Earth user so fucking weak and pathetic that he needs others to fight for him. Let me guess, you asked to discuss the Morteferi because you want protection from a leader who can keep your people safe. You are pathetic."

"She touched me. That's a gross breach of our rules, and you know this. Do you dare to think that this isn't worthy of an apology?"

Penelope ran over, her eyes frantic. "Sir, I informed Daniella of the rules, and I told her, I explicitly told her."

"Penelope shut your fucking mouth and piss off," I snarled, my eyes trained on Kayden.

Jackson walked over. "Drake, this isn't the time. Be logical."

"He insulted my bonded consort at my Coven's event. That equates to death. This solstice was planned by my Coven, and thus the rules still fucking apply. He needs to apologise before I incinerate his fucking pathetic existence."

Kayden's lip trembled. He was no match for me, and he knew it. I was scarred and abrasive, but that was the way I was raised, and I'd never back down from the fucking fight, even if sometimes

I knew that I wouldn't be able to win. He bowed his head, dropping to his knee.

"Forgive me, Arcansire," he said, using the term of mutual respect between High Mages. "She disgraced our kind by living among humans for so long. She's unaware of our rules, and I apologise for my actions, but we know that she must also receive punishment for her disrespect."

"Rise and get the fuck out of here before I change my mind." I looked at the crowd around me. "Matter of fact, all of you fucking leave!" I shouted, watching them all run for the exit.

Melinda strolled over, her hand on my shoulder. "I'm sorry that *she* displayed a disgraceful act. If you need anything, please know that I'm available." She batted her eyes, flicking her long hair over her shoulder. I noticed the sheer gown she wore, showing her entire body

I grabbed her hand from my shoulder, twisting it in my grasp. She whimpered.

"You dare lay your hands on me. Do you think that because you gave the occasional unsatisfying blow job that it makes you something special? You never deep-throated. You were never going to be anything more than a placeholder to relieve my blue balls. Now get the *fuck* out of my face!"

She ran away, crying. I ran my hands over my face at the colossal disaster this event had become.

Screams echoed from outside, and I ran toward the exit, stopping at the sight of the Morteferi attacking, and High Mages using their powers to protect their people. I glanced across the street, seeing a line of them waving their hands around. They were about to suffocate them all. I clapped my hands, throwing up a wall of fire around all the Mages in the vicinity.

"GET BACK INSIDE NOW!" I roared, and they ran without question. Holding the wall until the last second, I then let it fall. I burnt the lock, making it unbreakable to anyone who tried.

"Earth users, cover the building in plants, hide their sight." They stood forward, using ivy to cover the glass, hiding us from them.

"Arcansire, here now."

Tyler, Logan, Kayden, and Aston trudged over, removing their masks. The formality of the event was gone. They stood before me: a Fire, Water, Air, and two Earth users.

"What's the plan, Drake?" Logan asked. Kayden crossed his arms, annoyed that he wasn't sought for the same counsel. Tyler nodded, and Aston was a flighty individual. I questioned whether he had any brain cells.

"We either wait them out or we attack. I spotted eight Morteferi, that's more than I've ever seen in the past. How they knew where this event was worries me more than them actually being here."

"How do we attack? The moment we step outside, they will restrict our air. We're powerless against them." Aston's lip quivered, a fellow Air user showing just how terrified he was of these fuckers.

"Kayden, you've taught your people proper defence. Are they not prepared for this type of attack?"

"Not this many. I've taught them singular, not an entire group. They won't fight."

This was pointless. I took the stage, holding up my hands for attention.

"I won't lie. We're kind of screwed, but only because of the fear they hold over us. We have the power. We can stop them, but who's brave enough to join me? Who wants to take the fight to them?"

I never expected the response to be silence.

"You're all fucking pathetic." I walked toward the back door, sneaking around the front, staying out of sight before watching them stand in a circle, planning. They were making it very easy. I closed my eyes, pulling my fire from deep within, allowing it to consume me before throwing it toward them and igniting them in seconds. They shouted and squealed before dropping to the ground. It was over, but not before I noticed another standing further back. His eyes glowed purple, another Syphon. I moved, wanting to question him, but upon seeing me, he ran.

I returned inside, burning the door and kicking it open once more. "You can leave." My heart was full knowing that she was safe. She wasn't here, but what would she think of me?

Chapter Forty-Eight

What Do They Mean?

Daniella

During the ride home, the itch in my arms became unbearable. I had syphoned too much power from Drake and his fire explosion that initially burnt my skin. It healed once I'd enough power in my system. I paced the room, waiting for Drake to return and for me to be told off. I picked up the notes from Penelope and read them over, knowing I was right. Had she told me wrong, or did I write them wrong? No, I wasn't. I knew I was right. Did she purposely tell me incorrect information so I would fail? But she was hired to be my second, to help me with this. I met her the day of my wedding. Surely she wasn't a snake in the grass.

Maybe I should give her the benefit of the doubt. I glanced at my watch. It was after ten. Drake still wasn't home, and I hadn't heard anything from him. I began to worry and kept checking my phone even though no messages came through.

"Fucking hell, Drake!" I shouted to the empty house. Was this my punishment?

I trudged up the stairs, walking into the bathroom to shower and remove the gown, makeup, and hair of the night, then crawled into bed. I picked up my journal, flicking through the pages to see if I missed anything. I could feel the crazy scratching at the inside of my brain. My eyes grew heavy under the weight of what I did and how much damage I may have caused. I wished I could take it back. I continued to work on the song that played in my head continually, words that just flowed: *A feeling of being complete, the knowledge of being whole, you are the one who matches my soul.*

I woke suddenly, my eyes flying open to see Drake sitting on the chair opposite the bed, his shirt buttons undone halfway, exposing his tattoos. His hair hung over his face, my journal in his hands.

"Drake." My voice was soft with sleep as I sat up.

"To be honest, I don't know why I doubted you." He tapped the journal in his hands before throwing it to the floor. "It's all right here. Penelope tried to explain that you misheard, but I doubt her platinum-infected skull would know the difference between right and wrong." His deep voice echoed through the room.

"What happened? How much trouble am I in?" I asked, playing with my fingers in anticipation.

"None. Kayden likes to have dick-measuring contests, but he always fails, and honestly, after the Morteferi attack, your little stunt means nothing."

"Wait, they attacked? Are you okay?" I stood, making my way over to him, kneeling before him to see his face. I ran my thumb over the scar on his mouth. He had told me how he got them. He didn't speak much, but our walls were slowly crumbling. His heart was open, even while mine remained closed.

His beautiful brown eyes locked onto mine, and he took my face in his hands, staring at me in a way that I never expected. His thumbs stroked my cheeks, and he kissed my forehead.

"You are my everything, Daniella. I love you. Even if you screwed up with Kayden, I didn't care because I only care that you're by my side with every single fucking step that I take." His words caused my heart to ache as he kissed me with an intensity I had never experienced.

He lifted my shirt over my head, laying me down on the floor. His mouth was warm on my skin, leaving soft kisses along my collarbone. My breath hitched when he grabbed my wrists, his fingers wrapping around them, firm but gentle, pinning them above my head. He didn't want to hurt me. His eyes looked me over, like he wanted to memorise every inch of my skin.

"Eyes on me, *inferno*," he said gruffly, and I couldn't under the power of his gaze

Our eyes were locked onto one another, almost like he was peering into my soul and letting me know that he saw me and would always protect me. I'd never felt so exposed but safe in his arms.

He didn't thrust in roughly like he normally did. Instead, he slowly pushed himself inside me. I groaned, my body arching with the need to feel every inch of him as it adjusted. The slow torture almost knocked the breath out of me. I tightened my grip on his hands without meaning to, finding the pressure to keep myself within the moment. He built a steady rhythm between us—slow, but filled with desire and a hunger to feel each other like we never had before.

"Drake," I whispered, pleading with him for more.

He rolled his hips, slowly, deeply, having me feel every single inch of him inside. I could feel my walls tightening. He groaned, the sound like music to my ears. Our gazes stayed connected, my mouth opening with small moans of pleasure, which elicited a smile from him every time. The tenderness in his eyes made it hard to think, hard to breathe, impossible to know what was behind it.

Every thrust sent pleasure through my entire body. This wasn't just sex—this was the definition of making love. The way he held me so tenderly, his forehead occasionally touching my own, his hands trembling while they held mine. Almost like he had an internal struggle, holding back part of himself, but wanting me to feel everything he felt for me.

"You're going to be my undoing, Daniella, and I'm here for it." His words broke that barrier between us, opening up the door to something else, something other than the physical connection we shared. It terrified me, wanting this and not sure if I could handle it.

My walls were tightening, feeling the sensation in every part of my body, not just down below but within my core, my chest...my heart. He was slowly becoming—

I shattered under him, the ecstasy of him seeing more than just the erratic, magically-crazed Syphon.

It didn't take long for him to follow, my name a whisper on his lips. "Daniella." It didn't sound like just a name to him. It was as if, in that moment, I was the only thing in his world that made sense. Hearing it made my heart flutter because I knew I needed him and would never give him up.

✦

I lay in his arms, safe and secure within his embrace, understanding the magnitude of his love for me. I wished one day to reciprocate the same intensity. My fingers traced his chest tattoo, a dagger with wings on either side, one angelic and the other demonic.

"Are you having fun?" he asked, capturing my hand in his.

"What do they mean? I've always stared at them in wonder, but never actually thought about the meaning behind them. I know that tattoos on Witches have a personal significance, a way to channel more power, or even just to symbolise what type of warrior they are."

"True, but I have to ask…what do you think it means?" he murmured as I traced the jewel on the handle of the weapon. "I think this symbolises your upbringing. You are the dagger, your mother the angel on your shoulder, and your father's stern demonic wings on the other. You try to be the best of both worlds, with your father's brutality and your mother's heart, which is how you care for every member of your Covn, but destroy with an iron fist those who threaten that existence."

"Oh, what else?" His eyes were sparkling, and I knew I was right.

"The swirl on your neck is a channelling mark—it helps control the magnitude of your fire. This triangle with a line through it represents Air magic. Flip it upside down, and you have Earth. Fire is a triangle pointing upward, while Water is the opposite—a triangle pointing downward. All four come together within the Star of Eve, each point carrying its own symbol." I searched his body for more. "Here is the sun symbol, a circle cut into eight sections like a pizza, grounding you within the Fire power that runs in your veins. Although I find it interesting that you have Hecate's Wheel here. Should it be so close to the sun when—" I stopped, thinking about my next words, but coming up short.

"It symbolises power and knowledge"—he took my hand, kissing a finger—"which is closely linked to the sun symbol." Another two fingers. "I believe they go hand in hand." Another finger. "One cannot exist within the other. A little rusty on your Mage training?" He took the last finger into his mouth, and the sensation of wanting to feel that mouth everywhere else on my body rushed through me.

"Ha ha ha. I didn't get a full education." I pulled my hand away and poked him playfully in the pentagram symbol on his belly. "But I'm not sure about your sleeves—the vines with roses. I truly don't know." They were beautiful, with leaves that contained numbers. They almost looked like dates.

He cleared his throat. "Every person I have lost is represented on this arm, while the other..." He went quiet.

"Those whose lives you have taken." He sat up, grabbing his pants and pulling them on. "Drake, why do you do that? Do you fear that I would judge you?"

"I've done horrible things, Daniella. I killed eight people tonight."

"They threatened our people. It was warranted," I stated, standing and pulling on my baggy T-shirt and moving to stand before him.

"Was it?" His eyes appeared glassy, holding back emotions I hadn't seen.

"Yes, without question. You saved countless lives at the cost of a few. What, did you think you could talk them down? You know they are increasing their attacks. Would you prefer the death of hundreds on your conscious? You made the tough decision, a choice, just as those hunters chose to attack our people."

He put his hands on his hips, staring at the floor and closing his eyes. He reached up to rub at his eyelids, his breathing growing erratic and hitching occasionally.

"You've shown me that life isn't just black and white—it's messy, complicated, and full of grey. And maybe I don't understand all of you yet, but I want to. I'm trying. I know you've done things…hard things…because you had to, because you believed it was the only way to protect what mattered. And I see how it weighs on you. You act like nothing touches you, but I know better. I see the fear, *your fear*, the worry you try to hide behind that mask you wear. But Drake…I see you. I see all of you. I accept you—as you are, not who you pretend to be to everyone else."

"You truly are *my inferno.* The one who lit a fire in my heart." He kissed me, pulling me into his arms.

"I have to tell you something, and I know you'll be mad at me. I'm sorry in advance, but I'm on birth control." I held up my arm. "I have the implant, so the chances of me conceiving are slim, and it's still valid for another year."

"That's probably a good thing. I truly don't think a child would be good right now." He chuckled, completely unfazed. "We need to sleep. I have a council meeting tomorrow to discuss moving your transcendence forward to the next couple of days."

I drew up the blankets, covering myself in his scent as his arm wrapped around my middle and pulled me against his body. I'd never felt more at peace than I did in his arms.

His tattoos were a journey of his life, representing his inner strength, resilience, and passion. A true message of his transformation and his journey through life. They were a reminder of what he'd endured and what he had accomplished. His was the fire that burned brightly in the night, the fire that kept the Coven secure.

Chapter Forty-Nine

Tainted Coven

Drake

This meeting had to happen after the attack at the solstice. I tapped my fingers on the table, waiting for the remaining council members to attend. Daniella sat beside me. We both felt the shift between us last night. Something clicked into place. I couldn't explain it in words, other than a deep desire for one another beyond all reason. I peered over at her. Her cheeks flushed as she glanced away. I snorted at her embarrassment, wondering what she was thinking.

The men entered, and the room stilled for a moment. Bracken Romano strolled in wearing a suit, his hair slicked back.

"Bracken." Daniella's soft voice flowed through the room. She covered her mouth, remembering the rules. I waved at her, giving her permission to see her brother.

They embraced. She hadn't seen him since our wedding. They hadn't had the chance to see one another since I burnt their father to a crisp like the piece of fucking shit that he was. She touched his face, speaking to him in hushed tones. He nodded, their exchange showing no animosity, just love. Had Giuseppe abused more than one of his children?

I cleared my throat, indicating they needed to separate. I noticed the way Bracken held her hand tightly. It was his first meeting on the council.

"Daniella, why don't you join your brother for this session? Help him settle into his new role on the council?" She turned her head, a beaming smile on her beautiful face. Fuck, I loved this woman.

The men sat, discussing the events of the solstice and the attack by the Morteferi. Nobody had any idea what to do about it. Their shelter, unknown. Members, unknown.

I slammed my fist on the table before standing. "How the fuck do we still know nothing about them, but they knew about our fucking celebration? That was top secret, only a few—" I stopped short, my eyes darting to Daniella at the realisation.

They wouldn't have known unless somebody told them. My hands landed on my chair, rocking back and forth with this information. A sickening feeling in my bones. How had I missed this?

"Meeting is concluded, you may leave."

The men filed out while Daniella walked her brother to the door. "Wait, you can stay." He wouldn't be tainted by the old, stubborn men set in their ways. He was a fresh pair of eyes, a new opportunity.

Four people were in the room—Jackson, Daniella, Bracken and me. The only people I trusted right now. I gestured for all to sit, waiting a moment to find the right words.

"We knew there was a rat within the coven, but they're closer than we think. The rat is in the fucking council." Screw the right words, I had to find the answers.

"What?" Bracken shouted.

"Who?" Daniella questioned.

"How?" Jackson asked.

All were valid questions that I wanted to know as well, but this investigation would have to be top secret to find the culprit behind the attack. We were lucky that only one person lost their life before it got any worse. We knew there was one, but after the attack at the solstice, it was clear—the council had been infiltrated by the hunters.

"All excellent questions. I only just realised it then, remembering that every single aspect of their attacks has been with knowledge from those closest to us. Daniella, how did they know what school you were at and what time your break was? Jackson, how did they know to attack at Craig's house? How have they known where we are going to be? It makes sense that somebody is feeding them intel, but who the *fuck* would be stupid enough to go against their own coven? What could they have promised?"

"Drake, these are big allegations." Jackson cleared his throat. "Wha..." He threw his hands in the air, speechless at the situation.

Daniella sat quietly, looking at her hands, her face pale, and those eyes missing their spark.

"What is it?" I asked her, wondering why she was so quiet.

"Whatever is said in this room stays in this room, yeah?"

I nodded, glaring at the two other men.

"Could…this is going to sound ridiculous, but could this be about me? They want me as a Syphon more than to harm you, or at least those are our assumptions. I was at all of those locations, and they attacked me at work." I scratched my chin while Jackson rubbed the back of his neck. Bracken just looked lost.

"I don't know, but the vampires know about you. I had an interesting visit the other day. They offered to train you to control your powers. It's an idea that I'm considering, if it helps with your situation, but one that can be discussed later. For now, we have homework. We are to each come up with a list of people that we have discussed certain things with, people that we might assume could have leaked intel. Jackson, I want you to look into their finances. Fuck the repercussions. I want answers. Bracken, keep an ear out. You are new and fresh, so they might approach you."

Jackson and Bracken left, leaving Daniella and me alone. She swung on the chair, her fingers on her lips. I could see she was thinking, so I sat beside her.

"What is it?"

"What would their aim be? That's the question that stumps me. Why, Drake? You are known for your brutality. You would kill them even if they did it under duress. Just why?"

"If it is because of you, Syphons are weapons. They can be used for multiple purposes. If it's another reason, then I worry about what is coming for us. But right now, I don't want to think about it. I want to plan your transcending ceremony. I like the idea of Sam coming."

Her eyes shot to me. "Yes, I know you would have told her. You needed a friend, and she has been one for a long time. But she'll be given a forgetful potion before she leaves."

"That's fine. She will be there. I'm so excited, but Drake, what power should I declare? You wanted to hide my existence."

"Which power came easier when you were younger?"

"Water, I think, because the human body has so much of it, so maybe that."

"Then tomorrow, we will start planning. For now, let's go home. I'm wrecked and need to be deep inside you before falling asleep."

"I have to please my High Mage." Her eyes sparkled.

"Fuck, I love you, Daniella," I said, kissing her lips before taking her hand and heading out to the car.

CHAPTER FIFTY

FRIENDLY CATCH-UP, YEAH?

DANIELLA

How do you plan to transcend to your powers when you technically don't have any? It was the question I continued to ask Drake daily, but his response was always the same. *'It will be fine.'* He knew something that I didn't, and it was frustrating as hell.

Drake had ordered my dress. It had to be white—some weird Mage rule to represent the purity of those finally receiving their powers. I questioned whether it was appropriate, being that I was significantly older than most. There had never been another like me, but he didn't seem to care.

It was now Tuesday, three days since the solstice celebration on the weekend. Drake was more concerned with the Morteferi, making sure there was plenty of security, and trying to find the rat within his council. I apologised to Kayden for the mishap, but Penelope remained close to me. Drake wanted to see if it was a mistake on her end or something else more sinister. He was testing everybody at the moment, and nobody knew. It worried me.

I slid into the ridiculous blacked-out Mercedes SUV. I had permission to see Sam and invite her to my ceremony on the weekend, but had to explain that her memories would be removed afterward to ensure the safety of our people. It was better than nothing, right? I watched the cityscape change to suburbia before the country spread. I sighed, loving the relaxed nature of being out here. The way the landscape was just constant green, and the air smelled fresh and clean.

Vince pulled into the car park, and I stepped out in the tiny town I'd called home for so long, a smile spreading over my face.

"DANI!" Sam screamed, and I turned to see her running toward me, her arms wide open.

I walked to meet her halfway, refusing to run in my boots. She was in jeans and her school jersey— you had to represent the school. I wrapped my arms around her, holding her tight. It had been two weeks but I missed her. We texted every day, but it wasn't the same as our banter in the office daily.

"I missed you," she said into my shoulder, as far as she could reach with her tiny stature.

"You have no idea," I returned. Sam slapped my shoulder. "Ow. What was that for?"

"You can't say you missed me when you're literally glowing. Is everything going well with Drake?" She wriggled her eyebrows, and I snorted at her, taking her hand.

"I'm starving. Let's get some food."

We entered the café, and it was bustling like usual for the small town, mostly with the single mothers and the elderly. We ordered our food with milkshakes because they weren't just the boring standard ones, but rather the deluxe milkshakes that gave you a sugar rush. The ones dentists hated. We took our seats, settling into an awkward silence.

She reached over the table. "How are you? I know it would've been hard to give up teaching."

"It's strange to not be working. I never liked the idea of being a kept woman, you know that. I have dreams and so much that I want to achieve, but we both know that I couldn't have stayed there. Another attack would've happened, and this time, it might have been students who got hurt. The idea of that makes me feel sick. I made the best choice for that school, not necessarily for me." I sighed, biting my lip for a moment. "But Drake has given me tasks as his bonded consort."

She laughed at the name. "I love how you're not his wife per se, but his *bonded consort*," she said in a fancy, mocking voice.

"It's a term of respect, though, and essentially means the same thing."

"What the hell do you do?"

"I plan events and speak to fellow wives on the council. I have an assistant. I'm a bit suss on her, but meh."

Sam punched her fist into her other hand. "What's her name?"

I snorted when the food arrived—a chicken and avocado focaccia with chips and sweet chilli aioli sauce.

"Are you going to ask about him?" Sam raised her brow at me.

"Him, who?" I queried, popping a chip into my mouth.

"Kris." I didn't expect that. I lifted the water to my lips, taking a sip to ease the spice in my mouth.

"There's nothing to ask. I'm married, and he was out of line kissing a taken woman twice."

"You know Drake went to his house to threaten him."

"Yep. Kris touched what was his. It's a big no-no in Mage culture."

"Witches. You are weird," she whispered to avoid anyone else hearing.

"That reminds me! You're invited to attend an event on the weekend. I'm transcending to my power, and Drake has agreed to you being present, but…you have to take a potion after to remove your memories once it's done. You're there to support me and—"

"Am I not allowed to remember for my protection or yours?"

"Both, Sam, both. I'm just happy you can come. Will you?"

"To see my best friend come into her power? Absolutely. Also," she paused, taking a bite of her food, which only added to the suspense of what else she would say next, "I've asked people from the office to come and say hi." My stomach dropped. That meant Kris. I wanted to yell at her. I knew seeing him would only add to my confusion over things right now. I shifted in my seat. "What is it?" she asked, her eyebrows coming together.

"Honestly, I was hoping to not see Kris. It's just awkward, especially knowing how Drake threatened him. How do I—" I stopped, not sure what to say.

"How do you look at him when you had a connection and you kissed multiple times?"

"Well, yeah. Seriously, Sam, how do I?" It's going to be so hard. "Can you text and cancel?"

Sam scratched her nose. "Too late," she mumbled.

I heard the door open behind me, shouts of my name echoing through the tiny café before the scraping of chairs on the concrete flooring. Kris sat beside me while the others surrounded us. I glanced up, meeting his gaze and feeling lost in the moment. Moving away slightly, to put some space between us, I focused on the way Drake made me feel and how confused I was from the other night.

The way he made love to me, the way he touched me, the way he was able to bring emotions to the surface that I'd buried for so long. I felt something for him, but never experiencing the full breadth of love, I wasn't sure if this was it.

Laughter exploded between all of them, breaking my thoughts and forcing me to place a smile on my face to hide the thoughts racing in my head. I enjoyed being part of a group of people who knew the human part of me and not the complexity of being a creature that could channel powers and emotions from Mages, or rather, any supernatural creature. We had discovered that I couldn't Syphon from humans, since I had no crazy, weird stuff happen around them.

They checked the time. "We had better get back," Alan said, clicking his tongue.

All of them stood, giving me a hug and leaving the café. Sam and Kris still lingered for a while. Sam and I were making small talk when her phone rang. She stepped away, leaving me alone with Kris.

My heart began to race at the fear of being alone with him.

"Dani, you're going to have to look at me to speak to me." His voice was low and close to my ear, sending shivers down my spine.

My eyes slowly peered up at him. "I have no issue looking at you, Kris. It's more what you expect from me."

"You still have a choice. We can be together, we can explore this. You know there is something between us." The weight of his words was heavy, a crushing sensation filling my chest, but I craved the safety of somebody else, the security and love from Drake.

"No, there's no future for us, Kris. There never was."

He slammed his fist on the table, shaking his head. "He doesn't get to win." A vein in his forehead protruded, his rage evident as his nostrils flared.

"I don't have to listen to this," I snapped at him, standing to leave.

He wrapped his hand around my arm, stopping me instantly and pulling me against him. I pushed him away, pointing my finger at him.

"NO!" I yelled. "You don't get to do this to me. Drake is my husband, he is—"

"Do you love him?"

"I don't love you," I retorted, knowing the question wasn't fair.

"But do you love him? Answer the question, Dani."

"No, you have no right to ask the question, and I do *not* owe you an answer."

I turned away from him, seeing Vince watching the interaction between us. I would message Sam and say goodbye, but I had to leave. I couldn't be here. Kris grabbed my wrist, but I yanked it away from him. He reached for it again before I spun and slapped him across the face and ran back to Vince.

He held the door open, and I slid in, staring at the floor. My arms itched slightly around Vince and his power. He must have been using it. Vince reached back, handing me a phone.

"Are you alright?" Drake's voice came through, and my body relaxed at hearing it.

"Y-yes. I'm sorry." Tears welled in my eyes, feeling guilt, regret, and frustration.

"You have nothing, and I mean *nothing*, to be sorry for. That pig is in the wrong. I'm sorry I wasn't there."

I chuckled, a single tear rolling down my cheek. "Yes, I heard you threatened him for kissing me."

"Just marking my territory."

"I think you have done that a few times." I heard his laugh down the other end of the phone. "Drake, I feel weird again."

"Close your eyes and sleep. I'll see you when you get home. Hand the phone back to Vince for me." I did as he asked, getting comfortable and closing my eyes. Would I ever feel normal again?

Chapter Fifty-One

Strange Alliances

Drake

I sent out an invitation through supernatural channels, wanting to speak to that vampire again. I needed to know what he knew to understand what else was coming for Daniella. What if the Morteferi were hunting her?

The sky was grey, impossibly dark, when the front door swung open. I stood, knowing what was coming. I waited in the foyer as a strong wind rushed through before the door slammed closed.

"Mr. Vatras, I did not expect to hear from you again."

"No need for your bullshit theatrics. We aren't allies. I need answers. That is all this is."

"Not very nice for our future friendship. My name is William."

"Fuck up and sit the fuck down. You will answer my questions, and that is all. Understood?"

"Crystal clear, Drake." The blood-sucker took a seat, crossing his legs and draping his arm over my furniture. "What is it you would like to know?"

"Why would the Morteferi want her?" I took a seat opposite him. I had let all remaining staff go for their safety and kept the fire alight beside me, ready to manipulate it if needed.

"She is power—raw, untapped, and unparalleled power. She can control all the elements and more. If she were near me, she would have my strength, speed and agility. The same with a wolf. All our strengths with none of our weaknesses. Her only weakness is being human." He snapped his fingers "Oh, and consuming so much power that her actions become… well, I'm sure you have seen already."

I tried to keep my face as neutral as possible, but the biggest tell would be my heart. I never had to master the skill of keeping it beating at a normal rate. He would know the second I lied.

"Let me guess, you are contemplating whether to tell the truth or to lie. Aren't you, Mr. Vatras? Shall I save you the trouble? Don't. If it isn't your heart, it's your sweat, your hormones. Only those like myself can mask such things to keep secrets."

"Why does the power affect them that way?" I blurted, now understanding that it was fucking pointless to keep any secrets.

"Syphons are like conduits. What happens when one overheats or is not placed correctly?" His hand started as a fist before mimicking an explosion. "The human body cannot regulate or contain that much power. They will explode in different ways. There is no telling how they could react."

I nodded, remembering the hex on the house as well as the day at her school, and even the outburst with her father escalated quickly. Fuck me! I rubbed my chin before standing.

"What makes you think those peasants want her?" William asked, his nose turning up in disgust. It didn't matter if you were a Mage or not—the Morteferi weren't respected within supernatural circles.

"Since she arrived in my life, they have made more vigilant attacks on my Coven, and even toward her and myself."

"Interesting, but that could also be a coincidence, or it could be about the *Firebound One*," William stated, which I had wondered, but it was still a worry either way. I had seen that term in my research.

"You know of the prophecy?" I queried, wondering if he would reveal more, as information on this was spotty and hard to piece together.

"I have heard of different aspects, whether it is the *Firebound One*, the one with unclaimed power, or the Syphons' fates."

"That tells me nothing." I stood, making my way to the fire and staring into the flames, my thoughts consumed by the multiple questions that had no answers.

"Every part of the supernatural world has discussed different elements, so it's hard to know what is truth and what is fiction. Just be wary of whom you trust and know that you have my allegiance. I cannot harm her under the oath that you both took. I only offer my services for *her* benefit."

Doubt swirled in my mind, knowing he wouldn't reveal his hand. Vampires were sleezy, advantageous creatures. Only willing to help when it suited them. "Her transcendence is happening on the weekend. Will that help her?"

"Hell no, that might even make her worse. Who gave you that idea?" He snorted, glancing at his nails like this conversation was below him.

"The Keepers," I stated, my brow furrowed.

"Ah, yes, The Keepers of knowledge. They would surely never be wrong. They would never give you incorrect information."

"Why should I trust you?" I snapped at him, frustrated that this conversation was leading nowhere.

William reached into his pocket, pulling out a black object and tossing it in the air before throwing it at me. A black obsidian bracelet, each piece of it uncut and jagged. "Raw obsidian—it will absorb the excess power while she wears it."

"H-how?"

"She isn't the only Syphon to have existed." He paused, a deep sigh coming from his chest. "Drake, she needs training." He placed a card on the coffee table. "Call me when she is ready, or rather, when *you* are ready to trust me."

The conversation I hoped would provide more clarity had caused the complete opposite. There was still a possibility of the Morteferi wanting her, but what was this prophecy? Embers and Ruin? *Firebound One*? Unclaimed power? Syphons? How did it all link together? I rubbed my temples, a pain starting in the back of my head.

Chapter Fifty-Two

A Small Token

Daniella

I walked into our home, removing my boots because heaven forbid I dirty the floor. The housekeeper would kill me for it. She liked to keep everything spotless.

"Drake!" I called out, putting my shoes into the cupboard and out of sight. There was silence. "Drake!" I reached the kitchen to see Adam moving about, cooking up a storm like usual.

"He's in the gym, and Daniella, he isn't in a good mood."

"Do we know why?" I wondered what had happened. He didn't tell me about every meeting he had, but I knew he had so much shit to deal with.

"No, he hasn't told me. He shut down, but he might open up to you."

I trudged down to the gym. It was on the lower level of the house, along with the impressive wine cellar that was the size of a living room, and the garage. My ears pricked at the voice through the door, pushing himself to go harder. Pressing against the door, I kept my eyes on him, his hands locked around the bar. His arms were taut, every muscle defined and covered in a sheen of sweat. His only clothes were the tight shorts, showing every inch of his fucking hot tattooed body.

The ball flew through the air, and he caught it with precision between his feet before he tossed it in the air once more. His body moved effortlessly, and the muscles shifted with such grace. I found myself mesmerised by the sight. He was controlled, powerful, and oh so fucking dangerous.

Every movement was a balance between restraint and strength, his arms never yielding. It wasn't like Drake to balance that line of control. I tilted my head slightly. His shoulders. His back. The way the muscles in his abdomen flexed when he pulled himself up. My temperature rose instantly at the ripples of his body moving in such an intricate way.

He caught the ball again, holding it for seconds, but it seemed longer. He lifted his legs with a grunt before tossing it once more. Watching him like this, so focused, unguarded, and strong—it was like a drug that I could get high from. His hands were turning white from the intense grip, and my mind drifted to that strong grasp that held my hands above me while plunging deep inside. Desire pooled between my legs.

Heat rose in my cheeks, flushing with embarrassment. I forced myself to look away for a moment to compose myself. I cleared my throat, glancing up and meeting his gaze. A small smirk played over his face, and he caught the ball before dropping it and landing on the mat.

"Enjoying the view?" he puffed out, taking a swig of water.

"I mean, it was hard not to with…with just how terrible you were." The words stumbled from my mouth, a little off balance after my perve session.

He laughed, pulling me into his sweaty arms. The most annoying part was the fact that he still smelled so amazing, not disgusting like people normally did after a workout. He didn't move for a while, holding me tight.

"I have a gift for you." He broke the embrace, grabbed his bottle, and took another drink before grabbing something near his phone. He hid it behind his back, wriggling his eyebrows. "Close your eyes and hands out."

"This isn't some dirty thing where you put your penis in my hand, is it?"

"Oh, Daniella, you're hilarious. No, I have this for you." He pulled it out from behind his back.

He dangled the black obsidian bracelet in front of me, each piece crooked and not matching the next. It was beautiful in a broken kind of way.

"It should stop your episodes; it will absorb the excess power if you have any. It's the best I can do for now."

"What do you mean *for now*? Is this what Adam was talking about? What did you hear today that has upset you?" I asked him, my hand reaching out to touch his arm.

"I'm not upset. It's complicated, Daniella. I spoke with a fucking bloodsucker, who said you're powerful and dangerous, and even when you transcend, it isn't going to settle things down. I'm lost, *inferno*. I'm not sure how to keep you safe." He hung his head, turning to grab a towel.

"You already have." I slid the bracelet on, feeling the excess power drain from my body in seconds. "Drake, don't doubt yourself. It's all going to work out. I will transcend, and everything will be fine. We will live long and happy lives where you will question your sanity daily with me by your side."

I leaned forward, his lips brushing mine before he pulled back. "Shower, now," he ordered. I knew what was coming. I ran up the stairs, giggling like a little girl, all my troubles fading away.

Chapter Fifty-Three

Transcendence

Daniella

S leep had eluded me all week. I paced the house endlessly, even asking Drake if I could file some paperwork—any menial task to keep my mind from drifting to today. Today, the day of my transcendence to my power, which wasn't a power, but more like a misdirection. How was Drake so calm right now?

I sat on the bed with my notebook in my hand, continuing to work on the song that had been plaguing my mind.

The nights no longer cold, A warmth that consumed my soul, The man never meant to be, Yet all I could see. The next steps, my feet heavy,

A knock at the door broke my focus, and I glanced up to see Drake enter, holding a white gown in his hands. The sun was beginning to set. The ceremony would take place when the moon was at its highest peak. I should've had a fucking nap. I fell back onto the bed, covering my face and wishing this wasn't happening. I almost wished to be pregnant and eighteen again.

"Careful, I have a few ideas with you in that position."

I snorted, sitting up and taking in his appearance. He wore a dapper suit that fit him, nice and snug, showing the outline of his muscular figure. How did so much sex appeal and arrogance fit into one person?

"Can that be the option instead?" I pleaded, wishing to do anything but transcend tonight.

Drake stroked my face, bunching my hair at the back of my head, a small growl escaping from his lips. He forced my head back to meet his gaze, his eyes alive with heat and desire.

"It's torturous to even put that option forward because I would love nothing more than to lay you out, tie those hands up, and worship every single part of your body. My cock is already hard from my brain replaying the sounds of you moaning my name and the sweet taste of your cunt."

"I'm sure we have time." I reached for his belt. A distraction might help.

"Daniella, this is important." He took a step back, restraining himself from his obvious desires, the tenting in his pants.

"Why?" I stood, my tone rising. "Why? What's so important about me claiming a power that I don't have?"

"It's to keep you safe. We don't understand this Syphon stuff, and I'm fucking terrified. If this gives me a little bit of peace, then fuck me dead, you'll stand up there and partake in the stupid fucking ceremony because that's what I fucking ask of you. To do one fucking thing, you got it?"

He threw the dress at me, storming from the room. The prick had returned, but the crease in his forehead and the throbbing vein in his neck as he shouted at me showed his worry. I threw the dress onto the bed, heading to the shower to prepare myself. My hair was wild, and there were bags under my grey eyes—evidence of what little sleep I'd had.

I sighed. "Let's get this show on the road." I spent the next hour getting ready—my hair, my makeup, and even hair removal.

I returned to the room, my hair having a wavy bounce with it pinned off my face on one side. My makeup was simple, just covering myself with a fresh and glowing look. The dress was stunning. It cut out around my breasts, showing skin on the side and plenty of cleavage, but it had wispy sleeves to add a touch of sophistication to it. The hem touched the ground, and I paired it with white and gold wedge heels. I stood before the mirror, looking like the perfect Mage, ready to take my position within this world.

"Are you ready?" Drake entered, staring at his phone and furiously typing away.

I placed the ivy clip in my hair and turned to look at him. "Yep, ready."

◆

"Daniella…Daniella. Time to wake up." Drake's voice was low and soft, and I registered his hand on my shoulder. My eyes flickered open, noticing the car was stationary. We were here. My stomach chose that moment to swirl, and Drake handed me a bag. I emptied the contents of my stomach, my hands shaking. "I'll be by your side the entire time." He stroked my face, and I leaned into his touch, a small comfort.

A knock at the door broke the small moment between us. He pressed his forehead against mine, placing a gentle kiss on it.

"I love you, *my inferno.*"

He cleared his throat, opening the door and walking around to do the same for me. I paused for a moment, steeling myself and trying to calm my racing heart. Swinging my legs to the side, they dangled above the ground, and I questioned my choice of white shoes on the wet forest floor. We had arrived at Red Wood Forest. Unbeknownst to regular humans, it was where a lot of rituals took place. A little area restricted with magic, and any who walked near fell ill very suddenly.

Drake linked our arms as we made our way to the Moonlight Ceremonial Circle. No speaking, just our breaths visible in the dark. It was cold, and Drake paused for a moment, removing his suit jacket and draping it over my shoulder. I smiled at him, a small gesture of thanks. Lights could be seen in the distance, growing closer with every step. My heart rate increased as we neared. I had this. I would be strong and resilient. My nerves were more from not being prepared. Drake had me practising with Matthew to learn and master small amounts of Water power for the day, but I worried that others might see through it.

The Circle came into view, the black stones in perfect alignment with the tree clearing above. Candles were placed strategically in between the gaps within the stones. The ivy and various other green protective plants were on the inside and outside of the Circle, with clear crystals that glowed. By a tree stump at the back, in the middle of the Circle, stood the High Ember, his face illuminated by the green flame roaring in the centre. He bowed his head. I took note of those around, holding a candle and a piece that represented their powers. It was about to begin.

Drake took my hand, squeezing it. "You've got this. You always did. You're doing this for that little girl who missed out all those years ago. Remember that."

He was right. This wasn't about the terrified adult, scared to screw up. This was about the teenager who missed out because of that abusive piece of shit. I stood straighter, determined to make it the best for her. I kissed his hand, stepping into the Circle, and all people disappeared from view. They were still there—I knew it—but no longer visible to the naked eye. Not until it was over would I see them again.

The moon sat at the edge of the clearing. The High Ember wouldn't speak until it lit up the entire area. He would say a few words, then I would show my power, and it would be over. The urge to shake away the cold pressed against me, but I stood firm, unwavering in my position.

"Are you ready, Daniella?" The same High Ember who married us stood before me, and I nodded.

He pointed to the Star of Eve in the ground. I took my place, my feet in the middle, the moon hitting its peak and lighting up the entire space in a cool, bright white. I now understood why he wore black robes, but the requirement of wearing white confused me.

"May Eve bless us today and all the days that follow. We bask in her light, the light of our creation, the light of peace, prosperity and power. Before us stands Daniella Vatras, previously known as Daniella Romano. She's ready to step into the light and begin her journey. Show us your blessing."

His voice echoed in the space, and I glanced over my shoulder, knowing that Drake would be anxiously waiting to see what would happen. The obsidian bracelet was securely on my wrist, there to avoid losing control or going crazy. I waved my hand, feeling the water power spurting from my fingertips, controlling it to surround me before thrusting my hand into the air, the water flying into the sky. I clapped my hands, watching the droplets explode into snowflakes and begin their descent to the ground.

"I did it!" I screamed with joy, knowing I'd finally transcended.

The light slowly dispersed, faces coming into view. My ears registered the round of applause, which grew louder with every passing second. Arms wrapped around my waist, lifting me from the ground before placing me on the floor once more.

"I'm so proud of you." Drake spun me around to land in his arms, dipping me down and kissing my lips.

He helped me to my feet, his arms pulling me against his body, holding me so tightly, like he never wanted to let me go. Safety wrapped around me in his arms, certain he would always be there. He had proven that, and I was blind to see that beneath his bravado and tough exterior was a man afraid to open his heart and feel.

"Drake, I need—"

"DANI!" I knew her voice before I saw her. Sam came running over. "That was incredible. You turned water into snowflakes, and they just floated to the ground! Can you conjure one now?"

"Yeah, if you want me to." I snapped my finger, and a snowflake formed in milliseconds before her eyes.

"Holy fucking shit, that's insane. I'm so shattered I won't get to remember this. The energy here is just wow, and the people are so friendly. The all-white is a little weird, like cultish. What is with the white? But then Drake is in black? Is that to represent his soul?" She cackled when Drake glared at her.

"It's a sign of respect. You would do well to remember that. You're here by invitation. That doesn't mean that I can't snap my fingers and remove the spell that allows you to see."

I held in my laugh. Knowing the man now, his threats almost seemed empty. He would absolutely break the spell, but it was still intriguing to hear him say the actual words.

"I apologise, Mr. Vatras. Can Dani show me around?" Drake kissed my cheek while Sam and I wandered off to the closest waterfall. Not too far away, but still close enough to see the lights.

I sat down, listening to the sound of the water rushing, and feeling the tiny droplets on my skin.

"Is this your life now?"

"Yeah, it is. I'm now officially a Mage within Drake's Coven." I beamed with happiness, knowing that I now belonged to someone and something. No longer tainted with the stain of the past.

"Are you okay with that?"

"When life throws you a curveball, you either run from it or you grow with it. I'd like to see where this goes. It wasn't what I had planned, but…" I paused

"Your son."

"Yeah, we know that I never wanted to be far away from him, but I'm alright with the knowledge that he has two parents who love and cherish him. They've promised to still send photo updates; there just won't be any more chances to see him in person. Life is what you make it, and I'm not about to let this bring me down. I had fun planning the solstice, you know me. My organisational skills are next level. Maybe this was always the life I was supposed to have, and teaching just taught me about myself. I've made peace with it, and I'm excited about my life for once, and what it can hold."

"Are you falling in love with him?"

I hesitated. "I honestly don't know. I've never felt what love is. I didn't really have a positive influence in that regard. What does it feel like?" I questioned, wondering if someone could give me an answer.

"It's different for everyone. Some say it's as simple as a flutter in their stomach whenever their person is around. Being vulnerable with them, being open and honest. The feeling of being safe and secure. More than anything, honestly, it's knowing that you can't live without them. The thought of not being near them would destroy you and your very foundations. Do you feel any of that for Drake?"

"I—"

Screams echoed, and fire burst through the trees. "Drake!" I moved to run before stopping, and turning back towards Sam. "Stay here and stay hidden. I'll come and find you."

The shouting grew louder as I dashed toward Drake. What was happening? The Morteferi…again? Please, no—this was my fault. They were attacking. A lifeless body blocked the way, eyes staring and skin white, and I forced myself past it. "Drake!" I shouted, moving through the ground, my wrist burning with the influx of power being used. My feet grew heavy. "Drake!" My screams echoed through the forest while searching furiously for him. Fire shot beside me. Following the trail, I ran into his arms.

"Are you alright?" He searched my face frantically, noticing a small cut on my neck.

"You are bleed—" Drake threw me to the ground, throwing fire and burning a hunter, his shouts reverberating through the forest.

"We need to get the fuck out of here." He grabbed my hand, pulling me to my feet. He reached for the bracelet. "We'll deal with the repercussions of that later. For now, we need all the help we can get."

"Drake, I—"

"You'll be safe with me," he said, pulling me behind him. We ran past people groaning in pain, others no longer breathing.

It was a massacre. Bodies lay everywhere, the sounds of people slowly diminishing. He never stopped, and we ran with all our might. Darkness covered our vision, but I trusted him. He knew where he was going.

"Oh, Drake." He stopped short at hearing the melodic voice, standing in the dark with nothing in view.

With my white dress, a beacon for any person close by, I would be easily detectable. He ducked, pulling me down with him. I could just make him out, pressing his finger to his lips, but keeping me close. My heart vibrated through my ears, the sound of blood rushing, the adrenaline coursing through my veins, the power itching my skin.

"The great and powerful Drake, hiding like a wimp. I never thought I'd see the day. What's that expression by humans? You're whipped." The voice sounded familiar. I'd heard it before, but couldn't place where.

"Can you conjure snowflakes to fall? We might be able to see them and figure out where they are located."

My fingers touched the ground, feeling the water in the earth, pulling it closer to the surface. It expanded into my hands until I cradled a ball of water. I threw it into the air, snapping my fingers and watching them explode into bright flakes of light, reflecting the moonlight.

"Smart, Daniella, very smart." The wind blew them away, but they gave away their position.

"This way," Drake mouthed. We crawled slowly along the ground, avoiding any objects that dared to reveal where we were located.

Light could be seen up ahead. The car! Our escape was within reach, but Drake froze. Vince sat in the front seat, dancing to music, completely unaware of the carnage that had taken place.

"*Inferno*." His voice was soft and tender. "I need you to get up and run to that car. Don't look back, just run. Get in and order Vince to drive."

"Drake, I c—"

"No, you will do as I ask. I can't concentrate with you here. Please, I won't lose you when I just found you." His voice faltered, and he squeezed my hand. I brought it to my lips, kissing it.

Drake stood, igniting his hands and forcing his fire out. "NOW!" he shouted, and I ran with everything I had before stopping. Fuck, Sam! I couldn't leave her. I had to go back.

Chapter Fifty-Four

Betrayal Always Hurts

Drake

Daniella ran in the opposite direction that I asked. Six men surrounded me, but I knew I could take them—there was no choice. When I saw men running after Daniella, my need to protect her was all-consuming. *FUCK!* I pushed myself harder than ever before, the heat from the flame warming my entire body. My hands spun, letting it fall around me in a protective circle. They wouldn't be able to attack with it in place. They moved closer, coming out of the dark and into view, wearing their cloaks.

"Ready to die, motherfuckers? Step forward now, and I'll make it painless. Fight me, and I will ensure you feel every single inch of your skin burning and understand what burnt flesh tastes like."

"Men, attack!" An ordered shouted in the dark. I threw my arms up, forcing the circle of fire out further, making it grow in size and strength. It didn't take long to hear the sounds of retreat.

I waited for absolute silence, allowing the fire to drop and watching the area for any movement. Six bodies lay lifeless on the ground, the flames still flickering to life. A smile spread over my face at their demise. Less hunters to attack our people.

My legs burned from how fast I ran, only to discover that she hadn't reached the car. Daniella. Fucking Daniella. She would have run for Sam. Fucking Sam. I knew it was a mistake to bring her. I fucking knew it. I had to find her. Daniella wasn't far. I thought about the proximity of everything. The waterfall. I was all turned around in the dark, unable to see which direction to go in.

"DANIELLA!" I yelled with everything in me, praying she would hear.

"DRAKE!" It was quiet, but I heard it.

I ran toward the sound, my feet crunching against the broken branches and tanbark on the ground. My heart was pounding. I had to reach her. I refused to lose her. She was my fucking everything. Fuck, I was spiralling the same way I did after the death of my mother. No, this wasn't the same. The Morteferi couldn't win.

I found my way to the waterfall, seeing Daniella pulling on Sam's arm.

"We need to go. Come with me now," she pleaded, keeping her voice low.

"No." She shook her head. "I can't. I have to stay."

"What do you mean you have to stay? It isn't safe. You'll die if you stay here."

"But he wants me here. He told me to come." Daniella's gaze met mine, and she let go of her hand, instantly backing away.

Sam had been spelled. She was the one spilling secrets. They had infiltrated her friend's mind. Daniella's legs faltered. All those deaths would feel like her fault. I reached her, lifting her to her feet. I wanted to hold her, but had to keep my eye trained on every single part of this environment.

"You should've left her alone, Drake. You should've picked another wife. This never would have happened if it weren't for you." Her words were hollow, like another was controlling her, the darkest of dark magic.

"Sam, you've been spelled. You're sick. I can help you, but you have to come with me. Daniella wouldn't want this for you. I'm sorry this has happened, but we have to go or you'll be killed."

Two men appeared. One removed his cloak. He appeared to be around the same age as me, with hair more thinned out and a lankier physique. He smiled, his teeth yellow, and wrinkles covered his entire face.

"Let her go!" I bellowed. Daniella reached for her friend, but I needed her close and pulled her back toward me. Prepared to jump in front of an attack for her. The other hunter kept their face covered, but my eye was drawn to a trinket that sparkled in my eye.

"Sam, please. Come here," Daniella begged, tears welling in her eyes. My heart yearned to hold her and protect her from this.

Sam moved backwards towards the hunters, shaking her head. "You shouldn't exist. You're an abomination. Eve made a mistake with your creation. Just accept your inevitable death." The words were cold, her eyes solely focused on Daniella, unblinking and almost alien. Soft sobs echoed through the night. Daniella was trying to hold back the wave of emotion with every last bit of her strength.

"Sam, please, if you're still in there, you need to come with me," she pleaded, holding her hands together, begging her to think for herself. I knew it was pointless. A human spelled had no free thought, and she would be dead soon. I only hoped it would be painless, as much as I didn't like the woman.

"Daniella, tsk tsk. You know this is your fault. She would be safe if you'd never joined the human world. Mages and humans can never mix—the oldest warning, but the truest. There are two options for Sam: a life in a mental hospital or death. Which would you prefer?"

"Do you have no shame? She has children! Have a heart." Her voice screeched, her hands shaking.

"That's your problem. Death it is." He stood before Sam, holding his hand out in front of her face and bringing his fingers into a fist. Sam coughed twice, holding her throat and dropping to the ground. At least she wouldn't have felt it. I took a step, ready to grab Daniella and run.

"No fucking further, *Firebound One*. One more step and I'll kill your wife." I froze, those words, the prophecy. "Yeah, I finally found your weakness. Who would have thought a girl could cause you to put on blinkers, not seeing what was right in front of you?"

"Fuck you," I spat at him, my hands igniting.

"No, fuck you. The *Firebound One* and his wife, without ordinary power. An unmaking—the sun will turn black, and the world shall shake. You will be the unmaking of the world; you will destroy us all. Take her away," he ordered the other hunter, the man's face still obscured.

I remembered finding evidence of a prophecy, but the page had been torn out, so it was hard to know what would occur. It reminded me of what the one who attacked my mother said, *'The Firebound One will destroy us all.'* Their eradication of those blessed with Fire magic made sense, but something important was missing.

I shot fire in their direction, but they waved it away as if it barely bothered them. I peered at my wife, a statue. How did our union signify the end?

CHAPTER FIFTY-FIVE

THIS CAN'T BE THE END

DANIELLA

"Daniella, run!" Drake shouted, but I stood frozen in place, staring at my friend's body, dead on the ground. She had three children, three young children, and her friendship with me had led to her death.

Fire entered my vision, which shook me from my thoughts. I moved toward Drake, but not fast enough. My hair was yanked backward, forcing me to the floor. Drake tried to burn the man, but I watched the fire avoid him, like an invisible shield was surrounding him. I used my own Water power, pulling it from the lake and forcing it toward the man. It, too, diverted in another direction, extinguishing the flames. A soft purple glow was hidden under the hood—the hunter was a Syphon.

"Drake, get out of here!" I yelled at him, kicking the man's knee, rolling over to get up and flee.

I didn't get very far before the air was pulled from my lungs. My hands clutched my throat, dropping to the ground and gasping for air.

"Let her go," Drake snarled, forcing flames at the man. Darkness covered my vision. Unsure how to fight this, my nails raked against my skin, desperate for some relief—anything to hold onto before succumbing. Tears slipped free as my heart slowed. This couldn't be my end.

Hands were around my waist, lifting me to my feet, and oxygen slowly returned to my system. I coughed and spluttered, searching for the sweet taste of life. The arms still held me in place, but I pretended to continue to struggle while preparing to attack. I threw my head back, smacking the face of the man holding me prisoner. Drake's knees buckled. I sprinted toward him, watching his Fire magic flicker.

A sudden pull dragged me back, the fabric of my dress ripping under the strain

"Drake!" I screamed, the sound echoing in the dark. His eyes found mine, holding all the fear and love he had for me. It hung between us, filled with unspoken words. We knew.

"No!" I shook my head, the world barely a whisper, the grip on my dress tightening, dragging me backwards. I clawed at the ground, in search of a weapon, anything to stop him.

"Take her. I'll finish him," the older man snarled at his friend, who was holding me captive.

"Drake, please get up!" I kicked, swinging my arms, desperate to get out of his grasp. "Fight this, Drake, please!"

I watched him claw at the ground, the faint glow of his fingers dimming with every desperate crawl, each movement agony to witness. The distance between us grew bigger by the second. Sparks flickered once more, hand arching upward toward my captor. He was weak, no flame leaving him, but he was resilient, trying over and over to get to me.

"Drake, please!" My voice croaked, full of emotions at watching this happen to him. "You can do this."

My heart tore apart at the growing distance between us—too far, too cruel. I needed him, needed his arms, that safety, that wholeness. A stick scraped into my grip, and I flung it behind me, frantic, wild, anything to get to him. The thud, the groan, yes, it worked. Legs buckled, the ground slammed into me, but I had to keep going, stumbling, falling, dragging myself forward, not stopping, never stopping. Drake was still gasping for breath. His hand was so close, I could almost feel his fingers. "Drake." I was desperate to touch him. If I could, I would be able to save him. I had to.

The old man approached, and my hand on the earth pulled water to my fingers, forcing it toward the hunter storming toward us. It brought us mere moments of relief. Drake gasped again, his skin turning pale. My eyes stung with tears. He stretched his trembling arm out, and I extended mine once more. We were so close.

The old man stood, veins in his forehead throbbing with rage. Hands grabbed my legs, pulling me back, and I dug my fingers into the ground to stop it. The old man reached Drake, lifting him into the air. No, this couldn't be his end. I just found him. I couldn't lose him. Not now, not like this, not because of me, not when…

"Drake, I—" Words were stuck in my throat. "I love you…please"

I said it. The words I was too afraid to speak, the words that had been dying on the edge of my tongue. Drake's gaze met mine—small flickers of light in his beautiful brown irises. Why did I have to wait? It seemed so stupid.

"A prophecy cannot be fulfilled with you gone." The hunter threw him backwards, his back hitting the tree with a savage crack.

"DRAKE!" His name echoed through the forest. He moved only slightly, lifting his head, a sly smile showing he wasn't done. The hunter let go of my feet, and I scrambled to stand, my face burning with the tears streaming down my face.

"Let him go, please," I begged, watching the only man I had ever loved lift his fingers, pleading for his power to work, to save us. His mouth opened, but I was too far away to hear the words leaving his lips. His hand outstretched once more before he face planted into the dirt. My knees buckled. I had lost two people tonight. A sharp pain tore through my chest. He was gone.

"No, no, no, no!" I shattered into pieces, collapsing to the ground, my vision clouded with black, my heart slowing. *Was this my end?*

Acknowledgements

Thank you to my cover designer Katelyn for the
fantastic cover, I adore it.
Thank you to Mel for creating the special edition cover.
Thank you to Krystal for just being an incredible person
Thank you to my beta team and street team for enjoying
this wild ride with me.
Thank you to all the readers for the continual support,
I hope you enjoy the story of Drake and Daniella.